Bronwyn Scott is a communications instructor at Pierce College in the United States, and the proud mother of three wonderful children—one boy and two girls. When she's not teaching or writing she enjoys playing the piano, travelling—especially to Florence, Italy—and studying history and foreign languages. Readers can stay in touch via Facebook at facebook.com/bronwynwrites, or on her blog, bronwynswriting.blogspot.com. She loves to hear from readers.

REVEALING THE TRUE MISS STANSFIELD

Bronwyn Scott

MILLS & BOON

First Published in Great Britain 2021
by Mills & Boon, an imprint of HarperCollins*Publishers*
1 London Bridge Street, London, SE1 9GF

ISBN: 978-0-263-28387-7

For my kids.
Never be afraid to be yourself.
Love, Mom

Chapter One

Seasalter, Kent—August 1820

'I can make you rich.' Gallant words from a gallant gentleman. Gallant enough to make Adelaide Stansfield look up from her painting and smile at the sight before her: Bennett Galbraith sprawled with informal élan on the picnic blanket spread atop the pebbly surface of a Seasalter beach, the sun flecking his blond hair gold, his skin the shade of warm toast from a summer spent outdoors. He was vibrant and handsome and, when he was in Seasalter, he made no secret that he was hers, a notion that made Addy's heart trip.

She shot him a teasing reprimand from beneath the brim of her straw beach hat. 'Yesterday, you said you could make me famous.'

Bennett was forever saying outlandish things. It was part of his charm and, while she was used to it after a year of his casual attentions, she certainly wasn't tired of it. Perhaps it was vain of her, but secretly, she thought it was refreshing to be the centre of someone's attention. That it should be the attentions of a *handsome* man made it all the sweeter.

Usually, it was her older sister, Artemisia, who held one's attention. It was Artemisia who'd stormed the masculine citadel of the Royal Academy of the Arts last year, asking for elevation to the rank of RA, and then stormed back out to form her own school when the Academy denied her. It was Artemisia who'd married Viscount St Helier after decamping to Italy and Artemisia who'd birthed the St Helier heir just a month ago, a sweet baby boy named Michael Caravaggio. Addy wasn't bothered by her sister's fame. Artemisia was made for centre stage. Addy wasn't sure she was, although sometimes she wouldn't mind trying it out.

'Well?' Bennett gave her a slow, lingering smile, his green eyes intent on her, making her warm with his perusal. 'I *could* make you famous and I *could* make you rich, Addy. I could do both, you wouldn't have to choose, if you would just let me.' He arched a blond brow in challenge. 'Sometimes I think you don't believe I can do it.'

'No, it's not that. I don't doubt you,' although she did wonder at times *how* he'd do it. She didn't actually understand what Bennett did for a living. He claimed to be a gentleman of independent means, but he owned no land that she knew of, which meant no rents and no tenants. Yet he always seemed to have money, he was constantly sporting a new waistcoat or presenting her with some little luxury. 'It's that I don't need the money, or the fame,' Addy demurred. 'My family is comfortably situated, my father and my sister have fame enough for us all.'

She'd grown up surrounded by that money and that fame. Her father had been a famous artist by the time she was old enough to know it. Addy had never wanted for anything money could buy. She'd held a paintbrush since she was four. Everyone had expected her to follow in the family footsteps and she had. Over the years she'd developed a talent equal to theirs, but not a passion, at least not for painting. She painted because she could, because she excelled at it, but it was art history that she loved—not that anyone had ever asked. The Stansfields weren't historians, they were painters.

Bennett scoffed at her response. 'Everyone needs money, Addy. Comfortable is not the same as being rich. Wouldn't it be a wondrous thing to have money of your own? Not to need to wait for your allowance from your father or ask permission to purchase something? You could be independent. Not even Artemisia is that. She has a husband,' Bennett said archly. Addy sensed a goad, a competitive nudge that played on the faintest flare of sibling rivalry—to have something that Artemisia did not, something that was hers alone. Bennett's ploy might have worked if Addy were the jealous sort, or if Artemisia was somehow unhappy in her decisions. Of course, neither was true. She wasn't jealous and Artemisia was happy, *blissfully* happy, in her marriage. Artemisia would not have married the Viscount if she'd felt it came at the expense of her freedom.

Independence, freedom. They were appealing prospects, the things fame and riches *could* buy, a chance to step out on her own.

The temptation niggled. What would it be like to strike out for herself? Addy couldn't pretend she'd never thought of it. What would it be like to stand beyond Artemisia's shadow and her father's fame? To know her own worth? To be perceived as a talented artist, a historian, in her own right? She pushed the idea away. She was not used to entertaining selfish thoughts. 'Maybe someday, but not now. Artemisia needs me too much with the autumn term about to start and the new baby to manage.' The term would take place in the newly refurbished dormitories. St Helier and others had spent the better part of the year turning an old fishery into the art school so that the school could move fully out of the farmhouse and expand its enrolment. Sixteen girls were expected this autumn, double last year's attendance. There'd be more classes to teach and this year it would be a full-length autumn term. Artemisia couldn't manage it all without her.

Bennett gave her a soft smile. 'There will always be something. If it's not the new students, or the new baby, it will be another new baby. You will spend your life assisting Artemisia's dreams at the expense of your own.'

He leaned forward, reaching for her, his hand cupping her jaw. 'Addy-Sweet, you should be in Florence this autumn, painting the Renaissance masters at the Uffizi with the other art students, not wasting away in Seasalter.' His infectious smile widened. 'Florence in autumn is spectacular. The tourists are gone, the air is cool and the new wine is in.'

'Stop, Bennett, you know how much I want to go,' she scolded him with a laugh, but it wasn't entirely funny. Italy was a dream of hers and his words made her hungry for it. She had not been there since she was a small child. What a fantasy that would be! She could see it in her mind's eye already: walking the Piazza della Signoria past the Palazzo Vecchio, sketching Ammannati's Neptune Fountain, lounging in the loggia, sipping coffees at the cafés, listening to street musicians. It would be a slice of heaven and it was out of reach, this year at least. She gave a rueful shake of her head as much for him as for her. She could not entertain it. 'Please, Bennett. Do not press me. I cannot go this year.' She could not desert Artemisia. Artemisia had raised her, given her years of love as a sister and as a mother figure when their own had died. Artemisia had been ten, still a child herself, and she'd only been two. She wanted to return the favour and be the best aunt possible to her new nephew and to support her sister as her sister had supported her.

Bennett leaned back on his elbows, considering. 'If you can't go to Florence, perhaps Florence can come to you.' There was an air of mystery about him now. He rose from the blanket and dusted off his breeches. 'I want to show you something. Walk with me?' He reached for the leather tube he'd brought along and slung the strap across his body bandolier style.

'But my brushes! They'll be destroyed if I don't wash them out first and the paint will dry,' Addy exclaimed. Whatever Bennett was, he wasn't himself an artist. Otherwise, he would know better than to ask her to spontaneously set aside her equipment. Ruining brushes was the eighth deadly sin in the Stansfield household.

Bennett waved to a servant, motioning for him to gather up the picnic and paints. 'That's what the help is for, Addy-Sweet.'

'My brushes need particular care. They're the Italian ones you gave me,' Addy protested. She didn't approve of the way Bennett ordered servants around, especially when they weren't his to order. They were technically St Helier's, but Bennett had no qualms about appropriating their services for himself. If Bennett had servants, they weren't here in Seasalter with him. She didn't think he even travelled with a valet.

'I am sure St Helier's man knows how to care for paintbrushes. If he doesn't, I'll buy you some more.' The footman came forward to pick up the equipment, and Addy gave him an apologetic smile as she took Bennett's arm.

'You're too soft, Addy, servants know their place and they need you to know it, too,' he scolded as they began to walk. 'You don't do them any favours by not letting them do their jobs. It's an insult to them.' Bennett was full of himself today. It made her prickly, but she didn't want to ruin the afternoon with a quarrel. He'd only just returned to Seasalter yesterday after a three-week absence to parts unknown. He never spoke of where he went, only that he was off on business.

She'd missed him, although she supposed she had no real right to. Bennett Galbraith came and went as he pleased. She had no claim to him. Who knew who he saw when he was away? He was the sort of man a woman looked twice at, a man who could have a woman in every port if he wanted. *Did he?* They never discussed it. She only knew that when he was in Seasalter, his company was all hers and she'd not asked for more than that. There'd not been a reason to. He was in and out of Seasalter like the tide. If he were to stay, if they were to be something more permanent, it would be different. She'd want to know. And maybe she didn't want to press him on it for fear of losing his attentions or being too cloying.

They stopped halfway down the beach and he drew her into a sheltered nook where the breeze didn't blow. 'I've brought you something.' His eyes danced as he slung the leather tube off his shoulder and removed the lid. He tapped the tube and out slid an oilskin-wrapped roll. He gave her a grin as he unfurled the canvas. 'Do you know what this is?'

A marvel, that was what it was, and far too fine to be displayed on a beach beneath the hot glare of the sun. 'You should put it away.' The historian in her was aghast, wanting to protect it even as it piqued her intrigue. She couldn't resist a quick perusal. Her breath caught as she studied the canvas's rich colours; the deep reds, the brilliant blues and the bright yellows of the Renaissance masters.

'Well? What is it? Tell me about it,' Bennett asked, impatient.

'It's old,' she said at last. 'Fifteen hundreds, perhaps. Italian definitely.' She squinted. She couldn't tell much more here in the harsh light. They ought to roll it up and take it back to the house. She would take just one more look.

Addy furrowed her brow. 'Look at the perspective, Bennett. The painter uses a two-dimensional plane and yet the use of aerial perspective creates a three-dimensional sense. That offers us insight into the date.'

'Do you think this is a Raphael?' Bennett prompted, more interested in conclusions instead of how she got to them. Addy smiled indulgently. Not everyone appreciated art history. Bennett was of the more practical sort.

'No.' Addy shook her head. 'Raphael used a vanishing point. This is something different, it's earlier. If I had to guess, I would say it's done in the style of Perugino, perhaps one of his students. That would be something.'

'How do you know it's *not* Perugino's own work?'

Addy rolled up the canvas carefully, reverently. Even if it was the work of a nobody, it was still history. It deserved respect. 'I don't recall seeing it in any of the catalogues.' She was mentally flipping through catalogues of illustrations about Perugino's work: *The Nativity*, *The Delivery of the Keys*, *Madonna in Glory with Saints*, *Pietà*. Certainly, the religious theme fit with his work, as did the style and colouring, but she did not recall this one. Of course, she could have overlooked it. How exciting if it was a real one. There were ways to tell. Her pulse started to race. 'Is there a signature? A provenance?' She ran her gaze over the corners of the painting, searching. 'Where did you get this?'

'From a French nobleman who has fallen on hard times. Old aristocracy, not Napoleon's new nobility.' Bennett shrugged. 'There's no provenance, but that's not important. It's for you. A gift.' He rolled the canvas back up and carefully put it in its travelling tube.

'For me?' It was a fine gift. It wouldn't have been appropriate to accept if they'd been in London, but in Seasalter such rules might be ignored. They were far from society. No one paid attention.

Bennett fastened the lid and passed the tube to her. 'This is what I meant if you won't go Florence, perhaps Florence can come to you. You can paint it, Addy. I know you can. Your work with colour has grown tremendously this year. Now you can hone your skill from a master's work without leaving home. I have others once you're done with this one, enough to keep you busy all autumn. Promise me, you'll paint it for me, that you will practise your skill.' He kissed her on the nose, a tender gesture. 'I believe in you, Addy.' He gave her a playful wink, 'While you paint, we can pretend we're in Florence.'

What else might they pretend? Florence wasn't only about art and her painting, it was about being alone with him, the two of them bashing around the Continent, every day an adventure, having Bennett all to herself. Hers alone. No more wondering about women in every port, no more wondering where he took himself off to when he wasn't here. His gaze was upon her, those clear green eyes of his, making her feel all sorts of things, not the least being a certain warmth in her veins, a certain wonder that somehow she should be the target of his regard. It was amazing that he wanted to run off with her, to have an adventure with her.

It prompted the question of why? How was it that a man so handsome, so mysterious and dashing would continue to be intrigued by her, a young woman who lived simply, who'd come to prefer the rustic environs of Seasalter to the civilised amenities of London. 'You are too good to me, Bennett.' It was hard to be angry at him for being high-handed with the servants when he looked at her like that—as though he wanted her above any other woman in the world. It was flattering in the extreme. No man had ever paid her such depth of attention. She hardly knew what to do with it.

'I missed you while I was away, Addy.' He lifted her chin with his thumb and forefinger, his voice soft. 'You don't give yourself enough credit. You are far more talented than any girl I know and far more selfless. Those are admirable qualities, *attractive* qualities. Then there is the issue of your hair, auburn in the winter, cinnamon in the sun, a curtain of burnished silk to sift beneath my fingers.' Her pulse skittered at the words. This was fast becoming a scene from a Mrs Radcliffe novel and she was out of her depth. Men worshipped Artemisia, not her.

'What are you doing, Bennett?' She offered a tremulous smile, not entirely comfortable with the direction things were heading, yet not entirely willing to put him off.

His mouth was at her ear, his voice soft, his teeth a gentle nip at her lobe, sending a frisson of excitement through her. 'I'm making love to you, Addy-Sweet. I had plenty of time on my trip to think, and I thought of you, of us, how we've known each other over a year and how I've not yet declared my intentions or kissed you and it's about time, for kisses, for more between us.' He kissed the bridge of her nose, 'I adore you, Addy, I adore your freckles and your sweet lips. How I've dreamed of them, of how they'd taste, of how they'd feel beneath mine.'

It was a slow kiss, his mouth lingering on hers, his eyes holding hers even when he pulled back. There was no reason to hurry. They were alone on the beach so they might take their time. His hands were warm and firm at her waist, holding her close, intimately even, hips to hips. It was not the first time he'd touched her. There'd been a year's worth of touches, a polite guiding hand at her back, the offer of an arm as they walked, dances at Owen Gann's annual 'Oyster Ball', which wasn't really a ball. But this was the most intimate they'd ever been and the intimacy didn't override her earlier misgivings. *What had changed? Why? What did he see in her?* Surely, when one was in love, love swept away such misgivings.

But her misgivings added to other warnings. Artemisia made no secret of her dislike of him. But Artemisia liked very few people and saw suspicious agendas everywhere. Her sister didn't know Bennett as she did. Hadn't Bennett given her the space last year to go to London with Artemisia? Hadn't he waited patiently for her to return to Seasalter? Artemisia had feared exploitation, but when had Bennett sought to exploit her? Never once had he taken advantage of her status as the daughter of a famed artist. Instead, he wanted only the best for her, encouraged her to better her painting. Perhaps in some regard, Bennett *was* right that Artemisia only disliked him because he sought to separate her from her sister and where would Artemisia be without her? Or she without Artemisia? They'd not been apart for any length of time except for a few months last year when Artemisia had left without telling her.

A traitorous thread whispered through her thoughts. Artemisia left without discussing it. Why should she now feel compelled to stay?

Why should you stay for her? Why wait? Perhaps Bennett is right, there will always be a reason to stay, why not go now while he is willing to take you?

Because it was too good to believe, really. Why would he do such a thing? Offer such a thing to one such as she?

'What do you want, Bennett?' She tried again to divine his intent. She smiled up at him, aware of his hands tight at her waist, holding her firm against him. His body implied one thing, but there'd never been any spoken expectation between them. He'd never once said he was courting her.

'Isn't it obvious, Addy-Sweet? I want you.' He bent his head to capture her mouth again. His hips pressed into hers, his voice low and hoarse at her ear. 'Can you feel what you do to me, Addy? You undo me.' The words were too much, too exaggerated like so many of his compliments. Amid the new sensation of his embrace, a murmur of doubt trembled: How could she undo him when she hardly knew him?

Chapter Two

London—October

Inspector Hazard Manning bent near the oil painting, eyes shut to block out any visual distractions, and inhaled. Deeply. He could smell a forgery like a hound smelled a fox trail. He exhaled. Forgery held no scent. It smelled like *nothing*.

The painting hanging in Lord Monteith's gallery had no odour to it. Proof that it was not old. Old paintings carried the scents of mould or mildew on them. This canvas carried nothing. He leaned in again and took a second inhalation, aware of Lord Monteith hovering in the background, anxiously awaiting his verdict. He exhaled again. Nothing except perhaps the faintest whiff of turpentine—a residue from the brushes, not the paint itself. Oil paint did not smell, contrary to popular myth. Of course, that didn't make the painting authentic. Monteith was pacing now but Hazard refused to be rushed. Perhaps if Monteith hadn't rushed his purchase, this situation would not have arisen. Or maybe it would have merely arisen elsewhere, on someone else's watch, perhaps someone who hadn't been called away from more important work on the East Docks regarding a murder case that had lingered since February.

So be it. He was here now. He might as well make good work of it to save having to come back later. Hazard took out a magnifying glass and bent to the details, muttering questions under his breath—the colour was off, or was that the paints themselves? Carefully, he lifted the painting to check behind it, searching for any maker's mark, but the back of the painting was as devoid of markings as the paint had been devoid of smells. At last, he stepped back from the purported Perugino—a long-lost minor work supposedly overlooked by cataloguers. Only a fool would believe that.

'What have you discovered?' Monteith was breathless with worry.

'It's not an original Perugino. The colours are right, but the paints are wrong,' Hazard launched into an explanation about how the cobalt blue on the Virgin Mary's robes was too new, a modern colour that wasn't used until 1802, how Perugino would have used azurite for the underpainting of the Virgin's robes if he was economising or ultramarine if he wasn't. 'Ultramarine was extraordinarily expensive, Perugino made his patrons supply it for him.' One of his Oxford professors had been a scholar of the Renaissance and had passed his passion for the intimate details of the lives of the artists on to him. It was a bit of impressive minutiae he seldom had call to use among the grit and the crime of his usual cases.

Monteith chuckled, 'You're wasted on Bow Street, Manning. Wasted on me, truth be told. You know too damn much. You should be at the British Museum where chaps care about that kind of thing.'

'Thank you, my lord. However, the museum wasn't hiring. Bow Street was,' Hazard demurred politely. To work for the British Museum overseeing authentication and the purchase of foreign art would be a dream come true, but that was work for gentlemen scholars, men with connections or titles of their own. He was on his own. He was the second son of a Sussex country squire with an interrupted Oxford education. Whatever connections he might once have leveraged, he had deliberately cut years ago.

'I'll want my money back, of course. That painting was expensive!' Monteith was back to business.

'We'll find him,' Hazard offered confidently as a means of reassurance, although he wasn't sure how he might begin the search at present. 'It's all in the details, milord, that's how we catch these bastards. A criminal always overlooks something. I don't. However, I have some questions for you, if you don't mind?' Details were what set him apart from other inspectors, private or otherwise. His reputation for them was why Monteith had hired him. This wasn't the first time he'd cleaned up embarrassments for the Earl. Details and discretion were his watchwords even if they weren't Monteith's.

They settled themselves in the Earl's office, healthy tumblers of brandy at their elbows,

Monteith drinking heavily in his distress. 'No one can know what I've done, Manning,' he insisted. Hazard nodded, not surprised that Monteith's first concern was for his reputation, not for the crime. The Earl fashioned himself a collector of Renaissance art. The man thought it made him appear intelligent and well rounded. The man had been to Italy once in his youth on a Grand Tour that pre-dated Napoleon's advance on Europe by decades.

'Of course, milord. I would not dream of announcing your misfortune,' Hazard assured him, although his assurances might not be enough. The Earl of Bourne, a true collector, had been the one to call the painting into question. He couldn't control who Bourne might tell.

Hazard took out his pencil and a small notebook for jottings. 'Tell me how you came by this painting?'

Monteith shifted ever so slightly in his chair. 'I was told it was owned by a French nobleman down on his luck, that it was part of his private collection.' It was a plausible story. French nobles had been selling artwork off since the Revolution, trying to keep their finances afloat, and it wouldn't be the first time a Perugino had come to English shores.

Historical precedence aside, Monteith was skirting the issue. Hazard was patient. He would have the whole story or nothing. Patience was how he'd broken ciphers during the war. He'd learned early that if a cipher didn't crack one way, to look at it from another and another until something slid into place. 'Did you meet with the Frenchman? Did you have any communication with him?'

'No, the sale was brokered by an agent.' Monteith was almost surly, as if Hazard ought to have known better than to assume he'd actually take charge of his own purchase. The Earl shifted again, crossing a leg over one knee. The man was positively fidgety with embarrassment or nerves.

Hazard took notes, asking his next question casually. 'Does this agent of yours have a name?' Given the fidgets, it occurred to Hazard that the Earl might be protecting someone. Himself, perhaps? Monteith loved himself above all else. He wouldn't want to admit he'd done business with someone of dubious repute.

'He's a finder, that's all I know,' Monteith offered at last. 'His man delivered the painting to my man.'

'Ah.' There were too many nameless men in this story for it to end well. Nameless men were harder to track. Hazard nodded and reached for his glass. He sniffed at the brandy and swallowed, letting his tongue confirm what his mind suspected. The 'agent' Monteith referred to was a free trader. He'd bet his father's pocket watch on it. The brandy was smuggled. No doubt the painting was, too. Potential pieces began to form and fit together. A Frenchman deliberately passing off a forged painting? Did the free trader know or was it an honest mistake? But the thought of a smuggler making an honest mistake was fraught with irony. There was practicality and economy in smuggling but not much honesty.

'Was there a provenance with the painting?' Hazard asked. This would determine how intentional the smuggler's role had been. If there was, the smuggler might have been fooled into believing the painting's authenticity. It would put the blame firmly in the Frenchman's camp. The origins and use of the blue paint marked it as a recent work, at most seventeen years old. But he doubted even that. He'd *smelled* the turpentine. To an expert like himself, it smelled *new*. Only a fool like Monteith would think the scent old. He made a mental bet with himself. There would be no provenance. Why would there be when there'd been no maker's mark?

Monteith shook his head. 'The papers were lost in the crossing. The boat ran into rough weather and some things were lost overboard.'

It was on the tip of Hazard's tongue to ask if that coincidence had not struck the Earl as odd, but he refrained. The dig to the Earl's intelligence served no useful purpose, and while his brain was often a sharp-edged tool, his tongue was a kinder instrument. Monteith was an old man. Hazard would not take his pride from him. Instead, he said, 'I see.' He did see. In the man's haste to impress people with his collection, Monteith had not done his homework. Acquiring classic art was a long, drawn-out transaction full of research and expert assurances to avoid situations such as this. Monteith, as usual, had rushed headlong into impetuous disaster. He'd not stopped to ask himself why a long-lost Perugino was offered exclusively to him, and privately, when it might fetch more if placed on auction among people who would appreciate it and drive up the bid.

'I want my money back and I want the man

who did this to be caught and punished. Forgery is a hanging offence,' Monteith fumed and poured another brandy.

'Sometimes,' Hazard felt compelled to correct the blustering Monteith. 'Only forgery, as in counterfeiting, is still a guaranteed hanging offence.' An art forger might get sentenced or face transportation, or, depending on the charges and who was pressing them, hanging. He was familiar with the law on that. The dead man on the East Docks had been a forger with wide-ranging skills. A counterfeiter for the London underground, he'd forged documents, deeds, pound notes, and who knew what else. They were just at the tip of that iceberg presently.

Monteith tossed back his brandy. 'His kind, whoever this forger is, will pollute the art world if paintings like these are allowed to infiltrate our collections.' Hazard thought there were certainly other ways in which the art world might be polluted by fraud, starting with the man seated across from him.

'I understand how you feel,' Hazard empathised carefully, wanting to get back to cultivating useful information and a useful direction for the conversation. He could take no action without a lead, minimal as it might be. 'But without a name, how am I to contact the finder?' He would need to question the man and that might not be enough. Sailing to France and tracking down the French noble might not even be enough. Convicting someone of fraud was tricky business. He would be hard pressed to prove the smuggler knowingly passed on fraudulent goods and the Frenchman had no obligation to be tried in an English court. 'How might I connect with your finder? How do *you* contact him?' By 'you' he'd meant Monteith's people, but Monteith took the reference literally.

'I don't know. *How* should I know?' Monteith waved a hand impatiently. 'When I want something, I tell my men of business to arrange it.'

Rich men like Monteith were never about the details. They made pronouncements and others followed through, others put the plans in motion and saw those wishes fulfilled. Men like him. Men like those who'd served with him, died beside him. He had not been able to keep them all safe, not even his own brother despite the promises he'd made his father. But those regrets were not for the Earl's offices. They were for the night.

'Then they would be the ones to ask,' Hazard prompted, leaning forward. 'I need to be clear with you. Without any leads such as the name of the finder, I cannot track your forger down. If you could make enquiries of your men of business or have your secretary make those enquiries, I could be of more service.' Hazard rose. 'Thank you for your time,' he offered, although it had been his time that had been requested.

He saw himself out, collecting his thoughts. Interesting indeed. Monteith told one story, but Hazard's instincts told another. Those instincts were seldom wrong—only the once had they failed.

Outside, the sharp autumn breeze freshened his thoughts. It was a long walk from Portland Square to his desk at the Bow Street offices, but his mind welcomed the chance to think and his body welcomed the brisk exercise in brisk weather. He breathed in the cool afternoon air, inhaling the changing seasons. The soot of London was not gone, but the stink of summer thankfully was. He enjoyed London in autumn with its crimson leaves and less crowded streets. He breathed out and let his thoughts come as he walked.

Was the French noble a fiction? The paint was too new. His mind kept going back to the cobalt blue. Not only was it not the blue preferred by Perugino, it was simply too new, a colour not in use until after the turn of the century. Why the fiction? Because Monteith would believe the story. It was the kind of tale Monteith could tell around dinner tables next Season. Hazard could hear Monteith now, regaling his guests as they trooped out to the gallery for a look at the lost masterpiece. *'It was hanging for centuries on a wall in a French chateau...my agent brought it to my attention...a lost Perugino...'*

He walked faster as his thoughts sped up. France was irrelevant for now. It all came down to the agent, who was clearly someone Monteith used regularly and who had a modicum of Monteith's trust, ill given or not. Monteith used this man blindly—not knowing a thing about him: not his name, not his address, nor where to find him. But someone in Monteith's employ did.

If he could find the finder, he would find the forger. The two were no doubt working together to pass off copies to unsuspecting, hasty buyers like Monteith. Whoever the forger was, he was good. This was no two-penny street artist. But forgers usually weren't. They couldn't afford to make mistakes. They were like him, all about the details. Details saved lives. Mistakes cost them—the dead man in the East Docks was proof of that. He would miss not being part of the team that brought that case to a close, but Monteith's business took precedence.

While he waited for the necessary details from Monteith's people, Hazard asked among his sources in Covent Garden and his comrades on Bow Street regarding any new forging games in town. A good inspector learned quickly that when one's eyes weren't enough, to use the eyes and ears of others. A good inspector, like a good soldier, left nothing to chance and he'd been a very good soldier before he'd been an inspector. But nothing had surfaced since winter and the death of the forger on the East Docks, who now had a name: Peter Timmons, a man who'd died, un-fortunately, with his secrets intact. No doubt a death arranged at the preference of the underworld for just that reason. The men Hazard had delegated the case to were up against another immovable wall. Sometimes one had to learn to live with cases that were never solved.

He could be of no use to them now; word from Monteith had arrived. There was no name, but there was a place. The finder used Seasalter in Kent as his point of contact with smugglers—assuming the finder wasn't also a smuggler himself. Hazard would make no such assumption. It was the first piece of information from Monteith that made sense if one bought into the smuggling premise. Seasalter, isolated among the marshes, was known for two things: oysters and free trading. No. Wait. He willed his mind to slow down. Seasalter was known for something else, too. Something recent.

He searched his mind as he packed, the answer coming as he threw a shirt into the valise. The new art school was there, headed by Viscount St Helier and his wife, the painter, Artemisia Stansfield, daughter of Sir Lesley Stansfield. St Helier was a leading art critic, his father the Earl of Bourne, Britain's leading collector of the English school and the very same man who'd questioned the authenticity of Monteith's painting. That would be a good resource for him, a benefit to his visit. Perhaps St Helier and his wife could be consulted while he was asking around. He would need a friendly connection in Seasalter. Smuggling communities were notoriously closed to strangers. He was honest with himself. This little trip was more akin to a wild goose chase. He was setting off with no name, only a place and multiple loose ends to tie up—with luck—into some semblance of cohesion.

He had spent the long day's journey running his mind through the various scenarios. All that was certain was that Monteith's supplier was in Seasalter. Was the smuggler bringing the forgeries in? Or was the forger already nearby? Or were there multiple forgers from various locations? That would be even more complicated.

He arrived in Seasalter and made his way to the Stansfield farmhouse shortly after four o'clock, his buttocks aching from a day in the saddle over rough roads. He might walk miles in London, but he did not ride in the city—something he missed. Classes were just getting out at the school and groups of girls ranging in age from ten to fifteen mingled in the yard, stretching their legs and enjoying the last of the autumn daylight. The simple joy of the scene tugged at him. If he was a painter, he'd want to paint that, to capture the innocence of their blue skirts and white blouses, their hair in braids and bows, their laughter as they giggled with one another. One of them had a smudge of paint on her chin. He caught snatches of their conversations as he rode past the fish factory-turned-school and up the trail to the farmhouse.

'I hope the *signora* will let the upper class try a Gentileschi to copy next.'

'We are doing a floral still life of Mrs Moser's.'

'I wonder when we'll get to paint a nude.'

Giggles followed. A nugget of inspectorly suspicion started to gnaw at the purity of the moment as he dismounted and made his way to the front door. He knocked, his card at the ready. There'd been no time to write ahead. What if the smuggler *wasn't* importing the pictures? What if there were various artists who were not spread out, but all in one place? What if there was a snake in Eden?

Chapter Three

They were in the farmhouse garden with baby
Michael, taking their usual late-afternoon
break between classes and supper, Michael
suckling hungrily, happily, at Artemisia's
breast when the message came. Mrs Harris, redoubtable housekeeper and formidable
gatekeeper, bustled out, full of purpose. No
one got past her. She guarded the family's
privacy like a dragon with a hoard of gold.
'There's a man here asking to speak with the
Viscount or Lady St Helier.' Displeasure over
the interruption was evident in her tone as she
looked from one sister to another, unsure who
to give the card to. Artemisia had her hands
full with the nursing baby.

Addy reached for the card. 'Inspector Hazard Manning. From London, Artemisia.' She

wrinkled her brow in curiosity. 'Is Darius expecting him, perhaps? I wonder what he wants? Do you know him?'

Artemisia shook her head. 'We can't possibly receive him. I am *busy*.' She switched the baby to her other breast. 'Darius is not home yet and we are not expecting anyone today. Mrs Harris, tell him the Viscount is out and we're not receiving. He should try scheduling an appointment tomorrow with my husband's secretary.'

'No, wait, Mrs Harris. I can see him,' Addy interrupted. She glanced at Artemisia. 'If he's come from London, he'll be tired and, whatever it is he wants, he obviously thinks it can't wait until morning. He's likely come straight here instead of stopping at the Crown.' She smiled. 'Besides, the last time an unannounced visitor showed up at the farmhouse, it was Darius, and see how that turned out.'

Addy rose, taking charge as she smoothed her skirts. She was still dressed in a dark skirt and a white blouse from teaching. 'You stay here with the baby, Artemisia, and go on up for a lie-down when the little dear is done feeding. I'll see to our unexpected guest. Have him put in the front parlour, Mrs Harris. Send one of the maids with a tea tray. He's probably famished. Be prepared to set an extra plate for supper and decant a bottle of that red the Viscount likes just in case.'

Artemisia adjusted the baby and reached out her free hand to take Addy's. 'Thank you, Sister,' she offered fondly. 'I don't know how I would manage these days, these *months*, without you. You've been my rock.'

'As you've been mine for so many years.' Addy squeezed her hand in assurance. 'That's what sisters are for.' It warmed her to see Artemisia happy, settled, after years of disappointments and struggles. The world was not always kind to women who stood up to it. Artemisia had fought bravely and tenaciously. She deserved this.

Artemisia smiled, the gesture softening the striking, often sharp features of her face. 'I forget you're grown up and then it occurs to me all over again that you're twenty-one.' She looked down at the baby who was nursing more slowly now, his little fist nestled against her breast. 'It's hard to believe this one will grow up, too.' She let go of Addy's hand. 'Thank you again for meeting our visitor.'

Addy made her way to the front parlour,

stopping briefly to check her appearance in the small hall mirror; good. No surreptitious paint smudges on a cheek or chin, no errant wisps of hair escaping from her workday chignon. Her nose still sported summer freckles, there was nothing to be done about that, the bane of being a redhead, she supposed. But all in all, she looked respectable enough. She straightened her shoulders and stepped into the parlour. 'Hello, Inspector, I'm Miss Stansfield, how can I be of service?'

The man on the sofa rose immediately upon her entrance. He was much taller than she'd expected and broader. The sheer rugged virility of him was intimidating and surprising. Somehow, she'd imagined an inspector being a smallish, barrel-chested man with beady eyes and a round face after a lifetime spent behind a desk. This man was the exact opposite. They both stood and stared in prolonged silence. Apparently, he was surprised by her as well. Of course. He was expecting Artemisia or Darius, the famous fury of the art world or the Viscount. She must be something of a disappointment by comparison, she usually was.

'Please be seated, Inspector. The Viscount

is not at home and my sister is indisposed.' She took the chair opposite the sofa, hoping she appeared confident. 'I will help any way I can and if that is not sufficient, you can apply to my brother-in-law's secretary for an appointment.' Mrs Harris herself entered on cue with the tea tray, arrayed with culinary delights—ham sandwiches piled amid the lemon cream cakes sent up on Thursdays by Foake's Bakery.

'Shall I pour?' Addy poured a cup for the inspector, meeting his dark eyes. Her brow lifted to enquire on milk or sugar. It was a piercing gaze and she could well imagine a suspect squirming beneath it. It seemed to miss nothing and see everything.

'Neither, thank you.' The inspector took the cup and saucer, the set looking tiny and overly delicate in his big hands. For that matter, the whole room felt small. He filled the space. She could smell the wind on him. He must have ridden the whole way.

'I trust you had a pleasant journey, although no doubt a long one.' Addy tried to make small talk as she sipped her tea, nearly white with milk.

'The weather was fine enough, thank you. I

savour each good day. One never knows how
many of them are left this time of the year.
The students seemed to be enjoying it as well.
I passed them on the way up. They were out in
the courtyard. The school appears to be pros-
pering.' He reached for a lemon cream with
a smile that revealed straight white teeth and
a streak of kindness that offset the intrusive-
ness of his gaze. 'These are delicious.'

'Yes, the bakery in town is quite talented.' Was he probing for information? She
couldn't decide if this was a quiet interrogation or small talk. She tried to divine his purpose. 'As for our students, Lady St Helier has
hand-picked every one. Is that what you've
come about? Do you have a candidate for the
school?' If it was about a prospective student,
Artemisia would want all the details. Perhaps
he had a daughter? Although he seemed too
young to have one of the proper age for Artemisia's school. She judged him to be in his
late twenties. Perhaps a younger sister, then,
although she'd have to be much younger to be
interested in the school.

'No...' He paused, having finished the
lemon cream in a single bite and already
started on a ham sandwich. The appetite

matched the man. There wasn't an ounce of fat on him. His largeness came entirely from his stature and muscle. 'I have come on business. I am hoping the Viscount might be willing to offer me counsel about some art issues that have arisen in London.'

'I'm sure he'd be delighted to offer whatever assistance he can,' although Addy wondered why he hadn't simply sent a letter and saved himself the journey if all he wanted was advice. Perhaps it was merely the urgency of his need that had prompted the trip? He could have his answer faster than a letter could travel. What prompted that urgency? 'Are you staying at the Crown?' Addy struggled to keep the conversation going.

'I am.' He ate another sandwich and drained his teacup. For all his apparent good manners, sipping wasn't in his repertoire.

'In that case, perhaps you'd like to stay to supper with us. Mrs Harris's cooking outshines the Crown's food any day and St Helier will be home to dine.' Maybe he was angling for an invitation to dinner? But what to do with the inspector in the meantime? She'd not thought about how to entertain him and there was easily an hour and a half before supper was served.

'That is very kind, if it's no imposition?' he asked. 'Perhaps I could beg a tour of the school from you in the interim? I read about it in the London papers and I would like to see it for myself.'

Addy leapt up in relief at the solution. 'Let me get a cloak and tell Mrs Harris where we'll be.'

Outdoors helped control the largeness of him. He seemed made for wide open spaces with his long stride. The skirts of his greatcoat swirled about his legs, his dark hair pushed back from his face by the breeze, showed off the strong, long jaw and the firm, square chin. Addy stole more than one glance as they made the short walk to the school. His face was changeable, depending on the angle, she decided. There was a rugged hauteur to it that walked a line between that of a working man and a gentleman, depending on how he was presented. It was probably a useful tool in his line of work, allowing him to blend in as situations demanded.

It was the hair that supplied the ruggedness, she decided. His dark mane hung loose below his collar, out of fashion with the closer cropped styles preferred by London men, but perhaps not so unruly it couldn't be smoothed into compliance when circumstances demanded it. Yet, the wind-blown rugged look suited him. He was no slave to fashion beyond what necessity required. Addy glanced at his boots. Not Hoby, just boots. Durable and decent. Beneath the dirt of travel, they were hardy, quality-made, sporting no holes or rundown heels, comfortable the way an old pair of shoes can be. As was the greatcoat. The inspector dressed as he chose, not as his budget limited. A man of decent means, then. And an honest one. He had not come in disguise, but as himself. *Not like Bennett*, came the errant thought. Bennett dressed expensively, excessively, quite often beyond what circumstances required.

They came to a rough patch in the foot trail and he offered her his hand. 'Allow me to assist, Miss Stansfield. I wouldn't want a turned ankle on my account.' His hand was warm, pleasantly rough where her palm met his. There was reassurance in the roughness, this hand knew how to do its job, knew how to hold on though ropes might chafe and cold might chap. This was a hand that wouldn't let go. It was not like Bennett's hand. This comparison was as unbidden as the first. Why should she compare the two at all? Bennett was pleasure and the inspector was business. The inspector wasn't even here for her. He was here for her brother-in-law. Suddenly those dark eyes were on her, catching her out.

'Well, Miss Stansfield? Do I meet with your approval? Shall you paint me?' The inspector chuckled and Addy blushed. 'I imagine artists look at everyone as if they're potential portrait material. I am afraid I might disappoint in that regard. I'm no great beauty.' Not conventionally, no, but there was beauty in him. An unfinished beauty, perhaps, noted for its rugged intensity instead of its smooth completion that made men like Bennett handsome. Bennett was a golden prince from a fairy tale. No one would mistake Hazard Manning for golden perfection.

'And inspectors? How do they look at the world?' Addy laughed, aware he'd graciously offered her a way out of being caught staring.

'Darkly through a glass, I fear. Occupational hazard.'

'Then your name suits you,' Addy smiled.

'Like a gardener named Gardener or a black-
smith named Smith.' He'd shown her polite-
ness today when she'd been gauche in her
staring and there had been kindness earlier
in his smile.

'Merely a coincidence, I assure you.' He
held the door of the school open for her. The
ruggedness of a labourer, the manners of a
gentlemen, she thought as she passed through.
Despite his appearance and ravenous appetite,
he knew how to call on viscounts and their
sisters-in-law. Perhaps he was one of those
men who existed between worlds. She often
thought Bennett must be such a man.

Hazard was on his best behaviour, every
instinct honed as he listened to Miss Stansfield tour him through the school. If there was
a snake in Eden it would be here, among all
the innocent Eves he'd seen standing in the
courtyard. The girls had moved indoors since
then. He could hear them laughing and talking
upstairs in the dormitory rooms in anticipation of the dinner hour. What a delightful atmosphere St Helier and his wife had created
here. It was difficult to imagine crime lurking
in its midst. He didn't want to picture it. But

he must. That was the first rule of investigation. No one and nothing could be above suspicion until logic proved otherwise. His was a dark world indeed so that others could live among the light.

Miss Stansfield preceded him into one of the downstairs classrooms, brushing past him with the scent of summer on her hair. He tried to ignore it and concentrate on the space. What clues might he find here? Any trace of the old fish factory the place had once been was entirely erased. The classrooms were outfitted with windows and light, easels and all the equipment for artists at work. The warm cream walls were lined with canvases depicting well-known scenes and popular works of the masters. 'Your students are talented,' Hazard complimented, studying the paintings while his gut tightened.

He rather wished the paintings had been of silly fruit baskets and flower vases like most young girls painted, or that the work was poorly done, but this work was skilfully executed. Artemisia Stansfield—Lady St Helier, he amended mentally—had chosen her students well. The excellence only made his scenario more plausible, assuming a young lady could be turned to such a cause. Forgery would not be undertaken lightly. Honour was no small thing, nor was fear of Lady St Helier.

He'd never met the notorious—or renowned, depending on whom one asked—Artemisia Stansfield. In either case, her reputation preceded her; a woman who'd challenged the establishment, who had uttered the word 'penis' in front of the entire assembly at the Royal Academy, would instil proper obedience in her students. She would not be easily crossed or duped. If there was something unseemly going on in her academy, she'd know about it and put a stop to it. Surely, Lord St Helier was of similar mettle. Such a scandal would bring their school down and their hard-won reputations with it. That was reassuring. They would not be tolerant of deviance. They would grab a snake by the neck and strangle it to death. Hazard's gut eased. It would not be easy for a snake to get into this unusual Eden.

'Do you teach as well, Miss Stansfield?' He knew that Sir Lesley Stansfield had two daughters, but it was an easy fact to forget in the wake of the elder's overpowering history.

'Yes, I instruct the younger girls in the

first class.' She swept past, leading him into a second classroom. 'These are my students'. I teach them art history and basic technique.'

He moved about the room, studying the books on the shelves. Vasari's *Lives of the Artists*, da Vinci, Michelangelo. All old friends from his Oxford days. He knew these texts, had spent evenings poring over them. 'Very impressive.'

'Thank you, I feel it's important that the girls understand *why* they paint. We don't teach technique for no apparent reason. Painting is about replicating and refining the skills of the masters.'

He could feel her passion for the topic and his heart thrilled to it. Here was someone who thought as he did, who appreciated the study of nuance and history.

Sweet was a word that came to mind when looking at Miss Stansfield. That sweetness transformed plain features—turning mere green eyes to a sparkling mint; a wide mouth to a generous smile; a freckled nose into a reminder of summer. She was an invitation to warmth, to empathy. There was a lushness a man would associate with home and hearth. It was not to be confused with a lushness of the body. Miss Stansfield was not curvy or broad-hipped. The lushness was in the comfort she exuded. Here was someone who was an instinctive nurturer. The allure of such instinctive goodness was potent. She would care for her students, she would know them uniquely. He found such warmth compelling. It was not a quality that peopled his world.

Hazard turned from her to take in the view of the courtyard through the window and to get himself together. He'd been without certain comforts for too long, too many nights doing Monteith's bidding or Bow Street's instead of his own. Seasalter could be no exception. He was here on business and a dalliance had no place on his schedule. Besides, Miss Stansfield was the sister-in-law of a viscount, daughter of a knight of the realm, a gentlewoman by law if not by birth. He closed his eyes, willing the image away. She was not a candidate for a dalliance and he could not be a candidate for anything else. He brought danger with him wherever he went. For that reason, he did not invite people beyond the periphery of his life.

She was standing behind him, all vanilla, French lavender and an undernote of turpentine. 'We should go before the girls come down for the evening meal. Mrs Harris will have ours on the table soon.'

'Yes, thank you for bringing me. I would like to come back and see the girls paint while I'm here, if that would not distract them unduly.' It would be a chance to see if anyone had skill enough, inclination enough, to test the waters of forgery. One of the older girls, perhaps. It was entirely possible whoever it was, whether that person be here at the school or elsewhere, was oblivious to what they were doing, that a crime was being perpetrated on them as well. That was a far preferable and more likely scenario—the unwitting accomplice.

If there was a forger who was deliberately hoodwinking the likes of Monteith, the forger would pay. If there was an 'agent' manipulating innocent girls, stealing their work and misrepresenting it, that agent would pay for both ends of his crime. It sat poorly with him as they started their walk back to the farmhouse that some scoundrel would take advantage of innocent girls, if that was indeed what was happening. In truth, he didn't know. The girls and the school might not be involved at all. He was aware he was spinning that scenario out of whole cloth. None the less, it had raised his protective nature. Justice would be done on his watch.

Dusk had settled and a golden autumn moon hung low on the horizon, ready to begin its ascent. He breathed deeply of the crisp air tinged with the brine of the marshes and fish. No soot. This air was unpolluted. A marshbird gave its night call. On the surface, Seasalter was peaceful. Too bad something corrupt likely lay underneath, hidden somewhere amid the calm. He *would* find it. He almost wished he didn't have to disturb that placid exterior. Almost. But right was always worth the disruption.

Chapter Four

Hazard's presence at the school the next morning was only a small disruption, generating the kind of excitement any man might at an all-girls' institution, no matter how unobtrusive he tried to be. He stood in the hall outside Miss Stansfield's classroom, his body angled away from the door so that he could watch her without being seen himself. She looked much as she had the day before, her hair neatly coiled, the lacy stock tied at her neck, as she delivered a lecture on Renaissance painting, her students eager with attention. He was, too, for that matter. She knew her subject well and presented it with impeccable clarity so that even the most novice of students understood the concepts.

'The Renaissance breathes fresh life into

painting by revisiting the presentation of the three-dimensional in a flat medium…'

She was clearly in her element, her face alive with her passion for the subject and her joy in sharing it. How lucky she was to have a job that suited her so ideally.

Her voice carried easily into the hall. 'The exploration of perspective is in itself an exploration that relied on the rebirth not only of an interest in painting, but in other fields as well such as science and mathematics.'

A hand shot up. 'Miss Stansfield, why is that? I like to paint, but I don't like mathematics. I don't see what the two have to do with each other,' a girl at the front asked as the class laughed and Miss Stansfield smiled at her honesty.

'That's a good question, Mary.' She was all calm affirmation as she responded to the girl's question. 'Mathematics provided artists with an understanding of geometric lines that led to the establishment of the vanishing point. From there, painters could begin to create the illusion of depth. Does anyone remember from the reading the two Italians credited with this development? Maggie, do you know?'

'Alberti and Brunelleschi?' came the tentative answer.

'Very good, Maggie,' she praised. 'To be fair, they weren't the first to experiment with it. As early as drawings on cave walls, humans have tried to depict spatial reality. That's a great place for us to end today. We can discuss this further on Monday. Class dismissed.'

The girls poured out into the hall, eyes wide at the sight of him. Hazard stepped cautiously to the side to avoid being trampled. He waited until they'd dispersed before stepping into the room and standing quietly at the back while Miss Stansfield cleaned up, erasing the chalkboard and wiping her hands on a rag.

'The girls are in high spirits today,' he offered as small talk.

'You must forgive them,' Miss Stansfield apologised. 'It's like that on Friday. It's a half-day. The girls have the afternoon off. It's something new we started this year. They'll go to the village and spend their coins at the bakery and perhaps sketch at the shore on their own. We find it's been a good exercise for them, a chance for them to discover their own sources of inspiration.' She set the rag down. 'Speaking of inspiration, I believe you've come to see our students' artwork.'

She led him through the upper-level classrooms, giving him a chance to study the paintings on display as the girls filed in for the last class of the day. Hazard finished his perusal just in time and stepped out into the corridor as Artemisia entered, calling her class to order.

'Is this all of the girls' work?' he asked, careful to keep his voice low until he and Miss Stansfield were out of doors. He held the door open for her, treating himself to a surreptitious whiff of vanilla and lavender as she passed. His eyes noted all the details of her: the auburn hair smoothly contained in a chignon at her neck, the small gold earbobs, the delicate detail of lace trim on her stock. At a distance or close up, Miss Adelaide Stansfield was the personification of a respectable woman in every way, from her scent to her clothes, to her polite manners. For a man who spent his days tracking down the worst of humanity in the worst of places, such sweetness, such goodness, was most certainly refreshing, bordering on outright intoxicating to a man who lived beyond the light.

'Yes.' The simple answer eased him. He'd not realised how tightly strung he'd been this morning as he'd looked at the paintings, hoping against hope not to find what he was looking for. He'd been hosted at St Helier's table last night, welcomed as a valued guest despite the unexpected nature of his arrival. He'd found St Helier and his wife to be excellent company, despite their titles, and Miss Stansfield as well. They were intelligent and well spoken. He'd enjoyed discussing art with them. He did not relish the idea of exposing a dirty secret at their school. It would be a poor way to repay their hospitality.

Beside him, Miss Stansfield gave an honest laugh. 'Is that disappointment or relief I see on your face?' He could tell from her tone she wasn't sure what to make of his expression.

'Relief,' he confessed. There was no harm in being honest with her. He'd shared his purpose in being in Seasalter with all of them over supper last night. Although he had not divulged specifics about the forged painting. He was here to catch a criminal. 'While your pupils are skilful, none of them have achieved the expertise needed to be a successful forger.'

'They are too young,' Miss Stansfield re-

plied, unbothered by the potential implication
that one of her pupils might have been guilty.
'Technique cannot substitute for passion and
experience. These girls do not have the latter yet.' She gave a slight shrug. 'They may
never have it. They lead conventional lives,
they come from conventional families despite
some of the families' artistic bents. Perhaps
this is why serious art is considered the do-
main of men. How can a proper young woman
have virtue and experience? But a man may
live less carefully and have both.'

He sensed she included herself in that conundrum of ineligibility. He did not know her
well enough to presume further enquiry. But
he knew enough to know the remark was self-
reflection as much as it was a reflection on
her students. It was the first glimpse he had
into the mind of Adelaide Stansfield. Such a
thought hinted at covert rebellions and secret
disappointments. Perhaps she was not so different from her outrageous sister who wore
her disappointment in the world of men as an
outer armour. Miss Stansfield's disappointment was more circumspect, but no less potent for its discretion.

'So, Inspector, your forger is not among our

ranks. You will have to broaden your search.'
Miss Stansfield smiled, her generous mouth
turning up at the corners, her mint-green eyes
friendly. He could see she'd not really thought
the forger would be here. It had never been
a consideration for her. But she wasn't an inspector. She did not live in a world where no
one was above suspicion.

As ludicrous as it might have seemed to
her, he was required to consider it. It fell to
him to hunt out connections anywhere, even
when they seemed preposterous. The world
was one wide web. His job was to follow the
threads and see where they went. He didn't
necessarily like where they led even with one
theory dispelled. If Miss Stansfield dismissed
the students so easily, was it because she knew
better than to suspect them for reasons other
than their lack of experience? Because if it
wasn't one of the students, it forced him to
consider the other artists in Seasalter. That
left Miss Stansfield and her sister. It made all
the soft comfort of Miss Stansfield suddenly
and more prominently suspect.

'Where do you look next?' Miss Stansfield
enquired.

'Smugglers' rings, the underbelly of Seasalter. Someone here knows something.' *I look at you, at your sister.* He didn't dare utter such words out loud. Not only because he didn't want to startle her and send her running for cover if she were guilty, but because he simply didn't want to know. Not yet. Not until he had some hint that such conjecture was well founded.

'Smuggling rings?' She gave a small laugh. 'Easier said than done. You will be here a while unless you have help. Smuggler communities are not accessible to outsiders,' Miss Stansfield warned.

He lifted a shoulder. 'Unless one has the right sort of introduction.' Through an open window, he could hear the noises of classes dismissing. Papers shuffling, the scuffles of students rising from tables and desks. 'Your students will head to the village. Perhaps you would like to follow them down and give this newcomer a tour?' He hoped she would say yes despite the boldness of his request. The sun was out again for a second day and autumn was at its best, warm enough even for a picnic. But perhaps she had papers to mark or lessons to plan?

Smugglers to warn...forgeries to paint.

If she was hiding something, she might easily refuse the invitation. On the other hand, the invitation was impromptu and, guilty or not, his request might be nothing more than a legitimate imposition. She'd already spent the morning with him. But hope flickered. Maybe, like him, she sensed the easy affinity between them and was loath to part because she liked him, because she had nothing to hide. Those were soft thoughts in a hard world. He didn't allow himself many of those. Too many soft thoughts had the potential to obscure one's judgement. He needed to remember the reason he'd invited her at all; more time with her was more time to ascertain the truth of her. This visit to the bakery was all business. Right.

'I would be delighted, Mr Manning.' She smiled and his spirits lifted even as his conscience warned he could not use her acceptance as a litmus test of her innocence.

'Call me Hazard, please, if you think it would be all right to dispense with such formality so far from London since it appears I will be here a while,' he suggested politely.

Green eyes lit with honest mischief. 'Then you must call me Addy—for the duration.'

* * *

She hoped he wasn't disappointed in the short tour. Seasalter was a rather dismal excuse for a village. There was no 'high street' with shops. There were only the huts of the fishermen, a few farmhouses like theirs, the Crown and Foake's Bakery with the town's one big glass window in which carefully designed baked goods or loaves of freshly baked bread were displayed. Up on the knoll, the steeple of St. Alphege Church rose. 'The Foakes have one of the only ovens in town besides our farmhouse and the inn,' Addy explained. 'They bake their own bread, but also the bread of others. Wives drop off unbaked dough in the morning and pick up baked bread in the afternoon.'

'Fish and loaves,' Hazard chuckled as they closed in on the bakery.

'Yes, quite literally true. Fish, oysters and bread are the usual diet around here. Anything else we need, we hope Whitstable or Faversham can provide it, although they're not much larger. Of course, our farmhouse and the school have the benefit of London. Darius sees that we are not isolated from luxury. If we want something, we send to London for it. We simply need to wait for it. Darius has a wagon come from town once a month,' she admitted.

'Or use the smugglers?' he queried. 'I imagine everyone does.'

'We only use them for wine. We buy it from the Crown, but it's no secret where the Crown gets it from,' she freely admitted. 'That red from last night, for instance.' She clapped a hand over her mouth. 'Oh! I shouldn't say things like that to you, I suppose.'

He laughed. 'I am no excise man. Your red wine is safe from me,' he assured her as the metal bell over the bakery door tinkled.

Inside, the little bakery was already crowded with girls. 'I should have warned you, Friday is ginger cookie day. It's one of the baker's daughter's specialities.

'Addy, it's good to see you! Are you here for the usual?' A buxom, curvy blonde, sporting golden curls beneath a white cap and a six-months-pregnant belly beneath an even whiter apron greeted them with a bright smile.

'Hazard, this is Elianora Gann, the baker's daughter.' Addy made the introductions. 'Elianora, this is...' She hesitated for a moment. Would he want to be introduced as an inspector? That might make his job even harder. 'Mr Hazard Manning,' she improvised. 'He's come to consult on some art matters with my brother-in-law.' She did not miss the enquiring glance Elianora tossed her way, or the womanly approval in her friend's gaze, despite her marriage to handsome Simon Gann and her pregnancy.

Hazard made Elianora a small, charming bow, exhibiting more of his manners. 'You must be the one responsible for the lemon creams I enjoyed yesterday. They were delicious, the best I can recall.' Elianora blushed at the compliment and hurried behind the counter to retrieve Addy's box.

'I'm impressed you remembered,' Addy remarked quietly. Although that wasn't quite the right word, was it? He hadn't remembered, he'd *connected* two facts. She'd only mentioned the bakery yesterday over the tea tray. She'd not said a thing about Elianora.

'Part of the job. I notice everything—what is seen as well as what is said.' Elianora returned and he took the white baker's box from her and held the door open on their way out. He was far more successful in pretending he was oblivious to stares of villagers and the students than she was. Addy was keenly aware of the girls' glances as Hazard passed, and the villagers' slightly more circumspect looks. New people in such a small, isolated place could not help but be noticed. New people who were large males had no hope of being undetected.

'I'm not looking to hide,' Hazard said when she offered an apology for all the open scrutiny. 'I want them to know me, become easy with me.' He held up the bakery box with a smile. 'What's in here?'

'Perhaps you should guess, if you're so good at solving mysteries,' Addy teased. Joking and laughter came easy with him. They spoke well together. Beyond the initial awkwardness of their first meeting, there were no uncomfortable lapses in conversation, no need for stiff formality, no sense of being caught off-kilter as she so often was by Bennett, uncertain of where she stood with him, or even where she *wanted* to stand.

He slanted her an arched look, managing to look offended. 'Very well, I will guess.' He took a long sniff. 'Ginger biscuits definitely. Fresh baked, probably still warm.'

'Yes. What else?' Addy prompted.

'Chocolate. I can smell the chocolate.' He passed her the box. 'I must conclude, Miss Stansfield,' he said with mock formality, 'you have a sweet tooth.'

'Guilty, Mr Manning.' Addy laughed. 'Shall we walk down to the beach and open the box?'

'Let's go one step better and stop in at the Crown for a lunch basket to take with us.'

Addy might have read more into the offer if she hadn't seen him demolish the tea tray yesterday and then polish off a full supper a few hours later. The man had a voracious appetite. He would not be satisfied with a few sweets.

Besides, what was there to read into? The inspector was an interesting man with good manners, but that was all. He was here on business. He'd not come courting and she was with Bennett, she supposed. Bennett had left again on his own business in September, part of which had been to see about framing her copy of the assumed minor Perugino copy he'd brought her. She'd finished it just before he left. She was uncertain when he'd return and she was even less certain anything had been resolved between them. The latter was mostly her fault. She'd not been keen to commit to anything just yet. Bennett had been upset.

The beach was deserted today, although one could see the fishermen out beyond the estuary that looked across to the Isle of Sheppey. There was marshland that ran all the way to the sea. They busied themselves picking out a spot from where they could watch the marsh life, laying out a blanket and the food. They settled on the blanket, the close proximity serving as a reminder of his largeness, although it was less intimidating today than it had been yesterday.

'Have you always been an artist?' he asked, carving the joint of cold chicken the Crown had found for him. No fish and loaves today.

Addy pushed back a loose strand of hair and took the plate he'd prepared for her: cheese, bread, chicken and half an apple sliced into slivers of equal size. Hazard Manning was a precise man. 'Yes, always. I learned to paint as soon as I could hold a brush.' It had been a foregone conclusion.

Hazard took his own plate and stretched out, propped up on one elbow to eat. 'Did you ever want to do anything else?'

'Yes. No.' The question flustered her. She

laughed at her own indecisiveness. 'I don't know that anyone has ever asked me that. My family are painters. Artemisia was already winning prizes by the time I was old enough to be taught, my father already had his knighthood and his fame. I think it was assumed by all of us, myself included, that I would paint, too. I didn't question it.' She'd done what she'd been told, what had been expected.

'Do you regret that?' Hazard cut a wedge of cheese for her to replace the one she'd already eaten. 'You enjoy history—perhaps you would have preferred to be an historian?'

'An art historian, yes, that would have been the dream. Art reflects history, it tells civilisation's story.' She smiled ruefully. 'But there is even less room for female art historians than there is for female painters.' Art history wasn't all books and libraries. If it was, she might have stood a chance, might have made some room for herself. But it required travel, ethical acquisition, even Parliamentary debate and negotiating with foreign governments, all of which were male domains.

'Perhaps that will change in the future. By teaching art history to these young women now, I am part of that change. Until then, thankfully, it turns out I'm good at painting even if I lack Artemisia's passion for it. I enjoy it. Painting soothes me.'

'You are happy with the compromise?' The question startled her. It was an even bolder question, yet another thing people had never asked her, or understood her well enough *to* ask. She answered as truthfully as she could.

'I'm happy enough as things are.' She *was* happy as things were. Bennett's offer had got beneath her skin, though, along with his accusations. Temptation whispered louder these days. Just a little adventure would be nice, some of that experience an artist craved to stay fresh. Here she was, twenty-one, still practising for real life, painting copies of another man's genius in Seasalter, a backwater if ever there was one, still trying to perfect her own style, her own uniqueness at a craft she liked, but didn't love, while the thing she loved went by the wayside. When would her own life begin? What did that life look like? What if she never got a chance at it?

She pushed at the thought, hard. It was getting more difficult these days to dislodge those thoughts, to remind herself that her life *had* started and it was a good one, running the school with her sister, staying close to her family, spoiling her little nephew. For heaven's sake, what was wrong with her? She was sitting on a beach, with an attractive man, eating sweets. Her life was *good*—but it wasn't hers, not entirely.

Addy shifted the conversation away from herself and her uncharitable thoughts. 'What about you? Have you always wanted to be an inspector?' She was not the only one who'd compromised. She'd heard him discuss art with Darius at dinner. He was well versed in art history and yet he spent his time solving crimes in London's underbelly.

He considered the question for a moment, his unfinished features thoughtful. 'Like you, want has had very little to do with the trajectory of my life. However, need is a different story, as you well know.' He held her gaze, his eyes dark, steady, full of compassion as if he knew all the little battles one fights with themselves as they go through life. In that moment, Addy felt as if someone had seen into her soul for the first time and understood *her*.

Addy tucked her skirts about her and fixed him with her gaze. 'Then, tell me that story, the one about need.'

Chapter Five

❧᠎᠎❧

A Bow Street interrogation could not have stunned him more than Addy's direct green gaze, demanding he answer out of a spirit of quid pro quo. He'd had her story and now she wanted his. She did not know what she asked for, this proper miss who hid her secret rebellions beneath a starched white blouse and perfectly coiffed hair. 'I imagine an inspector must be a master of all things like an artist,' she prompted, offering him the bakery box, perhaps to sweeten the request. 'But your knowledge last night at dinner goes beyond that. It made me wonder—how is it that you know enough about art to earn an earl's commission? Is that all you do? Hunt down art fraud, or do you have other things you investigate?'

She'd thought about him. It put him on high

alert as both a man and an inspector. Should he allow the man in him to be flattered or would that distract the inspector from what she was really doing—assessing her opponent? Or were both versions too egotistical? Was she simply offering him a place to start, a safe place that could be filled in with facts, objective and unarguable, that might not haunt him tonight when he closed his eyes? Sometimes, he resented the idea that his mind could never truly walk away from his job. Perhaps the question really was as harmless as it appeared. Perhaps, just this once, he could allow himself the luxury of treating it as such.

'I hunt down whatever is required: art, missing jewels, missing children.' *Bodies.* He refrained from mentioning the last. Instead, he gave her a wry grin. 'The wealthy can often be quite careless with things of value.' It was all true and only partially funny. Monteith's niece had gone missing for two days once. Hazard wasn't sure she'd been all that pleased to be found. 'I work for Bow Street, not Monteith exclusively.' If she wanted his measure, he'd just given her fair warning. The mention of Bow Street should strike a healthy dose of fear into a forger's soul. Bow Street didn't hire amateurs, nor did it dabble in crime. A guilty party might take the opportunity to retreat. But Addy offered no sign of guilt with words or actions. She didn't retreat. She pressed forward like a woman intrigued.

'But *why* did you become an inspector?' It was only a mirror of the question he'd asked her, but he felt his walls go up. It got too close to other things. How did he explain his answer without explaining everything? When he said nothing, Addy took a biscuit drizzled with chocolate from the box, considering his answer. 'You're very close-mouthed about yourself.'

He reached for another biscuit, something to distract them both from the conversation, but she pulled the box out of reach. 'No more for you. I see we'll have to do this the hard way.' She smiled mischievously and held up a sweet as a bribe. 'A biscuit for each of your answers, starting now. How did you get connected with the Earl?'

He chuckled despite himself. She was right. If this was an ordinary conversation, he *was* being stingy when she'd been so very open. But he didn't have the luxury of assuming this was an ordinary conversation.

You need to remember the real reason why you are here on the beach with her.

The inspector poked at the man in him, a reminder that he should not like her so much. It made it hard to be objective, to see what might be there. Perhaps that's what she intended.

Regardless, there was no choice for the inspector or the man, he had to play along. 'Well, I had to support myself after the war and I'd served under Monteith's son. He was my commanding officer. Afterwards, he was pleased enough with my service to recommend me to his father and to arrange a position for me with Bow Street.'

'But why an inspector? You might have been anything.' Addy held up a biscuit. 'He might have recommended you for whatever position you chose?' Ah. She hadn't missed that. No one had forced him towards the life of an inspector. That had been his doing.

'I've always been good at puzzles.' He bit into the ginger biscuit. 'Finding things is just another type of puzzle.'

She relinquished the second biscuit with another smile. 'See, that wasn't so hard. So, you were a soldier first. Where did you serve?'

Her smile faded as if she thought better of the question. She handed him the bakery box. As an apology? Had his face given something away? 'I'm sorry. Perhaps I should not ask. War is difficult. I didn't mean to bring up unpleasant memories.'

The immediacy of her empathy touched him. 'It's not all drums and pageantry,' he agreed. Had she known soldiers? It occurred to him that perhaps she might have had a young sweetheart who'd marched away. He stopped his thoughts, wary of the pathos such a thought conjured. Did she want his empathy in return? He would not give her the opportunity to take it. He left his question unasked.

'The war must have interrupted your studies.' Her head was cocked to one side, her eyes intent on him, perhaps trying to gauge his age or perhaps pursuing another angle for taking his measure. 'You would have been at university.' Miss Stansfield was good at puzzling, too. And she was tenacious. He'd not been able to shut her down.

'University assumes my family was a family of some means.' He was enjoying this, matching wits and decoding secrets with her. He should not be, though, not until he decided where she sat on Justice's scales; friend or foe. Even if she landed on the side of friend, there was nothing to be gained beyond the temporary enjoyment of her company. Friend or foe, Addy Stansfield was to be resisted.

'It's not an erroneous assumption,' she argued. 'A man who appreciates art, who has your depth of knowledge, is not likely to have been raised on the streets where there's no time for the finer things. Besides, you might look rugged on the outside, but you have excellent manners.' She held up an éclair stuffed with vanilla cream. 'The vanilla is from Madagascar, another of Elianora's specialties,' she tempted. 'Is your family gentry? Where do they hail from?'

Hazard would rather Addy be less competent at this game. They were getting close to topics he'd rather not discuss, yet he couldn't seem to help himself. He was drawn to her, he wanted to tell her his story. 'The Mannings have an estate in Sussex. It's really more of a farm, giant fields of wheat as far as one can see. My mother keeps an herb garden full of thyme and lavender, and other things, I'm sure. But those are the ones I remember most.' From lazy summers before it had all gone awry. Before he had failed.

'Remember? Do you not see them often?' She handed over the éclair. 'London is not terribly far from Sussex.'

'No, but I'm quite busy in London and it's best not to have them too closely associated with me.' That was the reason he gave himself most often for not visiting. He was on familiar ground here. He knew how to argue this.

Addy's brows knitted. 'Why is that? Is your work dangerous? I suppose I don't see art fraud as peril-fraught.'

'Then think again,' Hazard replied with stern sincerity. 'Before I left London, my team was investigating a body found on the East Docks. Turned out, he was a forger hired by bosses in London's underground. His hand had been smashed before he'd been stabbed.'

Miss Stansfield sucked in her breath at the graphic words, her left hand subtly covering her right out of reflex as it lay in her lap. 'Why kill him, if they'd already wrecked his hand? He would never be able to forge again.'

'He knew too much. Then again, why wreck his hand if he was meant to be dead anyway? That's the more telling question.'

He held her gaze steady. 'Because no one is without danger who puts greed above human life or humanity, whether that be a banker or murderer.'

Addy nodded, giving his words consideration. 'I am corrected then. Your work must be very dark.'

He'd meant to shock her into re-routing the conversation and, perhaps, if needed, into reconsidering her own position. If she was the forger Monteith sought, perhaps he could help her, perhaps he could find a pocket of mercy for her if she came forward.

Why not just tell Monteith you discovered nothing? his conscience pricked. He did not like thinking of Adelaide Stansfield in prison or worse. He could not do that to her.

You wouldn't be doing it to her...she's done it to herself. You've merely discovered it. Don't go soft now just because a pretty girl smiles at you and feeds you biscuits.

'While I am sure your family appreciates your concern for their safety, they must miss you. Tell me about them. How many are there?' Alas, he'd not been successful with his shocking diversion. Addy was relentless with her questions. It might have been better if she'd stuck to questions about his soldier-ing. 'I know about your mother with her herb garden...' she smiled warmly '...how about a brother? A sister?'

'A brother, older.' Rafe, older by two years and far more dashing, far more reckless.

'And your father?' Addy's tongue licked a spot of vanilla cream from her lips. A nascent flame of desire flicked low in his gut. How delectable she looked, sitting here on the beach, a proper lady with her chignon and high collar, and wicked, pink little tongue.

Hazard cleared his throat. 'No, he passed a year after we came home from the war.' *We*. Hazard winced. He'd not meant to give her so much. Perhaps she would not notice. But he was not that lucky.

'Two brothers off to war and both came home. Your family was blessed.' She dropped her eyes, her fingers playing with the fringe of the blanket. 'Many families lost sons, husbands, fathers.' She gave a sad smile.

'Did you lose someone?' he asked his earlier question carefully, aware of what it might reveal—one more way for Addy Stansfield to get beneath his skin.

'No, but we had friends who did. It was an

awful time. My father painted several post-humous portraits for families who lost sons. It was hard, especially when we seemed to prosper while so many around us faltered.'

Hazard nodded, the familiar lump threat-ening in his throat. He knew the feeling, the guilt that came with personal prosperity amid tragedy. How was it that he'd come home whole when his brother had not? When he'd been charged with his brother's protection, with one task only—to see that Rafe came home whole? He had difficulty swallowing the éclair.

He'd failed. He'd brought Rafe home, but not all in one piece. That failure had killed his father, grieved his mother, and left his brother facing pain-filled days. He could not bear to look at his brother, so broken, no longer the brother of his youth and see his failure re-flected back to him so completely. So, Haz-ard stayed away. It was better all around; he reminded his family of too much, as they did him. It was best to stay in a world where he could be of use, where he could offer a mod-icum of protection to others as a means of penance.

'Last one—shall we share it?' Addy held

up the final biscuit, a chocolate drizzle. She snapped it in half before he could decline. 'Take it with my apologies, Hazard. Despite my best efforts, I fear I've stirred ghosts anyway. It was not my intention.'

'Nor was it mine to have them stirred.' He took the biscuit. He'd thought the ghosts were safely locked away; he'd thought as long as he kept them in his sights they couldn't slip out. He'd been wrong. He wasn't usually like this, vulnerable and talkative, the one answering questions instead of asking them. He'd lost control of this interrogation after the first biscuit. Addy had effortlessly created the sense of genuine attention and interest, those green eyes intent on him, conveying the impression that she would have listened to him talk all afternoon.

Now that afternoon was over. The hours had passed in sweets and secrets, the breeze on the beach had grown colder, the sun hung lower in the sky. The bakery box was empty. There was no excuse to linger. If he did linger, he'd have to be honest about his reasons; that he was not ready to relinquish Addy Stansfield's company, to share her with her household, and that reluctance had nothing to do with his investigation.

Addy shivered and got to her feet, perhaps also realising that duty had been discharged. To stay longer would require other acknowledgements. 'Artemisia will be expecting me. I like to watch the baby for her so she can rest before dinner,' she explained. 'But thank you for the picnic.'

'Thank *you* for the baked goods.' He rose, too, and helped her shake out the blanket. He tucked it under one arm and looped the basket over it. His other arm was for Addy. They walked back towards the village and up the trail to the farmhouse, making no particular haste in the early evening light. They said little, but the silence was not uncomfortable. Perhaps, like him, she was busy picking out the best parts of today, going over them in her mind. The man in him tamped down firmly on the inspector, refusing any other interpretation to emerge at present. There'd be time for that later.

If Addy leaned into him a bit more than she had earlier in the day, he could attribute it to the uphill nature of the path, it would not do to attribute it to anything more. He was here on business and then he would be gone, back to London, to protect and to serve others, to continue his penance for those he had failed. He didn't have the right to someone as sweet and kind as Addy Stansfield. It was his job to keep someone like her from danger, not drag her into it. Unless, of course, she was already there. *Was* she capable of creating a forged painting? His gut did not think so. But his mind knew that wasn't proof enough to dismiss her yet.

Artemisia and Darius were in the garden, heads bent over the baby when they returned home, laughing together at something their little cherub had done. 'There you are!' Artemisia beamed at her sister but not before Hazard caught the flash of a question in her eyes as her gaze moved between them. He felt Addy's hand hurriedly slip away from his arm, perhaps suddenly conscious that it had remained there after it ceased to be a useful support. 'A package arrived for you today. It's in the parlour.'

'From Bennett?' Addy's excitement was immediate and it lit her up from the inside, shining in her eyes. Whoever this Bennett was, he meant something to her. Envy speared the man in him, sudden and unlooked for. When it eased, the peace of the afternoon was gone. He felt illogically betrayed; all that interest she'd shown him, all the questions she'd asked, and all the while 'Bennett' lurked in the wings. Hazard *knew* his reaction was ridiculous. This Bennett, who'd gone unmentioned all afternoon, could be nothing more than a cousin, or a family friend, and yet he didn't like him, or the idea that perhaps Addy had turned those green eyes on him.

'I didn't read the note.' Artemisia had the grace to look ill at ease over her sister's undisguised delight.

Darius intervened with a convivial clap of a hand on Hazard's shoulder. 'Do you have time for a drink before dinner? I want to hear your opinion of our school and perhaps we can talk a little business about your search. I have connections in Whitstable that might be of use.'

'Of course.' Hazard nodded and bowed as if he didn't know that the moment he was out of sight, Addy would race to the parlour, unwrap her gift and forget all about their afternoon on the beach. 'Ladies, if you will excuse me?'

Chapter Six

'He has nice manners.' Artemisia jiggled the baby on her hip while Addy studied the package, square, hard and long, wrapped in a beautiful shawl of printed summer silk, white flowers on a field of blue. Too bad she wouldn't be able to wear it until next year.

'Bennett spoils me,' Addy ran her hand over the fabric, feeling the solidness of the package beneath, trying to discern clues. Hazard would be able to guess, she was sure of it. The man missed nothing. His insights today had been astonishing.

'I didn't mean Bennett.' Artemisia's sharp tone caused her to look up. Of course. She should have known better. Artemisia didn't like Bennett. She never had a compliment for the poor man. 'I meant the inspector.'

'He does have nice manners.' Addy smiled,

remembering the little kindnesses that had peppered the afternoon. 'His family is gentry from Sussex.' Her attention strayed back to the package. It was too long to be a conventional book, but not too long to be an unconventional book like an atlas. 'Our inspector is a soldier and a gentleman.'

'*Our* inspector? Seems more like *your* inspector. You've learned more about him in one afternoon than you've learned after a year of acquaintance with Bennett.' Artemisia sat down in a chair and began to nurse. 'The inspector only had eyes for you. I trust your picnic was successful, at least right up to the point you squashed his pride with the mention of Bennett.'

'It was—who told you?' Addy laughed.

'Elianora. I took the baby down to the bakery after his nap.' Artemisia gave a wicked smile. 'Elianora thought the inspector was handsome. I think so, too, in a rugged way. Do you?' The probe wasn't even subtle.

'I don't know,' Addy stammered. 'I was merely being a good hostess and showing him around. Besides, Bennett and I have an understanding.'

Artemisia grimaced in disbelief and distaste. 'Bennett has an understanding in every port and village he frequents, Addy. He's the sort who will say and do whatever is necessary to get what he wants. Have you considered why he's hung about so long, getting so little in return despite lavishing you with expensive gifts? Where does he get the money for such things? What is he investing in here? With you?'

'Yes, of course,' Addy retorted. Hadn't she asked herself the same question? Under Artemisia's stare, the rest of it came out. 'Before he left, he spoke of wanting more, of moving our relationship forward.'

'Forward? Where might that be?' Artemisia spared her no mercy.

'Florence,' Addy shot back, irritated at Artemisia's questioning. 'He thinks I should strike out on my own.' There was an edge to her tone, Bennett's words finding purchase. Perhaps Artemisia did want to keep her tethered.

Artemisia held her gaze, unflinching, for a long studying moment. 'Is that how it is? He wishes to separate us, or at the least to separate you from your family. Why would he want to do that?'

'He says I have real talent.' Addy stood her ground.

Michael fussed at the raised voice and Artemisia softened her tone. 'You do have real talent, Addy, not that I expect Bennett Galbraith to know it. I suppose Florence is a tempting offer. If you want to go, you should go on your own, without him. Go as your own woman. You don't need a man, or is that part of the allure of Florence?' her sister divined. 'To go gallivanting around Europe with Bennett? How far have things gone with him?'

Addy blushed hotly. Artemisia's own experiences with men prior to marriage had left her fiercely protective of her little sister. 'Only a kiss, Artemisia. Truly, you know we've only been friends.'

Artemisia's dark brow arched. 'Bennett Galbraith doesn't know how to be "only friends" with a woman. Such nuance escapes him, like summer silk shawls in October. You can do so much better than Bennett Galbraith. Trust me on this. I know a cad when I see one.'

Addy felt compelled to defend Bennett yet again. 'He's not like that, he's more than you give him credit for. You don't know him the way I do. I might not be worldly like you, but you have to trust my judgement.'

'He's no gentleman, he's not born to it.' Artemisia looked as if she had more she'd like to say. She seemed to weigh her options and then settled for, 'I just don't want to see you hurt.' She smiled and moved the conversation on. 'I don't want to ruin your package either. It's a handsome shawl, what's beneath it?'

Unwrapping the shawl from around the package, Addy draped it around her shoulders, feeling pretty in the soft silk, even if it was out of season. 'He's sent me a book, it's a copy of Vasari's *Lives of the Artists*.' Her breath caught as she opened the cover. 'Oh, Artemisia, it's splendid, with colour illustrations, and look at the gold tooling on the spine and the bonded leather.' It must have cost a fortune. Artemisia's doubts rang in her head. Where did he get the money? It was large and colourful, a piece of art all on its own. It was the sort of book one set on a bookstand in pride of place in a grand library. It was far too fine for the farmhouse. But that was Bennett: ostentatious and over the top.

She turned the page, something catching

her eye, a loose page. No, not a loose page, but something inserted between the pages. She studied it—another Perugino to go with the canvas he'd brought her. *Madonna and Child*, one of his smaller works, fifteen by twenty, the dimensions of the book. A note was stuck deep in the crack between page and spine. Addy smiled to herself as she read it.

> *Addy-Sweet,*
> *This reminded me of you and your self-less nature. I would love you to paint it. I will look forward to seeing it when I return, but not as much as I look forward to seeing you...soon.*
> *Best,*
> *B.G.*

Addy closed the book, wanting to cherish the note without Artemisia's interference. She waited for a sense of warmth, of satisfaction to overtake her. It did not come. Perhaps she should blame Artemisia for that, for tarnishing her gift. Or perhaps it had something to do with the dark-eyed man who had held her attention all day on a simple picnic blanket without needing to spoil her with gifts.

* * *

Hazard hated the book, everything about it from the gold lettering to the expensive binding, to its sheer size and elegance—all of it screamed it was a princely book, a present not given lightly, and it was not an appropriate gift for a suitor to give. Perhaps that should be encouraging. Perhaps it meant the unknown Bennett was not a suitor. He studied the displayed page where the book lay open on the reading stand in the parlour: da Vinci's *Vitruvian Man*. The page next to it contained a biography of the artist.

He read through it as he waited for Addy. On Darius's suggestion, she'd offered to introduce him to the innkeeper at Whitstable for a brief interview concerning the possibility of a lead on the forger or an agent. He wasn't sure how effective the interview would be, but it was better than what he could get on his own. On his own, the connection was non-existent. He had no way to meet the innkeeper, who would surely turn away a stranger asking questions. Through the Viscount, there was at least a tenuous link. He worked through the connection mentally to exercise his brain. St Helier was friends with

Owen Gann, Seasalter's leading citizen, who was the one who knew the innkeeper.

As he'd said, a tenuous connection, but he needed to make headway on the trail. He had to have something to report back to Monteith. He could hear Monteith laughing when he told him his two prime suspects were Lady St Helier and her sister. Even that much wasn't true. Lady St Helier had no motivation to engage in illegality. She had a title, a doting husband, a child, wealth, a school, her own art which was widely recognised, even if controversial. There was no reason she'd risk forging. What it meant was that he had one suspect, Adelaide Stansfield, and that was only primarily because she was the only other artist in the area that he knew of. Guilt by process of elimination. And yet, nothing she'd done supported a case for that guilt.

What motives did she have? This was the conversation he'd held with himself alone at the Crown the last two nights, feeling it was better to distance himself from the farmhouse for the time being. She had talent and some recognition, although nothing as great as her sister's or father's. She had money through her family. She had her work. For all outward purposes, Addy Stansfield was a happy woman. But not entirely happy. He knew better.

He'd heard the wistfulness in her voice when she'd talked of her students lacking experiences to fire their passions. He'd listened when she'd talked of familial expectations. There'd been no room to be anything else but a painter in the Stansfield family.

He turned the page. Another da Vinci drawing, the ink bright and lines clear, cleanly reproduced. There was no denying the fineness of the book despite his dislike of it. He knew very well what roused his distaste about the book was the giver and all the book might stand for—that someone might have a claim to Addy's heart. It certainly seemed a possibility based on the reaction she'd had. Her face had lit up and she'd looked happy, excited. Perhaps this Bennett had understood her passion for art history as no one inside the family had.

What other passions did she keep hidden? Did she want to step out of the family shadow? Would that be enough to motivate her to forge a painting? Would forging be a kind of secret rebellion? There was no denying she had them—secret rebellions. He'd noted it from the start about her. Perhaps forging would be a cry for attention, for recognition as an individual. Yet, he didn't sense in Addy the kind of twisted cry for help that would prompt such an action. Still, people were always surprising.

There were footsteps behind him. 'I'm ready, sorry to keep you waiting. A student needed some extra help.' Addy arrived, breathless from rushing.

He turned, the book forgotten. 'I am in no hurry. No apology is necessary.' He smiled at the sight of her, pink-cheeked from exertion and autumn air, dressed in her dark skirt and white blouse. Perhaps he wasn't the one who should be jealous. Whoever Bennett was, he wasn't here. He didn't get to see Addy, flushed from hurrying up the path from the school. He didn't get to spend an afternoon driving her into Whitstable or eating bakery treats with her on a beach.

Of course, jealousy was an inappropriate response, he reminded himself as he helped Addy up to the gig's bench seat. Jealousy implied having a certain claim, *wanting* a certain claim. Jealousy, like the lady herself, should be resisted at all costs. He clucked to the gelding, one of St Helier's carriage horses, and set off. Better to concentrate on driving than on whether or not he wanted a claim to Addy Stansfield. He was here on business. She might even *be* his business, although he hoped not. Even if he were free of that complication, his stay was short. He ran through the list of usual excuses: he lived in London, his work was in London. There was no place for a dalliance. He had his code, after all: his work was too dangerous to bring others into it, for himself and for them. He did not want innocent people in peril because of association with him and he certainly didn't want to be in a position where he had to choose between those he loved and his professional integrity.

Talk about putting the horse before the cart. He touched the whip to the horse's flanks, pushing the thought away. Love after three days? To a girl he hardly knew just because another man had sent her a book? 'Were you able to help your student?' He took refuge in small talk.

'Yes,' she offered brightly, reaching up a hand to steady the hat on her head. 'She just needed clarification on some Renaissance masters.'

* * *

She had chatted away as the horse ate up the short miles to Whitstable. 'Oh, dear, we're here already and you haven't had a chance to say anything at all. I've talked too much,' Addy apologised with a laugh as Whitstable came into view. Too soon for Hazard's taste, he could have driven for miles if it meant listening to her talk. He found her conversation intelligent and natural. There was no dissembling, no fishing for compliments, unlike the few London ladies of his acquaintance. Addy was entirely their juxtaposition.

'I like to hear what you have to say. You're a natural teacher, I think, intelligent and caring combined into one. I had a tutor like that once. He was the one that recognised my love of puzzles and he made use of that in his lesson. I think that was the beginning of my own love of learning. Latin conjugations on their own aren't terribly exciting to an eight-year-old boy, but when they're presented as a mystery, a pattern to decode, now that's interesting.' He chuckled. 'You care for your students, you unfailingly put them first.' He pulled the gig into the inn yard and hopped out, coming around to help her down. How easily his hands fit at her waist, as if they were meant to be there. In truth, he liked it a bit too much.

She gave him a smug smile. 'Don't think you're off the hook, Hazard. I might have talked all the way out, but I'll be expecting you to talk on the way back. I have questions and I will have my answers.' He wondered what other questions she might have for him.

Hopefully he would have answers, too, not about Addy, but about the agent or the forger, he wasn't picky. Whatever the inn-keeper could supply he would settle for as a starting point. He could build a trail out of a single piece of evidence.

The inn at Whitstable was unremarkable, made from a combination of brick and wood, weathered grey, but Hazard knew from ex-perience that appearances were no determi-nant of the flow of information a place saw. Inside was dark with the exception of the fire in the hearth. They'd caught the proprietor between lunch and dinner and the place was mostly empty. Good. If the innkeeper knew anything, he'd feel more secure offering in-formation with no one around to witness the meeting.

Addy made introductions and the inn-keeper led them to the inn's private parlour. Hazard got straight to the point. In his experience, innkeepers were busy people and didn't have time for small talk even when their inns were empty. If the innkeeper did have anything to say, he wouldn't want to be seen saying it to an inspector. 'I am looking for someone who sold a piece of artwork they claimed to have got from a French noble. The painting came ashore in this area before making its way to London. I have questions for the seller.' He watched the innkeeper carefully for signs that he might feel uncomfortable answering in front of Addy. Perhaps he would look to her for guidance if she was part of this, but the man's eyes remained on him, thoughtful, his brow furrowing as he struggled to remember.

The innkeeper shook his head. 'I don't recall hearing any talk about any artwork or any Frenchman.' His distaste for the recent war was evident in his tone. He leaned forward confidentially. 'Look, Inspector, let me make this easy for you. Our boys in these parts are about spirits *if* they're engaged in free trade,' he added, not wanting to give too much away. 'A piece of artwork is too specific for our boys to deal with.' Hazard understood what he meant. Spirits were easily sold, there was a mass market for them. A piece of artwork would take too much effort to find a buyer for and produce little profit by comparison. A second sale would be unlikely.

They talked a little while longer, Hazard reframing his question a couple different ways, but the innkeeper had nothing to offer. The interview took twenty minutes at most. Hazard bought two fish pasties on the way out and handed one to Addy. 'It occurred to me that you didn't have time for lunch,' he offered. 'Shall we walk a bit before going back?'

'A walking lunch sounds delightful. We've been lucky, the weather has been exceptional lately. I don't recall an autumn with so many nice days in a row. The fishermen like it, too.' Addy took his arm. The beach was part shingle and part sand, making the way uneven as they ate their pasties, she nibbling, trying not to make a mess of the juicy fish, and he wolfing his down in two bites. She paused and took a bite, a droplet of juice lingering on her bottom lip. He wanted to lick it. 'I'm sorry the visit wasn't more insightful,' Addy said once they'd finished eating.

He shrugged. 'Disappointing in some ways, but not in others.' It did help mitigate—*but only mitigate*—the need to include Addy in his suspicions. She'd given no sign of being concerned over this interview, nor had the innkeeper seemed worried about dealing with her presence. 'The interview helped me confirm that I should focus my efforts exclusively on Seasalter and that there is likely no Frenchman.' In his line of work, no visit was ever entirely unsuccessful in his experience. The presence of nothing was often evidence of *something*, even if that something was a redirection. He'd hoped to learn something that would help him cast his attentions away from Addy instead of leading them back. Ideally, he'd hoped the Frenchman would resurface in some way, that someone had heard of him. Without the Frenchman, he was left focusing on who in Seasalter might have been the contact or the forger. And that, unfortunately, meant he couldn't erase suspicions of Addy yet.

'I never thought of it that way. I suppose that's the puzzle solver's gift, to be able to arrange and rearrange the pieces for new perspectives.' She cocked her head and looked at him from beneath the brim of her hat. 'Tell me more about that tutor of yours, the one who made you puzzles.'

It was a safe request. He found himself regaling her with stories not just about his favourite tutor, but about his childhood, running the rolling hills with his brother, flying kites, fishing, climbing trees. Summers at the seaside. 'We have smugglers, too,' he added in jest as they came to the end of the shingle beach. He looked back, surprised to see how far they'd come. He wasn't sure he meant that only literally. 'You've got me talking about myself, again. It's a rare feat although you've managed it twice now.' *On purpose?* He hoped not. Despite the warnings he'd repeatedly given himself, he could no longer deny that he was attracted to her. The warnings seemed to have no effect on his desire to act on that attraction. He liked her, plain and simple. It had been a long time since he'd genuinely liked a woman. The fish pasties were long gone and the blue sky was turning grey overhead, threatening rain, signs that they ought to turn back. He didn't want to.

'You and your brother sound very close. Rafe. He has a name.' Addy smiled. 'He didn't the other day.'

'We were close.' He picked up a handful of pebbles and spread them out in his palm, picking through them, looking for a smooth round one.

'Were? Are you not close now, other than the distance between London and Sussex?' Addy wrinkled her brow, trying to assimilate the pieces of the puzzle he'd given her. He knew what she was remembering. He'd told her he and his brother had gone to war together. She'd be remembering, too, that he'd been reluctant to discuss it. Despite her apology earlier for having brought it up, would she risk bringing it up again? He hoped not.

'My brother and I are not as close as we once were.' Hazard would give her that much at least. 'He served in the field during the war while I spent my time cracking ciphers for Monteith's son and acting as an aide-de-camp.' He selected a pebble and cocked his wrist to send it skipping across the little waves.

'Ciphers, a perfect calling for one with your skill. I'm impressed,' Addy mused.

Don't be, he wanted to yell. He'd broken all the codes but one and that made all the difference. To Rafe at least. He was the fastest, most accurate codebreaker on the Peninsula. It hadn't mattered. Just once. One mistake. He threw another pebble with too much force. It sank. Perhaps Addy sensed that she'd made a misstep, not that it was her fault. She reached into his palm and stole a pebble.

'Teach me how you do it. I've never mastered stone skimming.' Her tone bordered on over-bright. She was trying too hard for both of them, but he welcomed the effort. He didn't want to think about the war, about Rafe.

'First, you have to select the right pebble. It should be light and round.' He studied the one she'd selected and chose another and discarded the rest on the shingle. 'Try this one. Do you feel how much lighter it is? But the stone isn't everything. The water should be still. Today's a good day, the ocean is calm, the waves are small. Then, hold your wrist like so.' He shook his head. 'No, not like that.' How to explain that special cock, the special snap? There was nothing for it. He had to show her.

Hazard came alongside her, his body cradling hers, sheltering, enveloping, his hand closing over her wrist. He breathed her in, the last scents of summer mingled with the sharp brine of an autumn beach. Intoxicating. Out on the horizon, an erne wheeled and dived beneath grey clouds. Addy was all warmth and woman against him and she was not oblivious. He noted the quick skip of the pulse at her neck when his body came up behind her, when he took her wrist. He pitched his voice low at her ear, his hand gently manipulating her wrist into position while his body thrummed with the nearness of her. 'Pull back, like this, and let it go, just a sharp flick.' His voice was a husk as if this was a seduction, not a lesson in stone skimming.

The stone sailed across the waves, skipping once, twice, three times to Addy's great glee. 'I did it! *We* did it,' she cried and her excitement warmed him. He'd not given her a fine book, but he'd given her this. He was here, in this moment with her. It emboldened him to move beyond being the inspector, beyond being a man who carried suspicion with him like a calling card, to simply a man in the moment.

With no stones to throw, his hands defaulted to her waist, his arms drawing her against him. His mouth found her throat, also seemingly by default. His mouth fit there against the curve of her neck as surely as his hands belonged at her waist, as surely as her body belonged against his. He kissed her, along the elegant column of her neck, and she sighed as lightning crackled out over the sea where the erne had flown.

Chapter Seven

It was the most natural thing in the world to shift in his arms, to give him access to her mouth. Addy turned into him without thinking, only feeling, only wanting. The shelter of his body surrounded her, the strength of him flooded her even as the lightning cracked. There was no storm here in the circle of his arms, but there was fire, an electricity that leapt between them as his mouth claimed hers, or was it hers claiming his? It was hard to tell who had closed the distance first.

It hardly mattered. Her mouth opened to him, her arms sought him, looping around his neck even as her body pressed closer to his, revelling in this new warmth, new fire that burned through her. This kiss was not a game, as it had been with Bennett. That kiss had been meant to overpower her senses, to deliberately dazzle her. She saw that now. But not this kiss. This was thorough and honest, as if Hazard was burning, too, as though he, too, could not get enough. The kiss was mutual. That made all the difference. The fire burned between them as thunder rolled overhead, a reminder that they could not linger.

'We have to get home or we'll be drenched.' Hazard's murmur mirrored her own reluctance. Already, out over the sea, sheets of rain were visible, moving towards the shore, pushed by the rising wind. Despite the proof of her eyes, it was hard to believe anything could touch her when his arms held her.

She sat close to Hazard in the gig in part for warmth and in part to preserve the extraordinary feeling of closeness the kiss had engendered in her. Never had she felt so shockingly, immediately connected to another person. Her mind was a riot of reactions—sorting through them with any semblance of understanding was a task worthy of minding mice at the crossroads. What was she to make of this? Kissing Hazard had been nothing like kissing Bennett. Bennett's kiss had been a demonstration of prowess. And yes, it had been exciting in its own way. But it had been designed for her, not for him. Her excitement had stemmed then from uncertainty.

She pressed closer to Hazard, trying to drive a certain horror away. What did it say about her that she'd allowed two different men to kiss her? That she was comparing their efforts when two months ago, she'd not ever been kissed once? More to the point, what did it mean that she'd allowed Hazard to kiss her when Bennett had asked her to consider advancing their relationship? She'd not been true to Bennett. Worse, Bennett had hardly crossed her mind this afternoon.

He's asked you for no commitment, only to consider it, her conscience argued on her behalf, trying to soothe her sense of ethics.

Artemisia would agree. Artemisia would say she owed Bennett nothing. She would settle for that. It was the best counter-argument she could make at the moment without feeling like a hussy. Artemisia would suggest a woman was entitled to experimentation, to comparison. But Addy was not Artemisia. She believed true love would not need a comparison, nor had she ever considered true love to be something she might test for herself. It was something theoretical, something for others.

She did not intend to marry, at least not for a while. She had her life to live first. Travel. Perhaps her art history to explore if she could figure out how. Besides, what would she do with true love even if she found it?

The first of the raindrops caught them just a half-mile from Seasalter as the storm rolled southwards. They'd almost outrun it. Hazard pulled a lap robe from beneath the seat and put an arm about her, shielding her from the worst of it. They arrived at the farmhouse only a bit damp about the edges, feeling giddy at their narrow escape as they climbed down from the gig. The lamps were already lit in the windows of the farmhouse, lending the yard a homely glow. Perhaps they'd lingered longer in Whitstable than she thought. The smell of Mrs Harris's supper wafted from the kitchen as they shed their outerwear: roast and potatoes.

Artemisia met them in the foyer, the sharp look in her eye dimming Addy's spirits. 'You're late and we have a guest.' Her gaze was split between the two of them. She didn't get to finish.

'Hello, Addy-Sweet,' a voice drawled as

a form came up behind Artemisia. 'I'm home. Just got back this afternoon and I came straight here.' Bennett came forward, golden and sleek, a winsome smile on his handsome smooth-featured face, his gaze making her the obvious focal point of his attentions. 'I see you got my book.'

'Yes, it's lovely.' Addy blanched, awkwardness making her tongue-tied. She was acutely aware of Hazard bristling beside her.

'Not as lovely as you, Addy-Sweet.' Bennett closed the small distance between them and planted a kiss on her cheek, a hand going about her waist in a proprietary gesture. 'I've missed you. But I must apologise, I'm being rude.' He looked in Hazard's direction, as if noting him for the first time. 'Forgive me, I haven't seen Addy in over a month,' he said with his customary bonhomie and a laugh. 'I'm Bennett Galbraith and you are…?'

'Inspector Hazard Manning.' The two men glared at one another over the top of her head, one dark and rugged, the other smooth and golden. Addy shot a glance of appeal in Artemisia's direction. *Help me. Do something.* She was out of her depth here. All she knew in the moment was that it was true—one could indeed cut tension with a knife.

Dinner was a most edgy affair. Hazard and Bennett cut into their meat with all the vigour of men who would have liked to have cut into each other instead. What they refrained from doing, however, with knives, they managed to do with conversation; sharp words and slicing wit darted in between Darius's attempts to keep their blades sheathed.

'How do you like our unorthodox little community, Manning?' Bennett drained another glass of Darius's red wine, his third by Addy's count, and started on his fourth. It was quite a lot given that two glasses were considered the polite limit at Darius's supper table. 'We have a viscount in our midst who insists on living in a farmhouse and an art school for girls only.' He talked as if he were part of the family. It was a continuation of the proprietary air he'd exhibited in the foyer. Addy saw Artemisia stiffen at the foot of the table, offended by the labels Bennett applied to the school, to them, and perhaps most of all by his assumption of membership into this group.

'And an active smuggling community as well, if this wine is anything to go on,' Hazard remarked. Addy couldn't tell if he meant the comment to redirect the thoughtless remarks or as a needle to prick Bennett with. Perhaps she was putting her own construction on the latter. Why would Hazard want to needle Bennett? He didn't know the man. Except through her.

'Ah, well, the whole of Kent is riddled with them, it's hardly a unique occurrence.' Bennett speared Hazard with a piercing stare, sharp and dismissive. Sweet heavens. The men were posturing like two cocks in a hen yard. It was ridiculous really, when neither of them had a claim to the hen. She didn't want to be claimed, she told herself stoically. But the heat rising in her cheeks belied it. A delicious 'what if' began to uncurl. What if Hazard had a claim? What if he wanted a claim to her? Would she mind that? She certainly hadn't minded his kiss.

Across the table, Hazard gave Bennett's comment some consideration. 'That may be true, but this community seems to have high tastes, excellent wine and perhaps even aspiring art forgers.'

Bennett set down his wine glass. 'What did you say?' Bennett's shoulders tightened. She could almost feel the tension emanating from him at the remark.

Darius inserted himself into the conversation. 'The inspector is here to investigate a potential forgery. His one lead is that the operator is out of Seasalter.'

Bennett's body relaxed as he laughed, a derisive sound that said he didn't think much of Hazard's investigative skills. 'That's not much to go on, sir.'

Hazard met Bennett's cold gaze with a glacial smile. 'Not yet,' he corrected. 'Addy's been helping me meet people who would have knowledge of such goings on. She introduced me to the innkeeper at Whitstable today.'

'Has she? Well, *Addy* here is quite the helper.' Bennett shot her a glance she felt deep in her gut. He thought she'd been untrue to him, that she'd done more than introduce him to the innkeeper. She could have kicked Hazard for putting that thought in Bennett's mind, only it wasn't just Hazard manipulating words. She had been very much a part of the kiss on the shingle. Perhaps Bennett did have a right to be disappointed in her.

* * *

Dinner could not end fast enough for Addy, but even then, there was no escape. Bennett rose as she and Artemisia excused themselves. 'Might I beg a break from protocol and speak with Addy? It's been over a month.' He played the ardent suitor impeccably. *Played?* The word implied the role wasn't real. Would she have thought the role untrue a month ago? Why did it seem less than true to her now? Was it because she had Hazard's kiss on her lips, and on her mind? His kiss had felt nothing like Bennett's. It was clear, too, that his performance was for Hazard's benefit, not hers.

Bennett's hand was at her back, ushering her out of the room before Darius offered his permission or before she could voice a protest. Once, she would have revelled in the attention, the idea that this handsome man was so proprietary of her, so desirous of her company. But outside the dining room, his hand moved to a shockingly hard grip at her wrist. 'Let's go to your studio, we can be alone there. We need to talk.' His voice was low at her ear, a growl of displeasure, his step quick as he led her to the glass-walled conservatory at the back of the house, a place the women had turned into their private workspace. It was more hers than Artemisia's these days, Artemisia had a larger studio at the school now.

The familiar smell of turpentine and paint settled her nerves as she lit a lamp. This was *her* room. She would not allow him to intimidate her in it. She was the queen here. 'Bennett, it is good to see you.' She set the lamp on a scarred side table beside the old sofa and sat.

'Is it?' Bennett did not take the hint to sit with her. Instead, he prowled in front of the cold hearth. 'You and the inspector seemed very cosy when you came in.'

Had they? 'It was raining out, we were trying to stay dry.' It was true, but perhaps there had been more to it than that. She'd liked taking refuge in Hazard's arms, sheltering against the bulk of his body, but she did *not* like Bennett's insinuations. 'What exactly are you implying? You're bristling like a boar, Bennett.' She was prickly, too, and, she realised, not afraid to show it. That was new. Once, she might have worried over offending him.

It had the desired effect. Bennett changed his tack. He sat beside her on the sofa, taking her hands, his face transforming with a rueful smile that managed to convey a kind of apology. 'Forgive me, Addy. I am simply being protective. I worry for you with him. You are kind and giving and vulnerable, my sweet. He is a man who would take advantage of your good nature.'

'Why would he do that?' Bennett's case made little sense to her. 'I have nothing to offer him.' Nothing but a little company on his lonely search. She'd sensed today and even during their earlier beach picnic that he was a man who was not merely alone, but lonely as well. He'd taken pains to hide it and it had been those very pains that had given him away. Separation from his family had weighed on him, evident in the brevity he gave the topic.

'You need to be careful with him, Addy-Sweet,' Bennett pressed, not answering her with specifics. Perhaps Bennett was the one to whom Hazard was dangerous, a threat to Bennett's own claim.

Addy furrowed her brow. 'How? I assure you, he's been the perfect gentleman.' Right until he'd come behind her, holding her body against his to throw a stone. Right up until he'd kissed her neck, her mouth, on the beach today. 'You misjudge his interest in me.' The last was added as a salve to Bennett's pride in case that was the real issue. It was hard to be sure. Was Bennett's concern on a personal level or something more? She wished she had more experience in reading him. Perhaps if she knew more about him, she'd understand him better.

'No, I do not misjudge him. I know *exactly* what his interest in you is. But I think you do not, which is why I must tell you, his interest is purely professional.' Bennett's words surprised her. She'd expected him to say something about jealousy, about affection. 'He is mixing the medium to get you to incriminate yourself.'

Incriminate? For what reason? On what grounds? She wasn't following Bennett's line of argument at all. She tried to pull her hands away, but Bennett held fast. 'There is nothing to incriminate. This is crazy talk, Bennett. He is looking for a forger.'

He held her gaze, intent and warm. 'You must listen to me. You heard everything at supper tonight. He has only one scant lead. He will be conjuring a case and a suspect out of thin air at this rate. Where better to look than at an art school for a forger.'

Addy shook her head with a laugh. 'He's already discarded the school, you needn't worry. He concluded none of the students had the necessary talent.' But a little nugget of concern tightened in her belly. Bennett was right. This *had* been the first place Hazard had considered. Was he truly only looking for a quick solution to his problem? Would he really settle the guilt on the first likely suspect?

Bennett's grip tightened on her hands, his hair burnished and gleaming in the lamplight, his face dramatically planed, as handsome as any Drury Lane actor. 'But what of the instructors? Think, Addy. If the forger is not among the students, if there are no likely suspects out in the community, and there aren't, you know that—think how ridiculous it sounds,' he offered as an aside. 'It's only a matter of time before he runs back through his list of suspects and thinks about the instructors. Suspicion will fall on you and Artemisia. Think about what that would mean! At the least, scandal for the school and, at the worst, an arrest.'

His hands gripped her shoulders. 'I could

not bear it if he were to take you away.' He paused. 'It would be you on whom suspicion would fall. Artemisia has no motive and she has the Viscount to protect her.'

The supposition was completely outlandish, just like Bennett's claims to make her rich, to make her famous. Bennett was always dealing in hyperbole. 'No one is taking anyone away,' Addy assured him. His concern touched her, even though it seemed unnecessary and extravagant, like his clothes, his gifts. 'I've done nothing, Artemisia has done nothing. There are no grounds for him to think otherwise.' It was so cut and dried for her, so obvious, that it was hard to see Bennett's fear as anything other than fantastical. She might have wondered what inspired it if he wasn't always so hyperbolic.

Bennett released her, a soft smile on his face, relenting. 'I just want you to be safe, Addy-Sweet.' He stroked her cheek with a gentle hand, his voice a caress. 'I suppose I don't want to lose you. I can't always be here and I worry that someone else might steal you away.' He gave a charming, self-deprecating grin, as if he considered his own appeal quite humble.

'Have you thought about our discussion before I left? About us? I have. Constantly.'

The burn of his gaze set off alarms. She wanted time to stand still. She didn't want this scene to happen. It was like a dream where one knew what would come next, but was helpless to stop it. Addy froze and waited, unable to stop the moments unfolding before her.

Chapter Eight

It was a very pretty scene, a handsome man down on one knee, his every gesture, every feature illumined by the soft light of the lamp. She gasped as he pulled a small box from his pocket. 'Addy-Sweet, I want to spend my life with you, I want to marry you, but I cannot, in good conscience, ask you to wed me empty-handed.' He flipped open the lid, showing off an elegant, expensive marquise-cut emerald set on a gold band, surrounded by diamonds. 'This is just a promise, Addy-Sweet, a place-holder until I can come to you and make an honest offer.'

She was numb, her mind reeling from one of Bennett's shocking revelations to another; *Hazard was dangerous, Hazard might frame her for forgery, Bennett wanted to marry her.*

The night had swung from extreme to extreme. She needed time to get ahold of it all, to sort through it. 'Bennett, I am honoured, truly, but you needn't give me a ring. It is too much,' Addy stammered, her gaze split between the dazzling jewel in the box and Bennett's own emerald gaze. They matched. It was too much *and* it was too soon.

She gently shut the box lid and closed his hand around it. 'We will discuss it when you're ready to make an official offer, *after* you've spoken to my father.' She offered the reminder as politely as possible, her mind already making its usual excuses for him. How was he to know the proper way things were done if one did not tell him? But she already recognised her prompt as a means by which to postpone the inevitable. She wasn't going to marry Bennett. She wasn't going to marry *anyone*, at least not until she had her life sorted out. Her life hadn't even begun. She couldn't possibly hand it over to someone else without having sampled it herself.

Bennett's face fell, his gaze reflecting confusion. 'Don't you want to marry, Addy? I always supposed you did.' He did disappointment very handsomely.

'Maybe…someday.' She groped for an explanation. *Someday*. She was sick of that word. How long had she defined her dreams as something for later? Things to be postponed? If not now, when? When would she seize them? How much longer would she wait? Was Bennett the person she wanted to do those things with, this man who knew her so little? 'Is that why you asked, because it's something you thought *I* wanted?' Marriage needed to be based on far more than that. There'd been no protestations of love, of commitment, of dedication, none of the things a groom ought to pledge to a bride.

Bennett sat back on his heels, putting the ring in his pocket. 'I want to run away with you, Addy. I want to take you to Europe, to show you the world, to show you what you can be if you'd shake off the shadow of your family. I will take you there with or without a ring. I just didn't think you'd go without marriage. I'd leave tonight if you said the word.'

What gallant words. There was a certain romance to the idea of walking off into the night, even if she couldn't realistically act on it and even if she couldn't quite imagine walking off with *him*. The image of the man beside her on such an adventure was a rugged man in a greatcoat and sturdy boots, dark hair blown by the wind. It was perhaps poorly done of her to think of Hazard when Bennett was taking the refusal with more grace than she'd expected. Perhaps he was relieved? It helped to think that. She'd not wanted to hurt him. She'd not thought it was possible to do so. Bennett seemed impervious to regret.

He rose to his feet, shaking off the moment. 'We'll speak of the future some other time. I will not allow it to spoil tonight and coming home to you. Show me the progress you've made on the *Madonna and Child* I sent.'

She blushed and stood with him, grateful to have something else to discuss. 'I've only started. There's not much to show. I've just sketched it out. I've started mixing paint, though. I'm working on getting the red exactly right. I'm thinking a cochineal for the Madonna's robes. It would be authentic to the time.'

'When do you think it might be done?' Bennett interrupted as she went on about the trick of mixing historically accurate red paint. Hazard would not have interrupted. Hazard would have found it interesting.

'The end of the month?' she estimated. 'Perhaps sooner. Is there a rush?' She couldn't imagine that there was. This was only practice, after all.

He smiled, sleek and smooth in the light. 'Only that I have some news for you. I had wanted to tell you before dinner, but there was no chance.' His tone implied Hazard was to blame for that. 'You recall that I went to London to have your painting framed? While I was there, someone was impressed by the work and wanted to buy it.' He paused with a shrug. 'I wasn't sure what to do, Addy, and there was no time to consult you.' His eyes were dancing flames and she felt her own breath hitch with excitement, anticipation. 'I thought, why not? Addy can paint another for us.' His grin widened. 'Close your eyes, Addy, and hold out your hands.'

Her hands filled with paper—no, not paper. *Pound notes.* Her eyes flashed open, transfixed by the money in her palms. She'd never held this much money all at once. 'Someone paid you for my painting?' For her practice?

'I told you I'd make you rich.' He beamed at her.

He'd done more than that. She was not sure

she could articulate to him, a man for whom money was the ultimate standard against which all else was judged, that it wasn't just the money that mattered. It was what this money stood for. Someone had *liked* her work. It was a type of recognition she'd never had and that Bennett had been the one to make it happen—well, that filled her in a new way.

It made her ashamed of her reaction to him earlier. She was letting Artemisia's poor opinion of him sway her when she ought to make up her own mind, when she ought to stand up for him. She was no sort of friend if she let others malign him in her presence when he had done this for her. She reached up on her toes and pressed her lips to his cheek. 'Thank you, Bennett.' For the money, for not pressuring her about marriage or about Italy. Surely Artemisia had misjudged him.

Some gratitude at last. He took her chaste kiss with gallantry and decided to quit the field while he was ahead. Perhaps the chambermaid at the Crown would be more accommodating. Addy, the little minx, was proving difficult to please. What hadn't he done for her? Paintbrushes from Italy, pretty shawls, that damned expensive book about the artists, the promise of travel, of freedom, or of marriage if that's what she wanted. He'd made her a pretty proposal complete with a dazzling emerald ring that matched his eyes. He'd thought proper Addy Stansfield would have leapt at the offer of marriage. She hadn't.

That surprised him. He'd expected starry-eyed, plain-faced Addy to jump at the opportunity to marry him. Not that he actually *meant* to marry her. He just wanted to bind her to him with something more than work and friendship between them so that she would be inclined to believe him, to protect him if needed.

He might need that protection. The inspector had thrown a kink into his plans. The painting he'd sold to Monteith had been discovered after hanging for only a few weeks in Monteith's gallery. That was unfortunate. It might have hung for years if he'd been lucky. It was a lesson in patience, he supposed. He'd rushed Addy. The rumour in London had been that it was the paint that had revealed the fraud. Addy, thinking the painting was just for practice, had used a modern blue.

Clearly, however, that mistake wouldn't

happen again. She was already looking to match reds to authenticate shades used in the time period for the *Madonna and Child*. Addy could be counted on to take care of the details. To her, practice was not just copying a painting, it was practising with paint shades, with brushstrokes that reflected the original intent. It would be much harder for her next Perugino to be detected.

Addy would be good for business *if* he could get her away from Seasalter and her sister *and* if he could get her away from the inspector. Hazard Manning was known in certain circles for attention to detail. Bennett had not met the man in person until tonight, but he knew of him. The inspector was a man to steer clear of. To endure a supper across the table from him had sent a twisted thrill of competition through Bennett, knowing that Manning was looking for him and had no idea the very person he sought was in the room.

For the moment, Bennett held the upper hand. The night had become focused on getting his defences in order: binding Addy to him, sowing doubt about the inspector's honesty and encouraging Addy to finish the next painting. He already had a buyer in mind.

But the risk of a sale was certainly enhanced knowing that Manning was on the case.

Bennett laughed up into the sky. Let him come. Even if Manning caught him, he had so many ways to wriggle out. He could always feign ignorance, that he hadn't known, he was just passing the painting on. If Manning didn't buy that, he could hide behind Addy's good name. The Viscount would protect his wife's sister and Addy would protect him. The man she loved couldn't be attached to a scandal. He was banking hard on the last. If there'd been anything that had shaken him tonight, it had been seeing her with the inspector. Not because she was with the enemy, he could deal with that, but because of the *look* on her face. She *liked* the inspector. She'd looked happy, confident, at ease, as if she didn't need to earn the inspector's approval.

It wasn't at all how she looked when she was with him. When Addy was with him, she was all eager puppy dog, wanting to please, worried over putting a step wrong, adoring to the point of doubting herself. He liked that, he liked keeping a woman off balance. He was good at it. A woman off balance would never overplay her hand for fear of losing his attentions. Until tonight. She'd been assertive tonight and that bothered him. *Could* he lose Addy?

Once upon a time, he would have said Addy worshipped him. His good looks, his dazzling gifts, his kisses, his promises of a future together had been enough to keep her panting after him. Tonight, *he'd* been the one to feel off kilter, the balance of their relationship no longer so obviously in his favour. Would she turn to the inspector? That would be an interesting dilemma for Manning, a man known for his integrity and tenacity.

What would the inspector do if Addy was in danger? He'd seen the irate look in the inspector's eyes when Bennett staked his claim. How far would Manning go to protect her if bringing Bennett in put her in peril? He chuckled. Poor Addy, she couldn't win at this game. Either she came away with him and they forged their way across Europe, or she turned against him and became the leverage he would use to win his freedom should it come to that.

Bennett pushed open the door to the Crown, letting the familiar atmosphere of a smuggler's tavern flow over him. This was better, much better, than the Viscount's proper table. These were *his* kind of people. A serving girl scurried past with an empty tray. 'Ah, Alice, my love, come and give me a kiss.' He grabbed her about the waist.

She squealed and swatted playfully at his shoulder. 'Master Galbraith, you're back!'

He planted a kiss on her willing mouth. 'I most certainly am. When do you get off?' He was feeling decidedly better about the evening. He'd match wits with Manning and he'd win. Things were looking up.

Chapter Nine

Hazard's morning had not got off to a good start. He pushed back from the table he'd appropriated in the Crown's public room for breakfast and correspondence, leaving a half-eaten meal of eggs and bacon among the letters. His brother had written again, begging him to come home. He'd stuffed that letter in his coat pocket, not wanting to deal with it. He couldn't go home. Couldn't face his brother. What did Rafe think going home would accomplish except to reopen old wounds? It was best to stay away. In other news, the team he'd left behind was still mulling over the question who had Peter Timmons worked for right before his death? Had someone hired his services or had he worked for himself? His colleagues had written as well with no news.

There were no rumours of active forgers surfacing in London.

He should not be terribly disappointed. News from that quarter had been long odds to begin with. Men who bought expensive art, men like Monteith, who had more pride than good sense, were not likely to suspect they'd been cheated, nor were they likely to publicly admit it for fear of looking foolish. By the time a forgery was discovered, perhaps years had passed since the purchase and the forger's trail was cold. He might not, even now, be searching for a forger if Bourne hadn't alerted Monteith to the possibility so quickly after Monteith's purchase. It was a bit of luck it had been spotted early, but the trail wasn't exactly warm.

The lack of news from London reinforced the failing nature of his mission. He had nothing to show for his time in Seasalter except dead ends. He certainly knew where *not* to look. Hazard mentally checked those places off; there was no forger embedded at the art school and no forger in Whitstable. The free trade connection from France was also starting to look like smoke and mirrors.

In the time he'd been here, two smuggling

runs had come ashore late at night to hide their goods in the basement of the Crown. He'd subtly grilled Padraig O'Malley, the smuggling captain, over several tankards of ale about the contents, only to conclude there was nothing relevant to art forgery in the catalogue of previous shipments. That, too, had been long odds. He'd wondered from the start whether Monteith's reference to a French noble was nothing more than a story Monteith had been fed for 'ambience'. If there was one, the trail would have led through the smugglers. Right now, the trail led nowhere.

Except back towards Addy.

He dismissed the idea. The trail only led towards her because it had nowhere else to go by process of elimination, *not* because she'd done anything that had pointed the trail in her direction. Nothing she'd done uniquely raised suspicion. The only suspicion surfaced from Addy being in the wrong place at the wrong time. She was an artist in Seasalter at a time when a forgery was suspected of emerging from there. Pinning the blame on her was the epitome of guilty until proven innocent. It was very poor and dangerous logic.

Hazard shook it off and opened his leather-bound writing ledger and prepared to make his weekly report to Monteith, trying to frame the limited findings in a positive, encouraging light. He didn't want Monteith regretting the bill he was running up at the Crown.

The little devil on his shoulder whispered, *Be honest...you don't want Monteith recalling you to London. You want to stay. You're taken with the art instructor. You're starting to fall for Addy Stansfield.*

Hazard kept writing, wanting to force his thoughts beyond that one hiccup. No, he couldn't be falling for her. He didn't allow himself to fall for anyone. He wanted to argue instead that it was the clean air and the simple living of Seasalter that he found attractive, that it was the regular invitation from Viscount St Helier to join the family for a home-cooked meal that was the real appeal, a homely juxtaposition to his life in London where meals where taken haphazardly from a chophouse and consumed on the run or at his desk, where he faced all natures of danger in the pursuit of doing right. So far, there was nothing more dangerous in Seasalter than a pretty art instructor with a sweet tooth.

And her suitor, the little devil reminded him. *Don't forget him.*

There was no chance of forgetting Bennett Galbraith. It appeared the man shared everything with him, from sitting at the farmhouse dinner table—a table to which it seemed Bennett was invited less often than he had been, something Hazard liked to note in moments of petty pique—to the accommodations at the Crown. Apparently, they even shared Addy's attentions, although the nature of those attentions seemed less clear. He'd not had a moment or a reason to appropriately ask Addy about the standing of that relationship or even if there was one. Galbraith seemed to think there was though, based on his behaviour that first night at dinner.

Hazard wasn't sure Addy shared that view. The man had nearly shoved her out of the dining room in order to get a moment alone with her. His doting behaviour had appeared exaggerated with over-the-top charm and excessive sweetness. Addy had seemed surprised by it, too. There'd been moments at dinner when she'd looked at Galbraith as if wondering who this person was. Whoever he was, and whatever his intentions, he wasn't faithful.

Hazard leaned back in his chair, letting the morning serving girl pour him more coffee in the hopes it would help clear his head. A large part of his sour mood this morning was a lack of sleep last night, courtesy of another serving girl, who went by the name of Alice, and one rather *ardent* Bennett Galbraith. The man who brought expensive books to Addy and possessively dragged her from dining rooms was also tupping the tavern wench without guilt, not that he was going tell Addy. He'd rather Bennett show himself as a bounder on his own merits. For Hazard to do it conflated the business and pleasure aspects of his time in Seasalter.

Damn! He slapped his hand on the table, making his coffee jump in its mug. It wasn't just the lack of sleep that was muddling his active brain, it was the whole situation with Addy—Addy the only potential suspect he had, Addy the girl another man fancied, Addy the girl whom he had kissed in Whitstable, the girl who'd drawn him in from the first. She was at the heart of everything he experienced here. He couldn't keep his mind on hunting down a forger on a cold trail while his mind constantly veered back to her.

Unlike the cold trail with its single clue, his mind had plenty to pick from when it came to Addy: images of her walking beside him on the beach, Addy skipping rocks, her body pressed to his, Addy's mouth on his, Addy laughing at the dinner table with her family, Addy with her sister's baby in her arms, a smile of complete contentment on her face that was quite at odds with a woman who insisted marriage was not on her list of goals. Did she even know how her face changed when she was with her nephew? Addy was meant for family, for children.

The thought edged dangerously towards other fantasies, of the family he could not have for fear of placing them in peril. And yet, his mind had readily spent time contemplating setting that aside and playing the 'what if' game. *What if* he set aside his private, personal vow? *What if* he'd exaggerated the risk of his profession? It was entirely possible. It was a convenient smokescreen for not dealing with the family he did have. *What if* he could keep a family of his own safe? Then, anything would be possible: marriage to a girl like Addy, a family to replace the one he'd left, a second chance.

No, he would not tread down that path. He needed fresh air. During the wars, when a code eluded him, he'd take a walk, let his mind roam as freely as his legs, in order to loosen up his thoughts and let the answers fall through.

Hazard shrugged into his greatcoat and turned up the collar. The weather had turned officially grey and along with the greyness came a chilly dampness. He turned towards the marshy shoreline and began to walk, his mind turning over what he knew in review, starting at the beginning: Monteith's man had got the painting from a man in Seasalter who'd supposedly got it from a French noble. He posed himself the usual questions: What part of that statement was true? What part was false? The last was false. Question: How did he know that? Answer: the paint was too new. That was indisputable fact. This was not an heirloom gathering dust in a chateau. But what did that fact really mean? That's where it was murky.

Did it mean there definitely was no Frenchman? It certainly minimised the chances, but perhaps it did not eradicate them. Perhaps the Frenchman was passing the painting off. Perhaps the Frenchman was the guilty party, the forger? If so, that complicated Hazard's task immeasurably. But no one had handled the painting, no free trader had brought it in. Who had Monteith's man met with?

He looked up and recognised his surroundings. He was back to where he started. In more ways than one. His wanderings had led him from the marshy beach to the footpath and up to the farmhouse. To Addy. He had not seen her since the night of the rain storm. It had seemed the right thing to do in all ways at the time. Professionally, he needed to maintain objectivity until he was certain of his case. And personally...well, that was becoming conflated with the professional as well. Perhaps it was time to revisit that reasoning. Perhaps seeing her might take the edge off him, clear his mind, hair of the dog being what it was. Or maybe that was wishful, convenient thinking.

She was in the studio. Mrs Harris showed him in. He'd never been in the studio, his visits to the farmhouse had been limited to the parlour, the dining room and what passed for St Helier's office. This room was clearly private, beyond even Mrs Harris's touch if the haphazard mess of the room was any indicator. His gaze swept the room, noting the old sofa with its soft throw tossed carelessly over its arm, set near the fire, the wall of glass that looked out on to the back garden, the stacks of books piled on a small table near the sofa and, on the floor, canvases lining a wall. One had to pick their way across the room if one wanted to go further than the sofa and the fireplace. Perhaps that was the point of the scattered mess. It was designed to keep people at bay.

Addy was behind an easel, one more barrier, he thought. An artist was well defended in this place. She looked up when Mrs Harris announced him and bustled off for a tea tray. Her smile was sincere and it lit up the room. 'Hazard, this is a pleasant surprise!' She set aside her brush and began unbuttoning her smock.

'Please, don't stop on my account,' he offered, although the gesture touched him, assuring him that he wasn't an intrusion despite showing up unannounced.

She set the smock aside and came around the easel, smoothing her skirt. 'No, I need a break. I was going to stop anyway and Mrs Harris will have tea here in a moment.' She sat down on the sofa, keeping up a stream of chatter, only the high flush in her cheeks suggested his arrival had flustered her. For good reasons or bad? he wondered. 'You haven't been around. I assume you've been busy. How is your case going? Do you have any new leads? Perhaps Padraig O'Malley was some help?' She paused for a breath, her animated face taking on a look of dismayed realisation. 'You haven't stayed away because of the kiss, have you? Please tell me you're not going to apologise for it.'

Her concern was so genuine, Hazard couldn't help but smile. He felt his entire face break into a grin. He dared not laugh, but it was deuced difficult to hold back. She wouldn't believe he wasn't laughing *at* her but because of her, the honesty and directness of her. 'It did not occur to me to apologise for that.' He took a seat at the other end of the sofa. 'Should I, Addy?' he said more soberly. 'It was a liberty, although at the moment it seemed right. I don't regret it unless you do.'

Addy's blush deepened and she looked down at her hands. 'I don't regret it.' She glanced up for a fraction of a moment, long enough for him to see the question in her eyes. 'Although, I thought you might once we got home and Bennett was there. It wasn't the ending to the day I'd anticipated.' She fidgeted with her hands as she braved the uncomfortable subject.

'Me neither.' He'd imagined a quiet dinner with the Lord and Lady St Helier and Addy. Perhaps a game of backgammon with Addy afterwards in the parlour while the St Heliers played on the rug with the baby. The farmhouse was an unconventional oasis. He'd missed it these last two weeks. It had got under his skin fast just as Addy had. Both were intoxicating and dangerous, challenging the life he'd chosen and the barriers he'd constructed.

'Since you mention him, may I ask who Bennett is to you? Is there an understanding? I do apologise if I am not delicate enough with the subject.'

'No, not at all.' She was quick to absolve him, quick to flash him a smile. 'You have every right to ask. My conduct led you to believe...' *Believe*. Yes, it certainly had. But that had been his imagination's fault, not hers. He'd never agreed with the argument

that women caused men to behave a certain
way because of how they dressed or spoke.
His reactions were *his* reactions.

'There is no harm in a kiss, Addy, no harm
in getting swept up in a moment.' He would
offer her absolution as well. After all, he'd
started that kiss. No harm, unless it happened
again. Then they'd have some explaining to
do to themselves and to each other.

'You are generous and I should be, too. I
should tell you about Bennett. Only I don't
know what to tell. There is nothing and everything to say.' Addy shifted on the sofa. He
didn't want her to be uncomfortable. His protective nature surged. He wanted to protect
her even from herself.

'You don't have to tell me.' He could hear
the rattle of the tea tray coming down the
hall. He rose to help Mrs Harris with the load.
It was the perfect break. By the time a space
was cleared on the low table, the tray settled
and the tea poured out, they could move on
to another topic. Only Addy didn't see it that
way.

'Bennett was just a friend, always around
when he was here. I was new to Seasalter and
Seasalter is a lonely place to be new in.' Addy

poured a quarter-cup of cream into her tea-cup, turning it white, and tenaciously returned to the topic. 'Before he left in September, he asked me to consider escalating our relation-ship. He talked of us going to Florence.' She reached for a ginger biscuit. He was conscious of every move she made, how she fixed her tea, what she chose to eat from the tray, how many bites it took her to finish a biscuit. He could tell from the way she stopped chewing that she was thoughtful. 'I should have seen it coming, I realise that now. All the little gifts he was forever giving me: the Italian paint-brushes, for instance.' She blushed. 'I'm not very good with men. I didn't understand.'

'A woman is not required to be affection-ate because she is given gifts.' Hazard wanted to argue the point. She was good with men, good with putting them at ease, getting them to open up about themselves. At least she had been with him.

'No, but I allowed him to keep on giving me gifts. I couldn't quite believe he was in-terested in me like that.'

'Why not?' Hazard filled his plate again from the tea tray. Mrs Harris had remembered his favourite ham sandwiches with mustard.

'Well, he's so handsome and worldly and I'm rather plain. The sorts don't go together. Water and oil, you know.'

Plain? Who had told her that? Addy Stansfield was *not* plain. She was all the beautiful colours of autumn with those last-of-summer-green eyes and deep auburn hair, buttermilk skin broken only by spicy freckles across the bridge of her nose. It was a different kind of beautiful than the beauty showcased by London's blondes, but it was still beautiful, natural, untarnished. 'Do you go together, now?'

'I don't know. It has all happened so fast, I've had difficulty adjusting to the idea. I've asked him for some time to consider it all. I've never had a beau.' She blushed again. 'But this is unseemly talk. Tell me what you've been up to. How is your case?'

'It's going nowhere. In fact, it's the reason I find myself at your doorstep today. I can't seem to get beyond my one lead and then the trail dries up. I thought a walk would clear my head. All I know is that the man who sold Monteith's people the painting operates from Seasalter. But no one's talking. The idea of forged artwork seems foreign to them.'

'As it should. These smugglers deal with

wine and brandy and a little silk and lace—the innkeeper in Whitstable didn't lie.' Addy took another biscuit, lemon curd this time. 'Perhaps the man you're looking for isn't a regular? Perhaps he isn't here any longer.'

'That would be unfortunate.' The thought had crossed his mind, but he had no reason to accept it yet. 'It would make my job much more difficult.'

'Perhaps you're working the wrong end of the puzzle, Mr Inspector,' Addy teased. 'Instead of tracking the person who sold it, track the painting.'

It wasn't a bad idea and it certainly moved her beyond suspicion. She was far too ready to help. Hazard smiled, his day seemed less grey. 'Tell me, Miss Stansfield, how do you suggest I go about that?'

Chapter Ten

~~~~~~~~~~~~~~~~~~~~~~~~~~~~~~~~

Addy leaned forward in her eagerness to explain. 'The seller is likely to only be a middle man. He can easily vanish. But the painting won't vanish. So, work the other end of the equation. Are there other paintings this artist has done? You could comb London, look through other private collections, see if there's a match.'

'A match? There wouldn't be a second painting,' Hazard argued. Forgers were too smart to sell the same painting twice.

'No, not a match like a second copy,' Addy explained, 'but a match in terms of the painter's work. Painters all have their own unique style.'

Hazard's attentions went on full alert. It was a daunting prospect, a very small needle in a very large haystack. 'How would I know what I was looking for? How would I recognise a style?' He couldn't very well walk around London, chiselling paint shards off artwork in order to seek out a fraud. 'How would I do it without wrecking the painting?'

Addy was ready with an answer. She lifted a finger. 'Wait right there, let me show you.' She rose and rummaged around the studio, coming back with a long leather tube. She slid the tea tray to the side before unrolling the contents of the tube and used the sugar bowl and a biscuit plate to anchor the canvases.

His breath hitched at the sight of them. 'These are old, Addy.' He scanned them, his eyes rapidly assessing what lay before him, originals in their own way.

Addy slid him a smile. 'Yes, they are. As best I can tell, they are apprentice pieces from Perugino's workshop. See how the aerial perspective is used? I think they are practice pieces, copied from the master in anticipation of being transferred to wood panels or altar pieces. It wasn't an uncommon Renaissance practice for work from an artist's workshop to be attributed to the master even if the master only oversaw it while the apprentices executed it in the fashion of the master.'

Hazard nodded, letting the information settle over him slowly, determined not to miss a single aspect of it. 'These are Peruginos?'

'I am fairly certain they could be from his workshop. There are several stylistic elements that lean in that direction. There's a lack of ornamentation, the use of aerial perspective and many of them use a serene countryside as backdrop.' She paused, cocking her head. 'And there's that sense of purity that a Perugino has that others don't. It's indefinable, but I know it when I see it. Then there's the colours—his blue, for instance.'

'The ultramarine,' Hazard broke in with a smile, losing himself in the moment, enjoying discussing art until he remembered *why* they were discussing it: a forged Perugino acquired out of Seasalter was hanging in Monteith's gallery. And now a roll of possibly related works had shown up in Addy's studio.

'You know about it?' Addy smiled back, the current of attraction leaping between them as it had on the beach in Whitstable. 'Every artist has their own style. That's Perugino's, but others have specifics like how they paint hands or ears. Raphael's ears are different than da Vinci's, for instance. I've made a study of it. Maybe someday I'll write an article for a journal or present a paper for the Royal Academy.' She drew a breath and he was aware of her gathering herself, bringing her thoughts full circle. 'What that means for you is the forger would have a style of his own. You could take the painting you do have, study it for nuance and then see if there are other paintings that share the nuances. It could lead you to your forger if he's done more than one painting that resides in London. That's the risk, of course.'

That wasn't the risk he was worried about, though. 'Can I see the others?' he asked, carefully lifting the corner to look at the canvases beneath it, hoping against hope he didn't find what he was looking for, but there it was, at the bottom of the collection, the work that hung in Monteith's gallery. He swallowed hard, working to keep his emotions in check and his thoughts in order. 'Where did you get these canvases?'

He felt her gaze study him, her answer coming slowly as if she were suddenly wary. 'Bennett gave them to me as a gift a few months ago. He especially liked that one. He said he got them from a French noble down on his luck.'

The Frenchman. At last, and not where Hazard wanted him to be—connected to Bennett Galbraith. But the Frenchman hadn't done anything wrong. He'd merely sold canvases. There was nothing wrong with that. In truth, no one—not Bennett or Addy—had done anything wrong yet. 'Addy, did you paint this one?'

Please say no. Please say you've done nothing with these canvases.

'Yes, I've been doing a study of Perugino and I'd wanted to practise with the aerial perspective. I didn't bother to mix any authentic paints for it since it was perspective practice.' Addy's brow furrowed and she reached out a hand to place on his arm. 'Hazard, is something wrong?'

The damn cobalt paint.

Everything was wrong. His voice was thick when he spoke. 'Addy, where is that painting now?' He hoped it was here, that she was going to pull it out and show him and he would be able to breathe easy.

'I don't know. Bennett liked it so much he took it to London to have it framed, but then he said he sold it to someone who'd admired it. It could be anywhere. I suppose I'll have to paint it again after I finish the *Madonna and Child*. That one *is* a colour study. I'm mixing authentic reds for it. Bennett thinks he has a buyer already, although who would want to buy someone's practice work is beyond me. Come see it.'

Hazard let her lead him to the easel while his mind sorted and re-sorted the evidence, unwilling to believe the conclusions forming.

'It's one of Perugino's *Madonna and Child*. Even here, you can tell it's mine, though, and not his because I do hands like this.' She pointed to the lines of the Madonna's hands curved around the child, explaining her technique. She reached for a stiff paper printed in colour and held it side by side. 'This is Perugino's work, it's a reproduction from a book, but it's his work. Look at the hands on his Madonna, see how they're slightly different than mine? A novice wouldn't notice, but someone who knows would.'

His breathing hitched again. Dear lord. All the pieces were fitting at last and he didn't want them to. It had been here right in front of him all along.

'Hazard, are you all right?' Addy's hand was on his arm, steadying and worried.

He brushed it off. 'I need some air, give me an hour or two.' He wanted to move away from the farmhouse, somewhere where he could breathe, where he could think the unthinkable.

Addy was the forger.

He staggered outside, the very thought taking the wind from him like a punch to the solar plexus. He squatted down on his haunches, trying to breathe, trying to reconcile the facts with his gut. Sweet, kind, fun-loving Addy who'd never skipped a rock across the water, who ate bakery sweets with honest abandon, who'd kissed him with that same full-fledged abandon on the Whitstable shingle. His mind was a flailing, dark place. The inspector was immediately suspicious, *had* to be. There was no choice. Had she played him? Was the direct open freshness of her all a ploy, in preparation for this moment so that when it came he wouldn't believe the worst of her when he faced it?

Betrayal warred with reason. The inspector in him battled with the man, firing off questions designed to tie his gut into useless knots. *Why would she do it?* Not just the painting, but the kiss. Had she meant the kiss to protect the painting? To protect herself? Bennett Galbraith, who seemed to be the instigator? Did she think a kiss would bind him to her? To make it unlikely he'd accuse her if it came to that? If so, how much more was she ready to do to prevent those accusations? To make him think with his heart—or other parts—as opposed to his head? If so, the inspector in him scolded with harsh honesty, she'd succeeded there long before the kiss.

The man in him was not willing to go down without a fight. His pride wouldn't allow it. He'd been the one to do the kissing that day. *He'd* started it. She'd responded because she'd wanted to. The man in him believed that to his core. The man in him remembered other things, too, the day he'd toured the school and laid his hypothesis at her feet, that the school was sheltering the forger. How she'd laughed, unconcerned. Someone who was worried about protecting their secret didn't have that kind of nonchalance when inviting the wolf into their hen house. She'd gone on to spend the day with him, to share stories with him on the beach.

Those were not the behaviours of a guilty party. If she was guilty, it stood to reason that she'd want to get as far from him as possible. The inspector's cynicism was back—not unless she thought she could control him better by keeping him close, by seducing him with stories, smiles, sweets.

No one was that good at being guileless. Addy wasn't an act. The man in him refused to believe it. The question came again, why would she do it? This time the question was about the crime. Why would she commit forgery? For the love of Bennett Galbraith? Such depth of affection, an affection that ran so deep as to inspire a life of crime on Bennett's behalf seemed dubious based on their discussion today. She did not carry affection for Bennett. She'd said as much. *Unless she was acting, lying.* No, she'd been genuinely awkward with the conversation today—that blush of hers could not be feigned. A man knew these things whether he was an inspector or not.

His lungs were loosening as he walked, the beach coming into view. It was easier to breathe. He let the breeze bathe him in clarity. Once he was past the initial horror of his discovery, the horror of perhaps having been duped by a pretty face—the oldest game in the book—he was starting to see the cracks in the conclusion. He could see that it didn't quite make sense. Beyond affection for Bennett, she had no motive to risk conviction. Addy was the daughter of a famous artist, she was talented, able to have legitimate recognition in her own right if she sought it. Addy had practically led him to the forgery. That was not the work of a guilty person.

Hazard took his first deep breath since his mind had shoved the pieces together. He rearranged the pieces for a new conclusion. He knew why it didn't make sense. Addy was almost certainly the painter, but she wasn't the criminal. That role fell to Bennett Galbraith alone. Galbraith had sold her work without her consent and misrepresented it to boot. Was he counting on Addy to protect him? Hazard's mind began to run through scenarios. What would Bennett do once he guessed he was exposed? Would he try to hide behind Addy, or would he seek to take her down with him?

The warrior in him rose, hackled and bristling, his mind and stomach, roiling riots of emotions and actions on Addy's behalf. The man in him wanted nothing more than to march down to the Crown, pull Galbraith out of his bed and confront him with all his misdeeds. But the inspector in him counselled caution. If Galbraith suspected anything, he might run and that would make him difficult to find. There would only be the painting and the promise of profit to lure him out into the open. A disappearing Galbraith also put Addy in danger. Desperate men did desperate things: blackmail, kidnapping. He'd prefer to have Galbraith where he could see him, even if it meant being seated across from him at the dinner table. He turned from the beach and retraced his steps, wondering the whole way back how he should tell Addy. The news was going to devastate her. He had not been played, but she had.

She was waiting in the road for him, her blue cloak wrapped about her for warmth, the wind tugging at her hair. From the look of her chignon, she'd been waiting a while. He schooled his features as he approached. He didn't want to frighten her. He needed information from her if he was to protect her and bring Galbraith to justice. To do that, he needed her to trust him. 'Addy, we need to talk.' He was unprepared for her face, chalkpale and fear was etched into her eyes. Their fresh green light was gone when they studied him. While he'd been thinking, she'd clearly been thinking, too, and she'd come to the same conclusion.

'It's true then,' her voice trembled, but her chin went up a brave fraction. 'You think I'm the forger. I wish I could say you're wrong, but you're not.'

She hadn't meant to be the forger, but Addy doubted such an excuse would carry any weight. She clasped her hands tight at her waist, gathering her courage. Oh, sweet heavens, what had she done? Forgers could hang! At least, those convicted of counterfeiting hung. She wasn't sure if that applied to art forgeries as well. But it might. Hazard must hate her, must think her the worst sort of person, perhaps even that she'd misled him from the start. 'Will you arrest me?' She barely got the words out, her mind a turmoil of horrid images, of iron shackles, dark prisons, a courtroom full of onlookers witnessing her shame, a noose. Her sister, her father, would be so angry with her.

It was too much. She started trembling and couldn't stop. She heaped recriminations on herself. She'd been a fool, a stupid Icarus who'd been persuaded to fly high on wings of false flattery. She shouldn't have given Bennett the painting—somehow she should have known he'd intended it for evil. She should have listened to Artemisia.

Hazard stepped towards her and she stepped back on shaky legs reflexively, wanting to preserve her freedom, thinking he meant to take her in on the spot. 'Please, let me see Artemisia.' A sob welled up, the words came out choked. She hated her weakness, but she had no strength. The shock of Bennett's betrayal, the shock of her own culpability, was too overwhelming.

Suddenly, she was in his arms, helpless to resist him, helpless to run even though her life seemed to depend on it. She swayed against him, his words slow to penetrate. 'Addy, I'm not going to arrest you.' The last of her strength gave out, her mind a fuzz, aware only of him. 'Addy, it's not your fault. You're not guilty.' He murmured it like a litany, soothing her as she got herself under control.

'Bennett knew, though…' Addy gulped back a sob, unable to complete the thought.

'Yes, Bennett knew. He's a scoundrel and a criminal, but not you, Addy. He used you. I can protect you, but you have to help me.'

Another set of alarms went off now that she had the shock in hand. She drew back, suddenly reluctant to give in to the comfort of his arms. This was what Bennett had predicted would happen: that Hazard would look for any scapegoat, that he would piece together a patchwork quilt of conclusions simply to make a case and have a suspect. He wanted her to think Bennett had betrayed her so she would feel no compunction in betraying Bennett in return. He wanted her to turn to him, to rely on him and, in return for incriminating Bennett, she'd be safe and free. That was the implicit deal. Perhaps he'd even wanted her frightened enough that she would immediately start divulging everything she knew, which was maybe less than he anticipated.

'I inform against him and Bennett is convicted in my place.' Or alone, while she was safe beside Hazard. Betrayal or not, Addy couldn't bring herself to want that. Bennett's wide smile and golden good looks flashed in her mind.

'Addy, he is counting on you protecting him. He is using your innate decency to cover himself, that and your family connections, no doubt.' Hazard was patient. 'I don't want to frighten you, but I don't believe he'd have any qualms about pinning this all on you if given the chance. I'd rather not give him one.'

The fear leached back in. 'Perhaps I *am* guilty, though. Perhaps I don't deserve to be protected.' Addy paused, remembering something else. Perhaps she couldn't be protected. She looked at Hazard, holding his gaze. 'I took money for the painting.' Surely that made her complicit. It certainly made her vain. She'd been so proud when Bennett had put the money in her hands.

Hazard nodded, unbothered by the confession. 'But did *you* deliberately claim the painting was a Perugino?'

'No, I never even thought of selling it. Why would I think to pass it off as real? The paint alone gives it away. The blue is too modern. I didn't think it was worth investing in the ultramarine for a painting never meant to leave the studio.'

Hazard walked her towards the privacy of the beach, his long legs eating up the road as he explained. 'You're not even remotely guilty, Addy. Don't you see? There are three ways a person is guilty of fraud: they can deliberately claim a work is an original when it's not, they can sign their name to someone else's work and claim it as theirs, or vice versa—that's not relevant here—or they can misrepresent the artwork's date or origins, all for the sake of turning a profit, of course. Galbraith is the one who claimed the work was Perugino's. You didn't. All you're guilty of is being socially attached to the blackguard.'

And poor judgement, if Hazard was right. But Addy kept those thoughts to herself. *If* Hazard was right? She felt caught between the two men. Should she doubt Hazard or Bennett? Who did she believe? She'd known Bennett for a year. She'd known Hazard for two weeks, yet she felt she *knew* him far better than she'd ever known Bennett. Was that on purpose so he could gain her trust?

Hazard faced her, hands on lean hips, his greatcoat pushed back, the beach behind him. 'You do believe me, don't you, Addy?' His dark gaze studied her. She watched his throat work as if her affirmation mattered. Did he have any idea what he asked of her?

Chapter Eleven

'You want me to work against someone who professed to be my friend, who believed in me, who thought I could be more, who said they could make me famous, make me rich, who proposed to me. He claimed to love me.' *None of it was true.* The idea whispered around her mind even as her voice broke. What was it Bennett had once said about bold lies? They were easier to believe. And she had believed everything he'd told her because admitting they were *not* true brought the initial sense of betrayal rushing back. Never mind that her own feelings towards him had been unresolved, that she hadn't wanted to marry him. She didn't want to marry anyone. Still, it had been nice to think someone was head over heels for her...

That it had been a sham cut hard and deep. No one liked to be duped and she'd been more than that. She'd been used and she'd been gullible. She'd been *warned* by Artemisia and she hadn't listened, even when it had been so clear, even when her own feelings had warned her something was strange about him, that it was all too good to be true. Now she knew why—why she'd never felt quite comfortable with him, why those feelings of hers had remained unresolved. Bennett was a fraud—all he'd offered her, felt for her, was a fraud as well. And it hurt—oh, sweet heavens, how it hurt.

'I am sorry, Addy.' Hazard's voice was kind without being full of pity even as he pressed his argument forward. 'He is banking on you believing all that. He thinks you'll protect him if he's found out, if not out of fear for yourself, then out of love for him.' He'd stopped short of saying Galbraith had tried to buy her silence, her protection with his expensive gifts. Addy was grateful for that small mercy. 'I know it hurts, Addy.'

She looked up, her tone sharp. 'How do you know that?' She was unwilling to be patronised with platitudes. How dare he stand there and pretend he knew how she was feeling. She couldn't imagine anything or anyone hurting Hazard Manning. He was too big, a veritable wall of a man, and he was too smart. He saw *everything*. Nothing got past him. He saw people as they were, not as they presented themselves to be. 'You never would have been taken in by the likes of Bennett Galbraith.'

Hazard sat down heavily beside her on the sand and picked up her hand. 'It's not just feeling duped that makes you angry, though, is it? If it was just you, you would find a way to bear it. But it's not just you who is affected by this. It's your sister, her husband, the school, the students. They are all potential victims of your choices and the consequences. People were depending on you and you let them down. That's why you're angry. You should have known better, for their sake as well as yours. I know, because I've done the same thing.'

Addy swallowed. The insight was so complete, so correct, that it pushed her out of her shock, her curiosity awakened. Perhaps that was what he intended, to offer comfort in the form of commiseration. 'I don't believe it.' Addy smiled to offer him comfort. The reference clearly made him uncomfortable and yet he was willing to sacrifice his own comfort for the sake of hers, to let her know she wasn't alone. The effort touched her, drew her in with its sincerity even as the new raw edge of her called for caution. It wouldn't do to make the same mistake twice.

'Believe it. It happened on the Peninsula. Men were counting on me and I wasn't fast enough. I should have been, though.'

He could not recall ever telling this story to another in the years since it happened. Mostly, he tried to bury it along with his other worst moments, but sitting here beside Addy, watching her take herself to task for having been gulled by the likes of Bennett Galbraith, he could not hold back. If his story could help her, then it would be worth unearthing.

'We were with the troops Wellington was using to take Salamanca. He'd entered the city and had deployed men to take the six forts outside the city. Our division was assigned to take San Gaetano. It was supposed to be easy pickings.' He slid Addy a wry smile. 'That should have been our first clue. Nothing is ever easy. Our Spanish intelligence was flawed. I'd intercepted another coded dispatch from the French, but the code was new. It took too long to decipher. By the time I had cracked it and ridden for reinforcements, we'd already encountered casualties. Our commanding general had already sent four hundred men to attack the fort, thinking that would be sufficient, only to lose a quarter of them, some of them killed, some of them taken prisoner by the French.' He paused. 'If I'd been faster decoding, faster riding, a hundred men and more would have been spared that night.'

Addy wrinkled her brow. 'But the British took the fort.'

'Oh, yes, we did, but I doubt that matters to the one hundred and twenty who were lost. A fort is just brick and mortar. A life is something rather more substantial. It wasn't just their lives that were lost. It was the lives of the ones they'd left behind. Young widows, children, infants. They're on my conscience as much as the soldiers who died.' Looking back, the code seemed so obvious now, but at the time he'd struggled, using old understandings to decode the new arrangement. 'Men paid for my incompetence, including my brother. He was with the four hundred. He was wounded. Severely.'

'Oh, Hazard, I'm so sorry.' Addy's voice was soft, her hand squeezing his in support.

'I don't want you to be sorry, Addy. That's not why I am telling you this,' Hazard held her gaze steady. 'I'm telling you so that you learn from it and start to heal, to believe in yourself.' He'd had to do that alone. He'd rather Addy not have to. 'I carry those ghosts with me, I carry my brother's injury with me, as reminders to not allow something like that to happen again, to put protections in place where people are not at risk.' *This* was why he would not marry. Telling her the story now was a potent reminder, perhaps the resolve he needed to reassert his vow.

'What happened?' Addy's eyes were intent on him, all her attention focused on his face as she leaned towards him.

'It was a new code, the one we now know was the Great Paris Cipher. It was the first time I'd seen it. I was cocky, after all there were those who believed I was one of the best in the business. I'd worked with Major Scovell on breaking the Army of Portugal code the year prior. Clinton, our major-general and

Monteith's son, trusted me implicitly. But the Grand Paris Cipher was different, more complex. It didn't play the usual rules of patterns and frequency analysis. We wouldn't fully crack that code for a while yet. I'd only got the rudiments down, just enough to think we might be in for some real trouble.'

'No, not that, as interesting as it is,' Addy broke in gently. 'What happened with your brother?' Of course, she would want to know. Addy Stansfield was all about people first, it was why Galbraith's betrayal had rent her in two.

'When we came home from war, no one was sure Rafe would make it, not even the doctors. He was shot high in the thigh and the threat of losing his leg was very real, as was the threat of losing him entirely.' He breathed out, controlling the emotions that the memory of those days raised. His brother, so vibrant and athletic, stretched out and pale, a lifeless caricature of what he'd once been as his bandages seeped with blood.

'You didn't mention he was wounded the first time you spoke of him,' Addy interrupted softly. No, he'd only said they'd both come home from war and he'd let her draw her own conclusions. It hadn't seemed to matter at the time. Just a few weeks ago they were new acquaintances. Now, perhaps he and Addy were so much more and perhaps she deserved to understand him better.

'I brought him home by ship, battling fever and infection for days until we reached Sussex.' He'd been relieved to get home, thinking that somehow, magically, if he could just get his brother home, Rafe would be all right. He'd written ahead and all had been prepared: a bed in the parlour, doctors waiting who didn't have a hundred other men to look after, fresh bandages and good food. All the things a man needed to thrive. 'When it appeared Rafe would lose his leg, his fiancée, Violet, went to pieces, railing at the doctors for their incompetence until I had to remove her from the room.'

'My father lost himself in painting and drinking after my mother died. He forgot for a while he had two daughters,' Addy consoled softly. 'It's understandable, stress and worry combine to bring out the worst in people.'

Hazard grimaced. 'It certainly does. Violet was in my arms sobbing when my father came upon us, his own temper and frustrations and fears pushed to the breaking point. In his agitation, he was ready to think the worst of his younger son and the woman pledged to marry his heir.'

He could still hear the words in his head, the accusation and his disbelief that his father thought him capable of such treachery. *'Is this how you treat your brother? Hasn't he suffered enough without you taking his intended, too? You are no son of mine.'*

'I packed up my things and left in the morning. I've not been back since. My father died of a broken heart, believing his son had tried to steal his other son's bride.' He'd left to prove his father wrong, left so he didn't have to face his brother and see evidence of his failure every day in his brother's limp, in the cane that would be his constant companion, left so that Violet and Rafe might have a chance at the life they'd so carefully planned before Rafe had gone to war, left so that no one close to him would be hurt again. He'd not been back for any of life's occasions; not the wedding, not his father's funeral. So far, it had worked. He was usually good at pretending he stayed away for reasons in his present instead of admitting the reasons were in the past.

* * *

'Thank you for telling me,' Addy rose from the sand. Would he understand she was thanking him for more than the story itself? That she was thanking him for sharing something deeply personal with her? For opening up to her and, in doing so, demonstrating that he was different than Bennett? That she could trust him in the days going forward? But the story and its lesson couldn't entirely take away the sense of betrayal. She'd failed others and she'd failed herself, thinking she knew what true love looked like. She didn't love Bennett, had never loved him. She saw that now and he didn't love her. They'd been playing at two different games: she at a fantasy fairy tale spurred on by his attentions and he at something more criminal and nefarious. She let the enormity of that wash over her. She'd just wanted her life to start, just wanted something different, so badly that she'd jumped blindly at the first chance to get it. She'd been such a fool!

She wanted to wallow in her dismay, in the hurt of Bennett's betrayal which had wounded more than her heart. But she couldn't. Somehow, in her weakness, she had to find strength.

Her family needed her to clean this mess up. She couldn't do that locked in her room, crying her eyes out. She drew a deep breath and exhaled, breathing out hurt, breathing in fortitude as she faced Hazard. 'So, what do we do next?'

Hazard smiled, his eyes warm with approval. 'Good girl. I knew I could count on you to rise to the occasion. To start, you are going home and telling Artemisia to set another place for dinner. You can tell her what you'd like or you can wait and we'll go over it together at supper.' *Together*. She liked the sound of that. Only she could make things right, but she wouldn't have to do it alone. 'As for me, I am going to the Crown.'

Worry stabbed at her. She reached for his arm. 'You're not going to go after Bennett yourself, are you?'

'If he's there, it will make quick work of this situation. I can think of nothing more straightforward than to question him and take him to London on the strength of your testimony that you painted the Perugino for practice.'

Addy nodded. *Her testimony*. Everything rode on that. She'd have to endure it, the questions, the speculation, no matter how public it became, no matter how it might damage her career. It's what she had to do in order to make amends, to stop Bennett from doing such a thing again to someone else. 'I will see you at supper, then.' She would go home, find Artemisia in the garden with the baby and enjoy the time left to her. Her world was about to shift. In a couple of short hours it would be turned on its end, never to be the same.

In truth, it had begun shifting the moment she'd realised what Bennett had done and how he'd embroiled her. How dare he do that to her? Her hurt was starting to congeal into anger. *Good.* She would need that anger. It was stronger. 'Hazard, be careful.' She would not forgive herself if anything happened to him on her behalf.

'I will be, Addy. Remember, this is my job.' He covered her hand where it lay on his sleeve. 'I'll see you at dinner.'

Chapter Twelve

Hazard drew his pistol, the weapon hidden in the long folds of his greatcoat, as he made his way along the narrow, dark corridor of rooms on the Crown's second floor. Galbraith's room was two down from his. He hoped the weapon would be needed only to expedite Galbraith's acquiescence. He didn't want to have to use it. The taproom below was getting busy as evening approached. A pistol report would draw attention.

He'd rather use his fists if Galbraith chose to resist. It would give him an outlet for the anger in him, anger on behalf of Addy. She'd been sorely used by Galbraith. He'd abused her trust and several other emotions in order to profit from her talent. She deserved better. At the door, he knocked. Despite his baser instincts, he had a job to do and he would comport himself in the manner Bow Street and Monteith expected of their representative.

There was no answer. He knocked again, pressing an ear to the door to catch any tell-tale sounds. Galbraith was abed all hours of the day. But there was no rustling of linen or clothes. 'Galbraith, are you within?' Hazard called. He tried the lock and exchanged the pistol for the picking tool in his pocket. He had the door open in short order, revealing what he'd already suspected. Galbraith was gone. The question was, had he left permanently and how long ago had he left?

Hazard opened the wardrobe. Empty. No personal effects littered any surfaces. The ewer was empty. He'd left after breakfast, then, and he'd taken time to shave or wash. Hazard pulled out his pocket watch. It was half past five now. Galbraith could have up to an eight-hour lead on him and could have gone any direction. Hazard sighed and leaned against the door jamb. So much for straight-forward. While he'd been putting the pieces together, Galbraith had been on the move. Which meant one thing: Galbraith knew he was looking for him.

Of course he knew. Galbraith had known from the start. Hazard closed his eyes, forcing himself to think back. That dinner at the farmhouse, the day they'd gone to Whitstable. He'd sat there at the table, telling Galbraith about the case. Oh, how Galbraith must have been laughing on the inside. What a game it must have been to sit there, knowing he was the one Hazard sought. No wonder he'd been so eager to get Addy alone. He'd wanted to shore up loose ends, to make sure Addy was on his side, to warn her about the inspector, no doubt.

Hazard's eyes flew open. Galbraith had stayed until he wasn't sure of Addy. What had tipped him off that Addy would not side with him? Or was it that Galbraith had only stayed until he realised Hazard had figured it out? How would he have known? If he'd left for the latter reason, it called the man out for a coward. What sort of man left a woman behind to take the blame for him? He'd run without Addy or a concern for what his desertion would mean to her. Addy was nothing more than a pawn. In chess, pawns were expendable.

And he'd left her unguarded.

He'd sent her home, so sure he'd take Galbraith by surprise and that would be the end of it. He'd have Galbraith where he could keep an eye on him, where Addy could be protected. It took all his willpower not to give in to the urge to run full tilt all the way to the farmhouse. He needed to be more orderly. He needed to go downstairs and talk to Alice, the maid Galbraith had been tupping. Already, his mind was assembling the necessary questions as he took the stairs: When had she last seen him? Had he said where he was going? When he'd be back?

Alice was no help. She'd not seen him since last night and he'd not told her anything useful. Hazard was inclined to believe her. Galbraith would want to cover his tracks and he was clearly experienced at it. Self-preservation made a man extremely careful. Trust no one, love no one. Hazard knew precisely how a man like that thought. A man who loved only himself was a dangerous man and now he was on the loose, beyond Hazard's control.

Hazard quickened his steps once he was out of doors and on the path to the farmhouse. Galbraith could be anywhere: miles from here, on the sea to France, on the road to London, or gone to ground here in order to keep an eye on the farmhouse. Would he leave without the painting? Addy said there was a buyer for it. Would he leave without Addy? Just as he'd earlier postulated that Galbraith had run without her, he wasn't so sure in hindsight. Galbraith needed her painting for money and he could use her for leverage for protection. If he held Addy and threatened to harm her, it would be difficult to expose him. Blackmail could play out in so many different ways, but only if Galbraith got his hands on Addy. Hazard broke into a jog. He could not allow that to happen.

A plan was beginning to form. He had to get her away from here, somewhere Galbraith couldn't find her. There was only one place he could think of that would give her that safety. Addy had to be kept safe at all costs, even if it meant facing his own ghosts.

Addy met him at the door, her eyes searching his face and sensing his worry. 'What's happened?'

'Change of plans. Galbraith is gone.' Hazard took her hand and led her through the hall, never breaking his stride, his words urgent.

'Where's St Helier and his family?' He did not think Galbraith would be so bold as to go after the Viscount, but he could not yet rule it out as a means of getting to Addy.

'In the garden.' Addy tugged at his wrist. 'Hazard, stop. Tell me what's going on?'

Hazard turned, placing his hands on her shoulders. 'Galbraith is at large. He was gone before I got there. He could be anywhere, Addy. Far from here or close by. We don't know where he is and, as long as he's out there, you are in danger. You're the only one who can convict him. Without you, there is no case.' He watched her pale and he hated adding one more shock to the shocks she'd already endured today. But his Addy was strong. She would get through this, he would see to it. 'We need to talk to St Helier and your sister and explain what must be done. I am taking you somewhere Galbraith won't look for you—I am taking you to Sussex. We leave in the morning at first light.'

It was mortifying to listen to Hazard lay the specifics of the situation out to Darius and Artemisia over a tense supper. All she needed now was for Artemisia to say *I told you so.*

Except her sister didn't. Artemisia merely took her hand and held it tight. Addy thought Artemisia's pity might be worse. Once again, she was the little sister in need of protecting, the little sister not worldly enough to make her own way. At the first opportunity to strike out for herself, she'd fallen for a bounder and it wasn't only herself she'd put in danger, but her family, too.

'Now, we need to keep Addy safe until we can find him,' Hazard was saying. 'I am taking her to Sussex. My family is there. My mother and my sister-in-law can act as chaperons. It will be quite decent, I assure you.'

Darius nodded. 'In the meanwhile, how will we find Galbraith?'

Hazard shook his head. 'I'll have my men in London keep an eye out for him, but there's no guarantee he even uses the same name or that he'll surface in London. I think we must wait for him to come to us.' Hazard nodded in her direction. 'Addy tells me there's another painting she's almost finished that he has a buyer for. Criminals tend to return to the scene of the crime, especially when there's something they've left behind, something they haven't got. In Galbraith's case it's Addy and the painting.'

Addy watched Artemisia and Darius exchange a glance in their secret, silent communication. Darius spoke, 'What happens when Galbraith comes back and Addy and the painting aren't here?' Addy's gut clenched.

'Perhaps you should come with us,' Addy put in, panic in her voice. Would Bennett harm them? Her sweet little nephew? If he did, it would be her fault. The more this unfolded, the more she realised the depth of evil she'd brought into her home.

'There's the school to think about,' Artemisia refused gently before Darius could take the suggestion. 'We'll be fine here. It's not us he's after and, if the painting is gone, too, I think he'll realise there's nothing here for him.'

Hazard nodded. 'I agree with that assessment. He knows we'll be looking for him, he is not going to risk his freedom by taking on a viscount. He needs more direct action, although you're welcome to come if you would feel safer.'

'No.' Artemisia was firm on that point, her eyes spearing her husband, daring him to gainsay her. 'We will stay here.' She rose. 'Addy, let me help you pack. It will be an early morning.'

It wasn't until they were upstairs that Artemisia gathered her in her arms. 'Oh, Addy, I am so sorry. Are you all right? You didn't say anything today in the garden.'

Addy hugged her sister, not sure when she'd see her again. 'I wanted to wait until Hazard was here. We wanted to explain it together and he'd hoped to have Bennett by then.' It was all supposed to have been easy and safe. But the world had tilted once again into the unknown. 'I am the one who is sorry. I should have listened to you.'

'No.' Artemisia stepped back. 'Do not scold yourself. No one blames you. It could have happened to anyone. Everyone makes mistakes. I certainly did. The most important thing right now is keeping you safe and catching Bennett. Focus on that.'

'I worry for you and the baby,' Addy put in. If anything happened to them… It was unthinkable. She still couldn't fathom carefree Bennett possessing the level of evil that would harm a baby, but she'd been wrong about him. She had to consider the impossible.

'Darius can protect us and you can, too, by going with the inspector. He's a good man, Addy. He will take care of you.' Artemisia paused. 'You like him.'

'I don't think that's a salient point right now. These aren't ideal circumstances for such a consideration.' Addy reached beneath her bed and dragged out her travelling trunk. If circumstances had been different, she might have more than liked Hazard. But right now, she couldn't.

How could she possibly think of leaping from her folly with Bennett, a man she'd known for a year and still been so wrong about, into the arms of a man she'd barely known a handful of weeks? What a disaster that could be.

But you know so much more about Hazard than you ever knew about Bennett, the temptation whispered.

No. Maybe someday there would be a man she could trust, but not now. The wound was too raw. Whatever might exist between she and Hazard Manning must remain unexplored, a casualty of life and mistakes. She already regretted the loss of that potential.

Chapter Thirteen

He was taking her to Sussex. Home. *His* home. A place he seldom went, to people he never saw, never spoke about unless he was heavily prompted. The enormity of that choice settled on Addy as the coach covered the miles between Kent and Sussex at record speed, a testament to how thoroughly Hazard believed in the safety his home could provide. But she was aware that safety for her came at a cost for him. His was a haunted house, full of ghosts from his past: a wounded brother, the memory of a heartbroken father, perhaps lingering traces of betrayal. He'd left under his father's cloud of suspicion and had not been back since. There was hurt for him there and a past that waited to be confronted.

Yet he was willing to face all that for her.

He'd been willing to put her comfort above his own, her safety above his need, as he had done throughout the entire mad dash from Kent. He knew how to make a woman feel safe, even a woman who'd had her world torn apart, who thought she might never feel safe again.

Addy was in tune with every sacrifice, with each consideration, aware that he split his time between riding inside the coach with her to keep her company, to offer her assurances, and riding outside to scout ahead and make arrangements, or to ride behind to be sure they weren't followed. When they stopped for lunch, a private parlour was ready at the inn and another when they stopped for the night. While he saw that she slept snugly in a bed, he slept roughly in the hall before her door, another sign of how seriously he took the threat of Bennett's disappearance.

It made for a very haggard Hazard in the morning. The man who ushered her to the coach after breakfast wore the stubble of a two-day beard and his features were drawn, his eyes marked by dark circles. All on her behalf. Guilt swamped her. This was her fault. She could hardly complain about missing Artemisia and the comfort of her family. It seemed a small thing when she saw all that Hazard was sacrificing for her. Of course, that was his job and that was what she was now. His job. A job he was very good at.

Under other circumstances, she might have enjoyed watching him work. 'Under other circumstances' had become her motto of late. She'd used that phrase last night when Artemisia had asked her about her interest in the inspector. *If* circumstances were different, she might have indulged in more kisses on beaches, she might have trusted her own judgement. But now? Despite Hazard's efforts at keeping her assured, she'd had too much time alone with her thoughts and they were miserable company.

She was doubt-ridden. What did his care of her mean? Was it strictly because of his job? Was it because those kisses meant something more? Or had they been his job, too? Had he suspected her from the start or had that been as big of a shock to him as it had been to her? Had he used kisses the way Bennett had used his? Had she fallen victim to both of them? Had she been twice the fool? She hoped not, but she had little hope at the moment.

The coach came to a stop and the door opened, revealing a Hazard who looked slightly less haggard thanks to the crisp autumn air. 'We're just a few miles away. I thought you might like some time to freshen up. There's a stream nearby and I've sent a rider on ahead to prepare my family.' He'd thought of everyone. This stop was as much for her as for his family, giving everyone time to ready themselves for this intrusion. That's what she was—an intrusion, an imposition thrown on an unsuspecting family.

Hazard showed her to the stream and gave her privacy, retreating back to the road to keep watch. She didn't have much tidying to do. She'd dressed carefully that morning at the inn, choosing a forest-green carriage ensemble trimmed in black velvet at the cuffs and collar, a hat set at a jaunty angle, more decoration than head covering. She checked her hair in a small travelling mirror. Nothing was out of place except the jumble of her thoughts. She wanted to make a good impression on her unsuspecting hosts. She would be an unexpected guest whose visit would be for an indeterminate length of time. She would make herself useful. She would not let them regret having her.

'Addy, is everything all right?' Hazard's boots crunched among the dry leaves.

'Yes—no.' She turned with a little laugh designed to hide her nerves. 'I don't want to be an imposition to them,' she confessed. Hazard had cleaned up, too. He'd combed his hair and taken time to shave while he'd kept watch. He'd retied his cravat, but it was crooked. She reached out automatically to straighten it.

'You are no imposition, Addy. They are going to like you as I do.' He'd hesitated for a moment over the word 'like'. For a moment, she'd thought he might say 'love'. How that would have changed the sentence.

'You have to like me. I am your job.' Addy fiddled with the cravat.

Hazard's hands closed over hers where they played with his neckcloth. 'You are not my job, Addy. Is that what's worrying you?'

Addy shook her head. He was being nice, professional. 'You don't have to pretend. I understand, truly. You needn't worry that I think there's anything between us just because we shared a kiss on a beach.' They'd shared more than kisses. They'd shared picnics, long walks on the beach, suppers with her family, and she'd convinced herself it meant something.

She'd let herself forget who she really was: plain Addy Stansfield, the girl who would always be second.

When would she learn? Men didn't fight over her or about her. Bennett had not loved her. She'd spun her own fairy tale there and she'd done it again with Hazard. She was second-born, the 'other' Stansfield sister, the other Stansfield painter, the other instructor at the art school. Even for Hazard, she was second-best. He'd gone after Bennett and when he couldn't have him, he'd settled for her. She was the only link left to making the case, he had no choice but to defend her.

Hazard's voice was a low, husky growl. 'This is why I could kill Galbraith with my bare hands. I won't have it, Addy. I can see in your face that you're doubting yourself, doubting me, all because of what he did to you. I don't just mean the business with the painting. I mean what he did to *you*, how you think of yourself. How dare he make a smart woman feel as if she is not enough?' His grip on her hands was tight, his gaze holding hers with an intensity that wouldn't let her look away. 'He wants you to think you're weak when in truth you're the powerful one. He's nothing without you, but he doesn't want you to believe that.'

'You're trying to make me feel better.' Addy let a smile slip free. 'Is that part of your job, too? Making your clients feel better?'

'Only you, Addy. Let us be very clear. I do not make a habit of kissing my clients.'

'I was your suspect first, though, wasn't I?' She matched his seriousness with a gravity of her own. 'Did you suspect me from the start? I have to know, Hazard.'

'Will you believe me? I want your word, or I won't tell you.' The world was quiet around them, just the call of birds and the sound of the stream. Addy nodded.

'I am not Bennett Galbraith. I did not kiss you to get you to incriminate yourself, to trust a man that did not deserve it. I kissed you because I wanted to, because I'd wanted to kiss you almost from the first moment I saw you. But I couldn't. Shouldn't. Not until the case was cleared. But you were irresistible. You still are and it's killing me. I can't be distracted if I'm to keep you safe. All I want to do is give in to the distraction and see where it goes. But I can't, so I am doing the next best thing, I am taking you home.'

His words left her speechless. 'I distract you?'

A slow smile spread across his mouth. 'Yes, particularly right now.'

She dared to let herself smile, dared to let herself feel a bit of the old warmth he had stirred in her, just before his mouth covered hers in a lingering kiss that fuelled a slow heat in her, like whisky on a cold day, only better, sweeter. 'Addy,' he whispered against her mouth, 'always remember you undo me.' It was not an exaggeration coming from Hazard.

She would remember. It would be a delicious memory to draw on someday when all this was over. She would also remember that it was just a kiss. This time she would keep her wits about her. She could undo him, but he could not be allowed to undo her. She'd learned her lesson.

He rode with her for the remaining few miles. They'd been no more than a half-hour from the house when they'd stopped and they were soon turning from the road on to an oak-lined drive spread above them in a radiant canopy of scarlets and golds, the kind of canopy that took generations to grow. At the end of the drive stood a square sandstone manor house, ivy growing about the windows reaching up to the slate roof. She was already painting it in her mind: a grey-blue for the roof as it reached to the sky, a beige tinged with pink for the sandstone, a deep forest green for the ivy, a spring green for the lawn, light pinks and lilacs for the flowering bushes. She turned to Hazard and smiled. 'You said you lived on a farm. I think you lied. I live in a farmhouse, but this is far beyond that.'

'It's an old home with Tudor door frames and Georgian staircases all mixed together. My grandfather had ambitions when he had the staircase installed.'

'I can hardly wait to see it.' Addy reached out a hand for his. She ought not to touch him so easily. It was a habit she probably needed to break, but not in this moment. She was not the only vulnerable one. It was her turn to ask the question. 'Will you be all right?' He'd looked after her so exquisitely, but who looked after him? He should not treat himself as an impervious stone wall.

'Yes, but thank you for asking, Addy.' The coach rolled to a halt and she let go of his hand, uncertain of what her role was to be.

Was she here as a friend? As a woman in hiding? What had Hazard told them about her?

'I told them you were an artist in need of refuge.' Hazard slid her a grin. 'My mother will probably want portraits.'

She could do that. She saw the genius of Hazard at work beneath the words. She would have something to keep her busy and the family had grounds on which to understand her presence. 'I hope that includes you.' She'd like to paint him, to master the unfinished ruggedness of his face, the solemn dark eyes.

The coach rolled to a stop and she watched Hazard take a deep breath. She imagined what this moment might mean for him, the weight of it and the worry. What sort of reception waited beyond the coach for him? Hazard opened the door and stepped down, reaching back in with a hand for her. They would face his family together.

The Mannings had turned out en masse for them, despite the short notice. The small household staff stood to the left in a straight line, the grooms and gardeners on the right, the family between them on the low front step.

For a moment Addy felt like a bride coming to her husband's home for the first time.

Her gaze swept the assembled family, picking out members from Hazard's brief descriptions. The older woman, dark-haired and dark-eyed, must be his mother. The pretty blonde with a blanketed bundle in her arms must be Violet. The man beside her was undoubtedly Rafe, his brother. They looked similar enough to have been twins, the difference in their ages negligible. But where Hazard might be rough-featured, Rafe was all sartorial precision, his dark hair immaculate, his jaw smooth. His eyes were as sharp as Hazard's. Rafe's hand rested on the shoulder of a small boy, perhaps five years old. Blond like his mother. Addy smiled. What a delightful surprise. Hazard was an uncle. Had he known? He'd not mentioned the children.

There was a moment of formality as Hazard introduced her, 'Rafe, Violet, Mother, this is Miss Adelaide Stansfield.'

Rafe nodded. 'Welcome to our home, Miss Stansfield. We are delighted to have you.' He stepped forward, leaning on his cane to navigate the shallow step. 'Now, for a proper welcome, Hazard, my dear brother. Is this any way to come home after being gone so long? Standing on ceremony when a hug would be so much more appropriate.' Rafe opened his arms and embraced Hazard and the family flooded about them, laughing and exclaiming over what a phenomenal surprise this was and well overdue.

In the midst of hugs and admiring children, Addy slipped Hazard a glance. His eyes were suspiciously glassy as his mother hugged him and his brother seemed determined not to leave his side. He was happy to be here, but there was pain in his gaze, too, a piece of himself he was holding in check, that he wouldn't give to the pleasure of a homecoming. Perhaps, while she was here, she would see what she could do about that after all he'd done for her.

After all he'd done for her, she'd repaid him by absconding with the painting. How dare she! Bennett fumed over a tankard of ale in a dark corner of an inn, in an even darker corner of Kent. That tube of oil canvases he'd given her had been an investment against a lucrative return, so had that book, and that ring, and more. The list was long and expensive when it came to what he'd spent on curating Adelaide Stansfield's favour. Now, she was gone, spirited off by Inspector Manning to who knew where, and the painting was gone with them. He knew. He'd searched the studio when Artemisia had been down at the school.

He'd gone back to the scene of his crimes to get the painting and Addy, to woo her one last time with the lure of his kissing and Florence, confident that it would work. He'd been kissing his way to success since he was sixteen. Women in general found him irresistible. He'd kissed whores and desperate ladies into all nature of compromising compliance, flattered fading roses into giving him the expensive jewellery from their wrists, their ears, their necks. Some of his compatriots on the streets had to steal for a living. He'd bragged he didn't have to. He kissed for it, undressed for it, pleasured women for it. Women were easily beguiled creatures, no matter their birth. Addy Stansfield had not seemed any different.

He blamed her sister. Artemisia had never liked him. He blamed the inspector, too, for turning up so unfortunately, just when he had a good thing going—Addy eating out of his hand, painting for him, making him money and not asking too many questions. He blamed

Peter Timmons most of all. If Timmons hadn't got himself killed, he'd still have his forger. He'd not have needed Addy Stansfield. Of course, she was far superior to Timmons, but she also required much higher maintenance— as current circumstances proved.

He was going to get her back and the painting, too. His thief's honour demanded it and she owed him. She was a danger to him if she remained at large. She could lay testimony against him and Manning would hunt him down if he stayed in England. He'd not be able to sell anything. His plan was to take Addy and leave. He'd let Europe swallow them up and she could earn her keep by painting. He'd blackmail Addy into compliance and she would come with him if she thought her family was threatened. Addy was a sop for protecting others. Besides, she wouldn't remain angry at him for long. He was a very good lover. In time, she'd remember why she'd looked twice at him to start with.

All he had to do was find her, a task much easier said than done. He could no longer walk abroad in Seasalter. The Viscount and the inspector had given the word that he was persona non grata. There was a reward out for

his capture and there was no honour among
Padraig O'Malley's smugglers. Facing down a
long, stormy winter, they'd gladly turn him in
for money that would put food on their tables.
But there was one person in Seasalter who
might not, if he could reach her undetected.

Chapter Fourteen

'Those sketches are good.' Hazard's voice made Addy jump. She'd been so focused on her work, he'd been able to steal up behind her undetected.

She shuffled the papers, flustered, and shoved them into a folder, blushing. 'You shouldn't startle a girl like that. You might see something more than you should.'

Like the sketch I did of you, shirtless, from imagination.

Sweet heavens, how would she explain after all her protestations that she didn't expect his kisses to mean anything? Her mind might have accepted her dictates on the subject, but her imagination had not. It continued to run rampant with fantasies.

'You've been sketching my family,' Hazard

commented, unapologetically. 'I've been watching you in the evenings.'

'It gives me something to do and it's a way to show my appreciation for their hospitality.' Addy threw her arms wide to indicate the guest cottage that had been set up as a private space for her. 'They've given me an art studio. It's unbelievable. They don't even know me.' In the short time she'd been with them, they'd managed to make her feel special, unique.

'I told you they would like you.' Hazard strolled the space, stopping to run his hands over a jar of brushes. He seemed distracted. A rush of warmth went through her at the thought. She remembered quite well what had happened the last time he'd been 'distracted'. 'Portraits would make a lovely Christmas gift. I could pay you for them,' he offered.

She shook her head. 'I wouldn't want money. I'd be glad to do them, but I don't know that I would be able to finish them all.' She paused. 'Do you think I'll be here that long?' She was careful with the question. In the week she'd been in residence, they'd not discussed Bennett or the case. She'd busied herself getting to know Hazard's family and making herself useful. She helped Violet with the children, not that it was a chore. Little Max was a delight to play with in the garden, full of curiosity, and baby Caroline reminded her of Artemisia's Michael.

Staying busy took an edge off the homesickness. She'd not been away from Artemisia like this before, where she had neither her sister nor her home. She missed her sister and the school, but she was also finding joy in being on her own, being Addy Stansfield with no strings attached. The Mannings didn't know her sister or her father. They only knew her. Here in Sussex, ensconced in the bucolic delights of the autumnal countryside and wrapped in her newfound freedom, she could almost forget why she was here and that she'd eventually have to leave.

Hazard straightened the quire of drawing paper next to the brushes. 'You can stay as long as you like. You needn't rush off when the case is resolved.'

'I wouldn't have any reason to stay if the case was resolved. I couldn't continue to impose.' She fussed with her pencils, needing something to do with her hands. This idyll *would* come to an end. Hazard would return to London and his next job once Monteith was satisfied. She would be free to return to Seasalter, or perhaps to do something else if she dared. Perhaps this would be the perfect time to do some travelling of her own. She'd already effected a breakaway, she should capitalise on that. In coming here, she'd taken one step into her own life. Why not take another? 'Has there been any word?' Maybe that was why he'd sought her out, but a shake of his head answered that question even while it posed others. 'What if there is no word of him?' She couldn't spend the rest of her life waiting: waiting for Bennett to surface, waiting for her life to begin.

He knew what she was asking beneath her words. How long did she hide out in Sussex before she outstayed her welcome, before it no longer made sense to be in hiding? He didn't have a ready answer for her other than it was too soon to consider that option. 'I know criminals like him, he *will* make an appearance, Addy. He's been cheated of a painting he had plans to sell and money he'd planned on having. He will want to recoup his losses. The point is that when he does, we'll be able to track him down while keeping you out of his trajectory. You needn't worry. Galbraith won't hurt you, I'll see to it.' Even if meant prosecuting Galbraith in absentia.

'I have my statement written out.' Addy moved to a little desk set against the window and opened the drawer. 'You can include it in your next report to Monteith.'

'There is no hurry, Addy. We have some time yet.' For what? To wait for Galbraith? To prolong parting with her? He was treading a very fine line here between his professional endeavours where she was concerned and his personal. When this was over he had no excuse to keep her close, no reason to bask in her presence without admitting to his growing feelings. Letting her go and denying those feelings was the best course of action, certainly. There was no room in his life for a wife *and* his work. It was dangerous to mix the two. He could offer her nothing but the present.

'I want you to be happy here, Addy.' He wanted her smile back, her laugh, her easy openness, the freshness that made her uniquely Addy. Selfishly, he wanted to be the one who gave them back to her. He wanted Galbraith to pay for what he'd done, but the law didn't convict a man for stealing a woman's confidence. He would have to settle for bringing Galbraith in on charges of fraud.

'I want you to trust again, Addy.' With him. Despite their conversation that day at the stream, despite his assurances, she was holding back from him, careful with her feelings. He should be grateful. It would make parting when the time came simpler if there were fewer ties between them beyond the case itself, but he didn't like the reason for it.

'I think it will be a while before I trust a man again,' Addy answered honestly. She moved to the sofa set before the fireplace and poked at the flames, stirring up the dying embers. 'If I'd listened to my sister, none of this would have happened. I thought falling in love would be different for me, that I would learn from my sister's mistakes and I would be smarter about it.' Addy sat down and Hazard took up a spot at the mantel, patient, waiting for her to say more. 'Artemisia was hurt early in love. It had been a bad choice from the start, even I could see it, but she couldn't. She thought she had it all well in hand but she was eighteen and no match for a man of the world.' Addy made an apologetic moue.

'I saw what it did to her and I vowed I would not make that mistake. When or if I fell in love, it would be a fairy tale.'

He heard the self-condemnation in her voice as it trembled over the last words. Galbraith was a bastard. A fraud conviction was too good for him. It took all of Hazard's restraint not to reach for her, not to pull her close. Every fibre of his being wanted to be her port in the storm. She didn't want that, wasn't ready for it, not from a man. She'd made that clear.

'I wonder if Bennett knew that? It was as though he could read my mind. He gave me the fairy tale, the compliments, the attention, the gifts. I fell for it, everything I promised myself I wouldn't do.' She gave a harsh laugh. 'Do you know the irony of it? Artemisia warned me. I didn't listen. I was so sure I knew exactly what I was doing and who I was doing it with. I didn't know anything about him. Or perhaps I did and I didn't want to admit to it.' She shot him a quizzing glance. 'You're awfully quiet. Say something.'

'What would you like me to say? That everyone makes mistakes? You already know they do. Your sister made them, your father made them. I made them. You just didn't count yourself among them. You need to give yourself permission to be human, Addy.'

'I'd rather go back in time. I want to go back to that day on the shingle in Whitstable where we were skipping stones. I wish we'd never gone home.'

Except then he wouldn't have the memory of Addy leaning her head against his shoulder all the way back to the farmhouse. 'Maybe we can.' Hazard took her hand. 'Come with me. We might not have the ocean, but we do have a good lake.' A walk in fresh air would do them both good and the lake wasn't far.

At the lake shore he bent down and picked up a few pebbles. He pressed one into her hand with a grin, 'Do you remember how to do it?'

Addy was game. The brisk air had helped ease the tension that had gathered in the cottage as they'd danced around the issue of their burgeoning relationship. Did they give it life or smother it like the fire in the fireplace? Banked before it got started, before it could burn out of control? Addy cocked her wrist and threw, but the stone gave a disappointing plop in the water.

Against his better judgement, he stepped behind her, his hand taking her wrist, adjusting it into position. He should not have done it, especially now when he knew how such contact ended. Nothing had changed, only intensified. The old electric feel of her vibrated up his arm, a reminder that he wanted her, pending heartbreak and all, for how else could this end? There would be disappointment if he acted on his feelings and disappointment if he did not. It was not well done of him. She was hurting and vulnerable. 'Now, try,' he encouraged. The rock skipped twice and he stepped back, putting a respectable distance between them.

But it was too late. Addy closed the distance, her gaze soft on his face. 'Maybe it's not just the stone skipping I want back.' She licked her lips, tentatively gathering her boldness. 'You kissed me on the shingle, back when I believed kisses were sincere.' She took another step closer. 'I want to believe that again.'

He should absolutely refuse. He did not want to be the rock she clung to like a desperate limpet. He wanted to be more. But his good judgement seemed to be in short supply today. She was in his arms, her sweet, heart-shaped face tipped up to his, lips parted expectantly, eyes filled with hope. He ran a gentle thumb over her lips. 'Addy, it's not men you need to trust again, it's yourself.'

Nothing could come of this. He'd be gone in a few weeks. He could offer her nothing, not even a family. Yet, the arguments that had been forming all week came: if he could offer her a small piece of solace, perhaps it would be worth it to taste the sweetness of her mouth against his, the soft press of her body against his. Perhaps for a little while they could both dream and that would be enough.

He bent his head to hers then, taking the mouth on offer, the hope on offer. Addy wrapped her arms about his neck, the warmth of her held against him, a reminder that Addy kissed with her whole body; mouth, arms, hips, the kiss as honest and open as she was. He could not help but give her the same in return. He let her tongue explore him, let her taste him. She loved leisurely kisses and he loved them with her—the languid heat those kisses stirred, the slow burn that followed in their wake. Did she understand, though, that for a man a slow burn would not remain a simmer? That it would become a raging fire? Even now, he wanted more from her. What would it be like to lay her down on a bed, to strip her bare and kiss every inch of her in that same leisurely fashion? To have her do the same to him as if they had all afternoon? As if they had for ever, not just a few weeks.

'There you are!' Rafe's booming tones reached him from a distance, giving fair warning or at least the pretence of it. There was a respectable distance between he and Addy by the time Rafe reached them, but the glint in his brother's eye suggested he'd seen it all. 'I am sorry to interrupt, but the post has come for you, Hazard, from London. I thought you'd want to know right away. Perhaps I was wrong, though,' Rafe said, looking from Hazard to Addy.

Addy smoothed her skirts. 'You go on with your brother, Hazard. Read your letters. I will…um…finish gathering stones, for my…um…project.' He grinned at her valiant efforts although they weren't fooling anyone, certainly not Rafe who seemed intent on making them squirm as only a big brother could.

'Stones for what? What kind of project?'

'Painting?' Addy improvised. 'I thought Max might like to paint faces on them.'

Hazard took his brother by the arm and turned him towards the house. 'Come on, Rafe, let's go read my post—that is, if you haven't opened it already.'

Rafe waited until they were out of earshot to begin his interrogation. 'She's a splendid girl, Haz. I can see why you like her. I wouldn't let her get away.'

'It's not like that,' Hazard corrected, suddenly aware of how rough the terrain was between the lake and the house. Surely it was too uneven for his brother to be walking about. He could fall and be unable to get up. 'Couldn't you have sent someone with the news? You shouldn't be out here.'

'Why not?' Rafe pulled his arm away, defensive. 'I tramp out here all the time.'

'You could fall and really hurt yourself.' Did Violet know Rafe rambled about unescorted?

Rafe clapped a hand on his shoulder. 'Dear brother, it's been seven years since my injury. I limp, I will always limp, but I've found ways to manage. A lot has changed since you left. You would know that if you'd answered my letters.' There was a scold for him in that as they found their way indoors to Rafe's office. 'I'm not an invalid.' Rafe stopped at the decanters to pour them each a brandy. 'We've been dancing around that since you arrived and much else.' He motioned for Hazard to take a chair near the fire. 'Does the post have anything to do with why Miss Stansfield is really here? Is she work or pleasure? I admit to not knowing. I think the two have been quite conflated since you got here and then there's what I saw at the lake. *That* was definitely pleasure.' Rafe took the chair opposite him and passed him the post.

Hazard studied the markings. Bow Street had written. He slit the seal and scanned the contents, his alarm rising. His team had connected Peter Timmons to Bennett Galbraith. The man had worked for Galbraith and had likely been killed because of it, not because of his debt as previously thought. That explained why Galbraith had come looking for Addy. He'd needed another painter if he meant to pursue his illegal art dealing. It was more than alarming to consider the why behind the need. Had the underground killed Timmons? Or, the darker thought formed, had Galbraith done him in himself for whatever reason? Hazard could imagine a few. Perhaps Timmons had threatened to betray him? Such a threat would make it worth the effort of having to find another forger.

Suffice it to say, it was not the news that Hazard had been hoping for—on several levels. He would have preferred a sighting, something he could track. He'd rather go to Galbraith than have to wait for Galbraith to come to him. More than that, though, the news was unwelcome because it verified quite concretely the risk to Addy. If Peter Timmons had been killed because of his association with Galbraith, Hazard could not dismiss the danger that might also be posed to Addy. He set the letter aside as his brother picked up the threads of their earlier conversation.

'Are you going to marry her?' Rafe was persistent with his infernal interrogation.

'She's a client, regardless of what you think you saw at the lake.'

Rafe chuckled. 'I *know* what I saw at the lake. She's more than a client to you. So, marry her after this is concluded if you're worried about it. You can have the wedding here at Christmas. Mother would be overjoyed to plan it.' Rafe made it sound so simple, assuming Addy wanted those things, too. Did she? They'd never talked of marriage beyond the one reference to his job. It wasn't something one discussed with a client or a witness.

He had his usual answer at the ready. 'I can't marry her, Rafe. My work is too dangerous. I can't risk her being brought into it. The criminals I track could use her as leverage against me if our connection were discovered. She could be a kidnapping target.'

Rafe raised a dark brow, not quite believing him. 'Is that why you've stayed away so long? Do you think you're protecting us? I doubt we'd be at much risk out here in the country.'

'You have children, Rafe,' Hazard warned. 'Surely their safety is a paramount concern.'

Rafe laughed. 'Yes, two of them, that you've never even seen. You'd think I injured my cock in the war, not my leg. I think it's of paramount importance they know their uncle.' Rafe leaned forward. 'I have a family now, Hazard: the wife I've dreamed of since I was twelve and children. I have everything I want except my brother with me. If it's a choice between Miss Stansfield and your job, come home. Run the estate with me and marry her.

We can build you a house on the edge of the property, our children can grow up together. Little Caroline won't be our last. Did you see Miss Stansfield with her the other night? She's a natural with babes.'

Did Rafe think he was blind? Yes, he'd seen her with the children, last night and every day before. He'd seen her in the orchard picking up windfall apples with Max and teaching him to paint in the studio. He went to bed with images of what that other life could be. He woke up aching and hard for want of them, of *her*.

Hazard took a long swallow of his drink. 'Rafe, slow down. You have so many carts before the horse. Addy and I haven't even discussed what happens next week let alone what happens in a few months.' Except they had. She thought she might travel. If she didn't, she had the art school. Besides, taking Rafe's offer was more than making a life with Addy. Coming home meant living every day with the proof of how he'd failed Rafe. For all the happiness this current homecoming had brought, it was a happiness that floated on the surface of darker waters.

Yet, he could not deny he was hungry for the picture Rafe painted, of a life with Addy, with a family of his own, a son like Max, a daughter like Caroline. It was not an image he'd allowed himself to dwell on for years. It had been easy enough to subdue, burying it in work and danger, deliberately putting it out of his reach until he'd met Addy. She'd brought the yearning roaring to the fore. He tossed back his drink and picked up the post. 'I need to change for dinner and send a letter of my own.' Mostly, he needed to be alone where he could get his thoughts back into a more orderly fashion. The reality was, he had only a short time left with Addy. The two of them needed to decide how best to spend what time they had: acting on their attraction, or deciding it was best shelved. After all, nothing could come of it except a handful of nights.

Chapter Fifteen

She only had a short time with Hazard, something that was brought home to Addy each day. Leaves fell, the weather grew colder, reminders that time was passing. It was all Addy was certain of these days, that and the reality of the growing attraction between her and Hazard, an attraction that was having less to do with their circumstances and more to do with the man every day.

Hazard's laughter drifted back to her through the trees, followed by a little boy's giggle as she stood up straight and stretched from apple-gathering, Max's new favourite hobby. It was late afternoon and the weather was cold but fair, perfect for getting Max out of the house. The four grown-ups had made an outing of it. Hazard was sword fighting with Max with sticks. The sight of them in the distance made her smile. No longer was it enough to say 'under other circumstances'. Addy found the refrain was not enough to keep her attraction to him at bay, nor were any of the usual cautions. Hazard was not Bennett Galbraith, something he demonstrated every day in all that he did. It would be easier to resist the attraction if he was.

'Hazard's a good man.' Violet joined her, Caroline swaddled in her arms. 'The three of us grew up together. I've known him my whole life. A girl can do no better than the Manning boys.' Violet smiled and Addy blushed.

'Is it that obvious?' She'd not meant to be transparent.

'You don't need to hide it. He's clearly taken with you as well, but I sense something is holding you back?' Violet was easy to talk with, a kind ear in the absence of Artemisia.

At the gentle words, Addy's reserve broke, her questions and concerns flooding forth. 'I've never felt like this before, about anyone. We spend most of our days together and it still isn't enough. We talk and we talk and there's still more to say, to ask, to know. When he touches me, I want to surrender everything that I am and fall into him.'

She waited, feeling foolish. Those words only touched the surface of how she felt with Hazard. But Violet simply gave her a considering look as she adjusted the baby. 'Then why don't you? Why don't you surrender?' Violet made it sound so easy.

'I once, not too long ago,' Addy confessed hesitantly, 'thought I was in love with someone else who was…false. I don't want to be mistaken again,' but her heart knew differently, no matter how her mind argued. Her heart knew this was nothing like that. At best, Bennett had been an infatuation, an infatuation that had been cultivated and manipulated. 'And, I suppose I don't want to hurt him.' Perhaps more than her fear of making a mistake for herself, she feared making a mistake for him.

Violet smiled softly. 'It's natural to feel that way. Rafe felt that way when he came home from the war. I was still intent on marrying him, wound or not, but he did not want to disappoint me.' She paused and looked down at her little daughter. 'He was not sure he could be a husband to me in all ways, that he might cheat me out of having a family. He wanted me to be free to find another man, but I wanted him, only him, children or not. It took a while to convince him of that, though.'

'How did you convince him?' Addy glanced down the line of orchard trees, watching Hazard swing Max up on to his shoulders as he strode towards her, the sight conjuring up fantasies she'd never had before, never thought she'd wanted.

'Trust,' Violet said simply and Addy deflated a little. How was that a solution? 'Rafe realised that he had to trust that my love for him overrode all else. Real love, real concern, is not put off by disappointment. Genuine affection does not easily turn to hate when things go sour. But you have to take the first step and trust that it's there.'

Easier said than done. Addy nodded, wishing the solution was more concrete, like a recipe for paint colour that could be mixed to perfection with the right ingredients. 'Trust is difficult right now.' Hazard had said as much to her a few days ago, that she had to trust herself first.

Violet gave a half-smile, following her gaze in Hazard's direction. 'Of course it is. Most of us don't make it this far in our lives without a few bumps and bruises. Rafe and I have them, you have them, Hazard certainly has them, although he keeps them close. But you never know what can happen until you try. Certainly, trying is worth the risk.'

Was it? Would Violet think so if trying could only result in short-term joy and long-term heartache? Hazard had made it clear he didn't consider himself marriageable and she'd not ever entertained serious thoughts of marriage, never thought she'd be worthy of someone's attentions for ever, so she'd convinced herself she wasn't interested. Besides, marriage had never come highly recommended in the Stansfield household.

Hazard swung Max down from his shoulders and took Caroline from Violet. 'How's my favourite niece?' The sight of such a large, masculine man with a tiny bundle in his arms set the butterflies fluttering in her stomach. The fantasies his very presence offered generated fantasies she hadn't even acknowledged she wanted: fantasies of a home, a husband, a family. Hazard Manning with his dark hair and dark eyes was a different kind of fairy tale, the kind that went on long after happy-ever-after—a man who would get out of bed in the dark of night to see to a crying infant, who would treat his wife as a partner even as he dedicated his life to her happiness.

He handed the baby back to Violet. 'Come walk with me, Addy. There's something I want to show you.'

The orchard smelled of autumn, a fruity debris of windfall apples and leaves beneath their feet as they tramped through the rows, Hazard telling stories as they went, 'Rafe and I played out here growing up, Violet, too. We were knights some days, soldiers of fortune other days. We climbed trees and ate apples instead of going in for lunch.'

'It sounds delightful.' Addy laughed as he grabbed her about the waist and swung her around. He was in boyishly high spirits.

'You're delightful, you look like autumn itself.' He kissed the bridge of her nose as he set her down. His actions, his words, were as close to acknowledging the attraction between them as they'd ever got. Her heart thrilled to it even as her mind tried to steel itself.

Addy touched the bridge of her nose self-consciously. 'I get my freckles from my mother.

Artemisia says I look like her.' They started walking again, her arm tucked through his. 'I don't remember her, of course. I was only two when she passed. What I do know of her is second hand.' She kicked at a pile of leaves. 'I look like my mother, Artemisia looks like my father. I wonder what my brother would have looked like? I think about him sometimes. Would he have painted like the rest of us? How would our lives be different if he and my mother had both lived?' It was hard not think of her own family when she was surrounded by Hazard's, surrounded by small children.

'I didn't know you had a brother?' Hazard asked carefully.

'He died right after birth.' Addy shrugged to hide the emotion that welled up when she thought of it. 'I didn't even see him. I was still a baby myself. Some people say he doesn't count, that he wasn't really my brother, he was hardly here long enough, just a few minutes, but to me he counts. I was never too little to be beneath Artemisia's notice, so it's always seemed fair that my brother shouldn't be beneath mine.'

'I *am* sorry,' Hazard offered.

'Don't be.' Addy gave him a smile, an attempt to banish the bitter sweetness that had settled on her. 'Everything happens for a reason. I like to think that it was because of Mama's death that my father found his fame, that Artemisia is the painter she is today, that good things came out of the loss, that it wasn't for nothing.' Hazard took another right, moving them closer to the centre of the orchard. 'Artemisia says Father lost himself in his grief after Mother died, but it's in her nature to see the glass as half-empty. I think Father *found* himself in his grief. That grief transformed his art.'

'Because you see the glass as half-full?' Hazard laughed.

'It's a choice, isn't it?' Addy smiled and hugged his arm. She was about to say something more, but they turned a final corner and came face to face with a sight that stole her breath.

'I give you the Pink Willow,' Hazard announced proudly. It was the largest willow Addy had ever seen and, as the name suggested, the pinkest. The size alone made it an astonishment to behold. Long branches heavy with willow fronds cascaded like cataracts to the ground. Add to that the unique pinkness of it and the tree qualified as the eighth wonder of the world. 'I've never seen anything like it,' she breathed as he held back the curtain of drooping willow branches and ushered her through. 'It's magical. We might be the only two people in the world.'

She was aware of him in this silent, secret space, of his hands at her waist, his voice a murmur at her ear, 'Our land, Addy, our fairy land.' Where no one might make demands of them, except themselves. How she loved the feel of his hands on her, at her back, at her waist, the feel of his arms about her, enveloping her in the hard strength of him. What might it be like to run her hands over all the strength that lay beneath the layers of his clothes? To strip away his ever-present greatcoat, his jacket, his waistcoat, his shirt, to undo his cravat. What would all that muscle look like? Feel like, bare beneath her fingertips? She would not have to draw him from imagination then.

A wide orchard swing hung from the branches. Addy moved towards it, hoping to banish imprudent thoughts. Hazard stayed her with a hand. 'Wait, let me check the ropes first.' He tested them, pulling hard until he was satisfied they wouldn't break.

She tossed him a teasing glance as she sat on the plank that made the seat. 'I'm not sure if I should be flattered by your concern for my safety or insulted by your concern over my weight.'

Hazard grabbed hold of the ropes and pulled the swing back, then set it in motion while Addy's laughter filled the private world beneath the willow. He didn't know how long he pushed her on the swing. He only knew he was breathless with his own joy when he finally stopped. Addy made him playful, made him feel light-hearted. It had been years since he'd felt that way, not since he'd left for the war. The world had been a dark place afterwards.

'You're good at that.' Addy was as breathless as he, her cheeks flushed perhaps with the same joy that coursed through him, breathless perhaps for the same reason he was breathless. He'd brought her out here to see the swing, but for other things, too, and maybe she sensed that. Things had advanced between them and it was time to settle how those things were going to be handled.

'I'm good at a lot of things.' Hazard's voice was a low growl, a reminder that they were not children at play here in the grove, that children didn't kiss at the lake shore as if they were the only two people in the world, or on beach shingles as if they'd drown if they couldn't get enough. *He* couldn't get enough and very soon their time together would be over. It had occurred to him that it didn't matter if there was little he could offer her. Perhaps it was the offering, the thought of the long term that was needlessly complicating things between them. Perhaps it was the long term they were both shying away from. But the short term might suffice for them both without either of them having to break whatever promises they'd made to themselves. Even so, he would not seduce such a decision out of her. She would have to come to that conclusion herself. In short-term arrangements, he was very aware a woman had more to lose.

'Is negotiating seductions one of your skills?' Addy said solemnly. 'Is this the part where we define our terms of association so that I may discover what other things you are good at?'

'That's putting it rather bluntly.' And directly, Hazard thought, but he should not have expected less from her. Addy had been direct, open, from the start. It was one of the things he loved about her. Loved. Not liked. He tested the difference and found it acceptable. Here, under the willow tree, he could love Addy Stansfield.

Addy rose from the swing, pacing in their willow kingdom as she answered her own question. 'What *can* it be between us, Hazard? I think it over and I always come to the same conclusion. This "situation" we find ourselves in will be over in a few weeks. We'll have no reason to be thrown together after that unless *we* decide otherwise. I don't wish to marry just when I'm discovering my freedom and you have your work in London. Despite our natural affinity for one another, our circumstances will shortly be against us.'

Hazard sat on the vacated swing, watching her think out loud, her conclusions echoing his own. How many nights had he lain awake, thinking the same thing? *What could there be?* She sat down beside him on the swing, her eyes soft and entreating as the old swing groaned beneath the added weight. 'You're the puzzle solver, Hazard, solve this.' Circumstances could be changed.

'Do you want me to solve it decently or indecently?' Hazard put the variable to her. That was what it always came down to when he tossed it about in his mind. It was his turn to be blunt. 'Decently, we can have kisses, secret, stolen kisses, as many as we'd like.' Such a solution would finish the job of driving him mad. He'd continue to go to bed aching every night with wanting more. In a paradigm of decency he could not have more from her, because he could not give her more in return.

'And indecently?' Addy's voice whispered the temptation as the rope swing broke beneath their combined weight and sent them to the orchard floor.

She landed against him in a soft thump, a laughing gasp escaping her lips as the little fall stole her breath. 'Oh! Are you all right?' She struggled to sit up and hit her head on the dangling slat. 'Ouch!'

Hazard pulled her back down to him. 'Careful, let me see, are you hurt?' His fingers combed through her hair, searching for a cut or a bump. 'You'll be fine.' He laughed. 'We should have known it wouldn't hold two. I suppose we got what we deserved.' They deserved this, he thought, to lie in the orchard together and look up into the willow boughs, to laugh together. How he loved laughing with Addy!

'And indecently? You haven't answered my question yet,' Addy murmured softly, her eyes on him, her hand on his chest. 'Were you thinking something like this?' She kissed him, long and lingering, sending a very indecent charge of want through him.

'Yes, something like that,' Hazard managed a hoarse response.

'Something like one night and no regrets?' She sat up, careful this time to avoid the dangling wood. 'You're too much of a gentleman to say it, so I'll say it for you. Do you think I don't know what our indecent options are?'

He sat up beside her, letting her brush the orchard out of his hair. 'I would not ask that of you, Addy.'

She looked at him with eyes that understood he was giving her the privilege of deciding for them, that the decision could only come from her. 'What if *I* asked it of *you*?'

Perhaps he should not encourage it, but he was thinking with his body, not his mind. He leaned towards her, capturing her with a kiss. 'It would have to be that way. I will not seduce you.' For so many reasons, not the least being that he refused to take advantage of her vulnerability. Rather, he wanted her to step into her power and come to him from a position of strength.

She laughed softly. 'You already have.' She ran her hands through his hair. 'If I asked, would you say yes?'

'You know I would.' These were dangerous words and even more dangerous promises. They should not make them to one another, but they seemed incapable of doing otherwise.

Chapter Sixteen

He was dreaming of broken promises and the war. Of the shattering boom of cannons as his horse galloped beneath him, sweating from fear, and the summer heat of Spain as he raced towards Wellington's headquarters at Salamanca, the hopes of Major-General Clinton's Sixth Division folded in his coat pocket, a plea for help. He'd intercepted intelligence last night that had belied the original report from the Spanish that the fort at San Gaetano was lightly manned by the French. That had not proven true. On the contrary, reinforcements for the French were on the way and Clinton was low on ammunition. His brother, Rafe, was there, *his brother* was low on ammunition.

Hazard kicked at his horse, asking for

more speed. The tops of the cathedral rose in the distance. He was nearly there. Thank goodness. He was exhausted, having spent the night wrangling with the French cipher to decode the information. Lives had been risked for that intelligence, lives were still being risked. Lives would be lost if he didn't reach Wellington and claim reinforcements for Clinton. They would be up against a superior French force and they'd be slaughtered.

His horse pounded through the narrow streets of Salamanca. He cried out to soldiers, 'Where is Wellington? Where is headquarters?' The dream blurred, a jumble of events. Wellington was there, nodding, barking orders. He was on the road again, sweating— the summer was for siestas, not sieges—a new horse beneath him. But he was too late. Men pulled at him, shouting news as he arrived back to camp. One hundred and twenty men were lost. Rafe was hurt, dying, grapeshot in his thigh. Rafe was on a pallet in the hospital tent, sheet-white and unconscious. *He was too late.*

Hazard woke, breathing hard, body bathed in sweat, dream and reality merging as he swallowed a harsh cry. His hands gripped the sides of the bed. Where was he? It was dark. Quiet. It unnerved him, setting his panic off again. He forced a deep breath. When one couldn't see, couldn't hear, one could smell. The whiff of coal in the banked fire wafted through the room.

Home. The forged-but-not-forged painting. Addy.

He took a deeper, slower breath, willing his body to settle again as his mind calmed. When he could trust his hands, he struck a match and lit the lamp beside the bed. He padded to the basin by the window and bathed his face, poured himself a cup of water from the pitcher. His mind knew the rituals from long practice—little routines to restore order after the nightmare. He pulled up a chair to the window and waited for the sunrise.

Why had he dreamed of Salamanca last night of all nights? Last night had been... calm. Everyone had retired early, worn out by an afternoon outdoors chasing Max around. Addy had gone up earlier than the rest. He could guess why. He'd put the decision on her shoulders today at the willow tree. Did she trust herself, did she trust *him* enough to see this attraction through? It wasn't just Addy, though. Darius had entrusted her to his care and he'd given his word not to hurt her. If her heart broke over this, it would be on his head.

Others had trusted him before. Major-General Clinton had trusted him to get help, to bring ammunition, to protect his comrades. His own father had trusted him to bring Rafe back, Rafe the gallant daredevil, Rafe his father's heir, his father's delight. Other men had trusted him—Monteith, sending Hazard out to save the family from themselves with their elopements, forged artwork and missing nieces.

Hazard sipped at his mug of water. Was that what had prompted the nightmare? The idea that Darius's trust or, more importantly, Addy's, might be misplaced? He had not lied. He did not intend to hurt Addy, indeed he'd done all he could to remove her from hurt. He'd given her the decision, it was Addy's to decide what she could stand. They need not pursue any of the fire that sparked between them. He would gladly burn on his own if it spared her disappointment and heartache over what could never be.

You want her to come, though, admit it, his conscience challenged.

Yes, dammit. He wanted her to knock on his door, to shut the door, the worries behind her, and say, *I want you, Hazard. For now... for however long.*

There was much he could protect her from—Bennett Galbraith's unscrupulous, criminal behaviour, an unwanted consequence of any passion they might engage in—but he couldn't protect her from a broken heart. If Addy came to him, she would come with all of herself. She would hold nothing back, because that's how Addy was. It all came down to Addy. He'd given her the key and the match, to unlock and ignite. He'd seen her eyes last night, she knew she held both their hearts in her hands. He'd done all he could.

The painting, the one Bennett had purportedly had a buyer for, was finally done. There was no real need to have completed it, Bennett didn't know where she or the painting was. But she'd needed to do it for herself. It gave her a sense of closure on the episode and, she supposed, there was always the chance they might need it if, or when, Bennett surfaced again.

Addy stepped back to survey it. There

wasn't another stroke she could make, or another colour she could add. Under other circumstances, she would be proud of this work. It was as perfect as she could make it. The attention to the historical replication of paint colours had been a challenge. 'Hazard, come and see.' Addy set aside her brush. It was colder out today and Hazard had spent most of the afternoon in the cottage studio with her.

He unfolded his big frame from the sofa and covered the distance in three steps. 'I'm being invited into the sanctuary at last,' he teased, a friendly smile on his lips, but something deeper moved in his dark eyes. Today, she thought there was a sharper edge to his words, a secret message wrapped in the teasing. It was not a cruel edge, nor was it meant to goad or push. It was only the edge of a man who was in the throes of desires restrained while temptation dangled. It had been two days since he'd put the question to her.

Hazard came around the easel and stood beside her, arms crossed over his chest, a move that, sans coat as he was now, served to emphasise the muscles of his arms beneath the sleeves of his white shirt. He was silent for a long while and she marshalled her impatience long enough to give him time to study the painting side by side with the copy she'd worked from. 'Well? Say something.'

'I am stunned, I don't know what to say. This is amazing. Honestly, Addy, this is beautiful on its own merits, there's a serenity in the Madonna's face that evokes emotion, that draws the viewer in, I just want to stare at her face, she's enrapt with the child.' He paused and she felt his gaze slide her way. 'It's the way Artemisia looks at little Michael, the way Violet looks at Caroline in her arms,' he said quietly. 'You've drawn on real life for this and it is all the better for it.'

Addy blushed at the praise, touched by his insight. Those were things people said about Artemisia's work. Not hers. There was no time, though, to bask in the praise. There was still an important task to do. 'I thought I would mark it. I had an idea about how to do it.' She laid out a few small squares of canvas already painted and dried. 'I got the idea from da Vinci.' She picked up a rag and dipped it in turpentine. 'Look at this.' She gently rubbed the cloth over the painted scrap, removing the first layer of paint. Beneath it were the initials

A.S. She handed him the rag and motioned towards a second scrap. 'You try it.'

'That's brilliant,' Hazard complimented, watching initials come to light. 'I am assuming your initials have been hidden away on the painting?'

'In the lower right-hand corner,' Addy nodded. 'I wish I'd thought to do this with the last Perugino.' She drew a breath, her words shaky. 'Hazard, what prevents him from saying I put him up to it? That I told him to represent the painting as original?'

'I do.' His gaze was strong on her, compelling. 'Your co-operation does. If you were instigating this, you wouldn't have laid down information. You are clearly not the leader in this gambit. Monteith's secretary has a receipt for the first painting. You were not paid the full amount Galbraith received for it. I won't allow any harm to befall you. You do believe me?'

This was the leap of trust Violet had spoken of and a leap it was. Trust was not about small, gradual steps. It was all or nothing. 'I do, Hazard.' She wished her voice didn't sound small, that it matched the enormity of her pledge and the enormity of what he was promising.

'Enough of worrying then.' He smiled and something warm flickered low in her belly. He helped her gather up her brushes and followed her to the sink, the jar of turpentine in one hand. 'No one should worry on her birthday, which, by the way, you didn't tell me was coming up, Minx. I had to hear it from Artemisia via letter.' He gave her a wink. 'She sent a small package for you.'

'It's hardly something one advertises. It's of no note.' Addy dismissed the idea. It was hard to be away from her family, today especially. Artemisia always had a special supper for her and her favourite dessert. But perhaps it was best to skip it this year. There'd been too much on her mind, too much confusion, too much fear. It seemed wrong to celebrate while the situation with the forgery hung over her.

'You should let me be the judge of that.' Hazard's voice was low at her ear, sending a wicked tremor through her even as it startled her from her thoughts. She turned sharply, misjudging the distance, and came up against his chest and a jar of sloshing turpentine.

'Oh! I am sorry!' Proof of her clumsiness

spread on Hazard's shirt. She reached for a rag and began to dab at it, trying to clean it up. 'It can leave a stain…' But her rag was no match for the turpentine as it soaked through.

He stilled her hand and laughed. 'Addy, it's all right. I have other shirts. I'll go wash out at the pump and perhaps you might send for one of them.'

She should have given him the privacy to wash. She should have kept her eyes averted from the sight of Hazard washing shirtless at the garden pump, but she didn't. She'd become very good at not doing what she ought to. Instead, she'd allowed herself one glimpse and found she couldn't look away, the spare shirt held forgotten in her hands. A single thought ran through her mind: shirts were overrated. Followed by: Hazard was a well-made man. The muscles she'd felt through the layers of clothing had only hinted at the masculine beauty beneath. But knowing that strength was there had not prepared her for *seeing* the evidence of it.

Her mouth went dry and her hands clenched involuntarily in the folds of the forgotten shirt at the sight of the carved perfection of sculpted shoulders and chiselled biceps that called to mind Michelangelo's masculine depiction of *Day* on Giuliano di Lorenzo de' Medici's tomb in San Lorenzo. She gave her eyes licence to study the rest of him, the atlas of his chest, da Vinci's dream to sketch—a study in the perfection of human anatomy, abdominals etched into his torso like steps in the side of a cliff, the sharp incision of muscle that framed the iliac girdle until it disappeared beneath the waistband of his breeches.

He turned, caught her staring and smiled, unabashed with his dishabille, unbothered by the autumn cold. 'Ah, you found a shirt, good.' He held out a hand for it and she had no choice but to walk towards him, towards all that masculine beauty on display, just for her. Perhaps she was walking towards other things, too, other decisions that she no longer wanted to put off.

He shook his head, sending droplets into the air, and slid his arms into the sleeves, leaving her feeling deprived as his fingers worked the buttons. Too late, she realised the missed opportunity. She ought to have done that for him. No, she *would* do that for him. Addy stepped forward and took over. 'Let me.' She smiled at him as she worked, trying to pretend she was comfortable dressing a man. She reached the last button and gathered her courage. Her hands stilled on the fabric. It was now or never. 'As you know, it's my birthday,' she said, letting the slow words hang between them.

'Yes, I am aware,' Hazard drawled, something sparking in his dark eyes, something that suggested he suspected what she was up to.

'It is sometimes customary for the birthday celebrant to make a wish.' Her tongue ran over her lips. 'You said you'd come to me if I asked. I'm asking.' She ran her hands up over the fabric, up over the planes of chest. She could feel his heart thump beneath her palm. 'Will you come to me, Hazard? Tonight? I don't know…' A finger pressed against her lips, followed by his mouth against hers, taking away her words.

'Yes, I will come to you. Leave the arrangements to me. I'll take care of everything. Your birthday wish is my command, my lady.'

By the time birthday supper was over, the anticipation of making love had honed Hazard to a finely tuned point of readiness, every nerve pulsing in awareness of Addy, his eyes riveted on the details of her. How the soft pink reminiscent of petunia petals complemented the auburn of her hair, the petal pinkness of her lips and the porcelain smoothness of her skin; how his nostrils caught the faintest scent of her every time she moved. Everlasting summer, that was Addy, all sweet vanilla and lavender. He wanted to bury his nose in her hair and breathe her in until she filled him.

Violet brought in the cake, alight with twenty-two dancing candles, and Addy gasped. She'd been visibly moved by the entire evening and the simple party the family had put together in her honour. Even Max had been allowed to sit at the table for the special occasion. 'Make a wish, Addy,' Violet instructed. At the suggestion, Addy's gaze slid surreptitiously his way, sharing the secret and the anticipation with him.

Addy closed her eyes and blew. When she opened them, Hazard felt himself rouse with the knowledge that she had wished for *him*. Very soon he'd make that wish come true. Even now, a groom was setting up the last of the supplies in the bower he'd created. He'd been busy in the interim between leaving Addy at the studio and returning for supper. Time had flown in those few hours, but now it was starting to drag. He was selfish, wanting to steal Addy away from the loving attentions of his family.

He declined a second piece of cake from Violet and waited patiently while Addy received her birthday presents: a mahogany paint box filled with brushes and all nature of equipment from Artemisia and Darius, and a delicate shawl of hand-done needle-lace silk sent on from her father.

Hazard pushed his own small gift forward, humbly. 'It's nothing. Just something small I thought you might like.' He was regretting not having something better to offer against the backdrop of such elegant gifts.

Addy smiled warmly at him as she untied the ribbon around the little box. She peered inside and her smile widened, recognising immediately what he'd got her. Addy held up a smooth stone. 'Skimming stones from the lake, hand-picked for success, no doubt. Five of them.' Her eyes were soft when she looked at him. She'd understood why. They'd skimmed stones the day of their first kiss without excuses, on the shingle in Whitstable and again at his family's lake. 'Thank you, Hazard. I'll treasure them always.'

His eyes held hers. 'At least until you learn to pick stones for yourself.' A reminder of impermanence. Skimming stones were only used once and then they were gone, falling beneath the waves. He didn't want to think about that tonight. He rose from the table, sensing that at last the birthday celebration was concluding. 'The moon is bright tonight. Perhaps we might take a birthday walk?'

'On the count of three you can open your eyes. No peeking, promise.' Hazard removed his hands and stepped away from her in the dark. 'Do you know where we are?'

'The orchard. We're at the willow, I can hear you fussing with the branches.' Addy laughed, playing along.

'All right, three, two, one!' He drew back the boughs of the willow tree like a curtain and watched Addy gasp in delight as the scene beyond the boughs was revealed: rushlights twinkling like stars in the space beyond, an arbour bed of fresh hay and sheets at the base of the tree, a hamper beside it. Addy stepped through the boughs and he let them swing shut, enclosing them inside. This was their private bower where they were safe from view, safe from the world, where they might be alone without ghosts and expectations. The night was for fantasies.

Addy spun in a slow circle, taking it all in. 'Oh! You've fixed the swing!' But when her circle came to completion it was on him that her gaze rested, making it clear he was the real attraction in the fairy glen. The knowledge warmed him, roused him. This beautiful woman wanted *him* and, dear lord, he wanted her with an intensity that surpassed anything he'd ever felt. She stepped towards him, wrapping her arms about his neck, drawing him down to her so that their foreheads touched one another. 'I have no words, Hazard,' she breathed softly, the tips of her teeth toyed with her lower lip. She was the complete conundrum of virgin and vixen here in the fairy bower, Lilith and Eve together, untried but eager. Unabashed and unafraid, yet unsure how to go on.

'You were beautiful tonight at dinner.' Those were not the words he wanted to speak out loud. *I love you.* The words he wanted to say shot across his mind like shooting stars. He should not say them, they were too new. She would not believe them. They were words that should not be uttered easily or taken casually.

'So were you. I couldn't look at you for fear of giving away every thought in my mind.' The rushlights caught the blush of high excitement on Addy's cheeks. Apples of passion, he thought.

Her hands worked the knot of his cravat. He stilled them. Not yet. He needed to give her one more choice before they were past the point of no return. 'Addy, are you sure?' His own voice was raw with wanting. Somehow, he would stand it if she said no.

Her eyes held his, sea-glass-clear with sincerity in the candlelight, her voice a quiet murmur. 'Yes, absolutely sure. I think I've wanted this since that day at Whitstable when you kissed me.' If he was not fully roused by her yet, he surely was now. There was no aphrodisiac as potent as whispered honesty beneath a willow tree. He let go of her hands, letting them slip loose the knot and slide his cravat from his neck. 'Undress me, Addy. Touch me...learn me. I am yours to do with as you please.'

Chapter Seventeen

She made divestment into a leisurely seduction; cravat, coat, jacket, waistcoat, shirt, all fell away slowly, methodically, as she stripped him, each layer removed driving his arousal continuously and thoroughly until at last her hands were on him, tracing the lines and muscles of his torso, circling the flats of his nipples, her voice a throaty exhalation, 'Hazard, you are very handsome. I did not imagine a man could be so...*beautiful* and I haven't even seen all of you.'

He was not used to such accolades. Women liked him, women had praised his strength, his size, his power, but he could not recall a woman telling him he was beautiful, nor with such reverent tones as if disrobing him was a form of worship. His body quickened to it, proud that she found him pleasing. He helped her with his boots, but left his breeches entirely to her. Addy did not disappoint, taking quite to heart the invitation to do with him as she pleased. Her hand pressed against the length of him, tracing him, testing him, tracking the firmness and size of him through the fabric until he thought such touch might send him over the brink. 'Do I meet with your approval?' he growled at her ear.

'You exceed it,' Addy breathed. 'I had no idea a man might be so large.' She gave a flutter of a laugh. 'I think David is not so well endowed, after all.'

For a moment, in his passion-addled state, he missed the reference. 'David?'

'Michelangelo's statue.' Addy shook her head, flustered. 'That was silly of me.' Her hand made to move away from the fall of his breeches. He captured it, holding it in place.

'No, not silly. No man minds being told he's larger than another.' Hazard chuckled. 'But perhaps seeing is believing?' He was growing increasingly eager to be out of the tightening confines of his breeches.

She undid the fall of his breeches then and he kicked them off, revelling in her green eyes going wide as he stepped into the light. 'The better to see you,' she breathed in appreciation, taking a step back and coming up hard against the arbour bed. She sank down on to the hay and stared, eyes riveted on the rigid core of him. 'I've never seen a naked man before, not a real one anyway, just statues and paintings. They don't do you justice.'

'That pink gown, lovely as it is, doesn't do you justice, either.' He held his hand out to her, drawing her up once more. 'Time for you to join me in the garden, my darling.'

The pink gown slipped away, leaving her in silk and shadows as he worked the pearl-tipped pins from her hair, each pin freeing a length until it all hung, heavy and loose, down her back. Hazard's breath hitched at the sight of her, the candlelight playing seductive tricks with the curves of her body beneath her undergarments. Was she shameless to glory in the response? Of rendering Hazard speechless as he brought a hand to her breast, tracing it, cupping it through the thin fabric of her chemise? Was she a wanton to not feel an ounce of shame when he pulled the chemise over her head and tossed it aside, rendering her as naked as he?

Just to be with him like this was a thrill all its own, but his touch was intoxicating: his mouth on hers, his hands at her breasts, his hips pressed to hers leaving no doubt to his desire. She moved a hand between them, low at his hip, finding her way to the length of him and closing her hand around it. 'Addy.' Her name was a guttural moan from his lips.

'You drive me to distraction, should I not do the same for you?' She smiled, coy, filled with knowledge of her own power to rouse him beyond measure. There was pleasure, too, in knowing that her touch pleased him.

He lifted her then, taking her up in his arms, and laid her on the bed. The hay crackled and gave way as he followed her down until they lay length to length, his hand on the curve of her hip his fingers splayed against the flat of her belly. 'Your body would tempt a saint, Addy.' His mouth was at her ear, leaving a kissing trail that tracked down her jaw, her throat, the pulse at the base of her neck, the valley between her breasts where he breathed her in, his breath warm against her skin. His mouth moved again, onwards, downwards, and she trembled for him, her body rousing, wet and hot and wanting.

'Please…'

Please, what? She did not know. She knew only that it was the one word that made sense. Please, would he make her burn, please would he only bring relief for that burning, for the yearning that welled up at her core?

He kissed her belly, his hands gripping her hips gently as his mouth sought a lower destination. 'Yes, Addy,' came the whispered, raspy answer to the unasked request, part of the conversation of their bodies. His mouth moved against her mons, against the dampness of her curls and she gasped in sensation, in delighted shock. Who knew people did such a thing and that it felt so *good*, so naturally right as if mouths belonged there at the most private juncture of another?

His dark head came up at her gasp, his eyes obsidian stars. 'Do you like that, Addy?'

'Heavens, yes,' she breathed, but moments later she discovered something she liked even more. His hands parted her folds, his tongue finding the treasure within, laving it with delicious strokes, her desire ratcheting with each pass across the tiny nub. A pearl within the oyster, she thought vaguely as a small cry escaped her and then another, the pleasure of his mouth coming in ever-increasing waves until the sensations in her built to a breaking point, pushing her towards some cataclysmic conclusion and she went willingly, her hands in his hair, her thighs clenching as she rode the waves to their crashing conclusion, the willow tree bower taking her cries as she crested.

She was still breathing hard when Hazard looked up at her from the cradle of her thighs, his eyes glistening as he laid his head on her belly, his own shoulders heaving, her pleasure was his pleasure. 'Is there anything as wondrous as this?' Addy murmured.

'There is, Addy,' Hazard promised, moving to cover her, his muscled arms taking his weight as he levered himself over her, his body positioned between her thighs, the hardness of him against the soft wetness of her core. The intimate juxtaposition sent a trill of new anticipation through her. *More.* Was it even possible that anything could rival what had just happened? 'Shall I come into you, Addy?' His breathing came ragged and she sensed the effort such a question cost him.

'Yes.' She moved against him, her hips rising to him, urging him on. 'I want you, all of you.' The largeness of him thrilled her, the power of him, the strength of him unleashed. She felt it against her leg, saw it in the corded tautness of the muscles in his arms.

He entered her then, slowly, considerate of his own size and the untried nature of her body, no matter how game her curiosity or desire. She felt her own body shift and answer to him, stretching, moving, accommodating until the fit was complete and then... Oh, then the wonder began—the fit and flow of him, of *them* together, bodies rising and falling in a rhythm as old as the Garden itself. Adam and Eve in Paradise in passion, the honesty of their desire in every exhalation, every movement as their bodies grappled with one another, clenching and clutching as desire swept them, pushing them, pulling them once more towards completion's cliff, only this cliff was much higher, the temptation to fall much greater. Hazard would be there—this time she would not fall alone.

She felt his body gather, cueing that his fall was near. Instinctively, she tightened her own legs about him, holding him close, while the muscles of his arms strained, his body pumping furiously. Hazard groaned, gave one last thrust and they fell, her cries filling the arbour as they tumbled over passion's edge, into its warm abyss, his seed spilling warm against her thigh while his body shuddered.

Her thoughts were as fractured as her body in the aftermath. *Life. This was life. This was all that mattered. Lying beneath a willow tree with this man. Nothing else mattered, nothing else existed, nothing else could reach them—not when Hazard's arms were wrapped around her and she slept in the safety of his embrace.*

The rushlights had burned down when she awoke, the bower dark except for the slivers of moonlight that found their way between long, weepy boughs of the willow tree. She did not need to see. She felt Hazard beside her, deep in sleep, his arm slung across her belly, cradling her in the nest of his groin, his phallus stirring gently up against her buttocks. Glorious, it was all glorious from beginning to end, from undressing one another, the touches, the caresses, the honesty of being skin to skin, the profundity of lovemaking, the sweep of wild feelings crashing over her like a wave. *He* made it that way. *They* made it possible.

She did not need a plethora of lovers to know this was not something lightly replicated, or that these feelings would not be the result of just any joining. This was unique to *them*. To Hazard and Addy. He'd promised to take care of everything and he had right up to the end. Even in the throes of his own pleasure he'd seen to her safety, her protection. There would be no child as a reminder of this night, this extraordinary moment out of time just as she'd asked.

Hazard murmured in his sleep, his body shifting as he settled, his arm about her tightening as if he sensed, too, in his sleep, the import of that last thought. Once only. A moment out of time not to be repeated. It was what she'd asked for. Now that she'd taken that action, as she lay in the soft wake of passion satisfied, she wanted to renegotiate those conditions, wanted to turn back time, to reclaim those days spent in agonising contemplation of how to go forward.

Addy sighed. She could not turn back the clock. But she could ask for more time. What would Hazard say to that? What would he say if she wanted to extend their acquaintance beyond the conclusion of the case? What more could they have? She began to spin fantasies of Hazard living in Seasalter, a little house near the school, of herself walking to the school in the mornings after nights spent in his arms.

Full stop. Fantasy indeed. It would never be anything more. In what sort of world did such a thing happen? Women did not carry on with men openly and hold respectable positions teaching painting to gentlemen's daughters. Her behaviour would bring scandal to the school, Artemisia would have no choice but to have her resign. That assumed Hazard would allow such conduct to continue. She was acutely aware that calling this one night out of time was a means of avoiding any talk of future commitment. If it were to continue, to become something more than their agreement, Hazard would require something more as well. She knew very well what the something more would be. Marriage.

Would it be so bad? temptation whispered, a snake in the garden of her assumptions. She'd not been raised to embrace marriage, intentionally or unintentionally. Marriage had brought her father grief when he'd lost his wife. He'd not sought it again despite his own eligibility. Many women would take pride in being married to Sir Lesley Stansfield. Artemisia had taken lovers before taking a husband and before that had seen the worst men could offer in terms of betrayal. Her sister's experience had not recommended romance or marriage.

It was no surprise, when Addy looked back over her own early adulthood, that she had not sought a Season like other women her age, had not sought to make a marriage despite her advantages—her father had a title, was well known among certain echelons of the *ton*. She could have married decently three years ago. She had not wanted it. She'd grown up believing marriage would give her nothing and take everything.

Only recently, that last assumption had been tested daily with Artemisia's happiness, with what she saw between Violet and Rafe, Elianora and Simon. Did it truly give her nothing? It gave her children, it gave her a family of her own, something she'd not fully understood she wanted until she'd held baby Michael in her arms and watched Darius and

Artemisia coo over him, exchanging longing looks over his head. But it came with a cost. Would she trade her freedom for that? Perhaps she would, with Hazard. He made her feel that even if she wasn't centre stage in the art world, she was centre stage with him and the sense of that was overwhelming in a way nothing ever had been in her life.

'Are you awake?' Hazard murmured. 'What are you doing?'

'Thinking.' She turned in his arms to face him, her arms about his neck, her body pressed to his.

Hazard shook his head, the moon slivers highlighting the dark stubble of his beard. 'No thinking allowed, Addy. We have better ways to spend our time.'

He rolled her beneath him and she had to agree. Better ways indeed.

Chapter Eighteen

The little minx was in Sussex. He'd found her! Actually, Alice had found her. Bennett kissed the Crown's serving girl hard on the mouth in his excitement outside the inn. He didn't dare go in. Meeting Alice at all had to occur by the dark of night.

'Alice, my love, you have done me a great service.'

'You're leaving? I thought you might stay the night,' Alice offered coyly.

But Bennett shook his head. He wasn't usually one to turn down a woman's offer and a free bed, but he also knew when danger lurked.

'Another time, my love.' He offered a charming smile to convince her and slid into the darkness. In truth, this would be the last time he was in Seasalter. He had what he needed. Now,

he could move forward, his plan intact: retrieve the painting and Addy and set out for
the Continent. Only the location had changed
and perhaps Addy's willingness to be wooed.
He'd seen how the inspector had looked at
her. No doubt, the inspector had vilified him
to the extreme, likely to help Manning's own
personal cause more than anything.

Addy would be filled with guilt and horror
over what she'd inadvertently participated in.
He knew how Addy worked. She'd be em-
barrassed, she'd want to make amends for
what she'd done, and she'd want to protect
her family from scandal. Bennett whistled in
the dark, feeling more hopeful than he had in
days. Addy was in luck. He would give her a
chance to make amends and more. He would
make for Sussex at first light.

Hazard had hoped for a better morning,
one spent lingering over coffee and memories while he ate breakfast basking in the glow
of an evening well spent and a woman well
pleasured. He'd seen Addy safely back to the
house before dawn, cleaned up the remnants
of their bower until there was no sign of what
transpired the night before, no sign of the fairy

glen with its rushlights and hay bed except that which he carried in his mind, of a beautiful woman in his arms, Addy with her name on his lips, her eyes wide open, locked on his as climax claimed them both, Addy's body curved into his in the drowsy aftermath of pleasure claimed. He'd not wanted the night to end, had not wanted to relinquish her to the dawn and the jumble of reality.

In his room, Hazard splashed water on his face, made the effort to shave and dress for the day before heading downstairs, his mind barely registering the routine, too busy contemplating Addy. She would be going through her routine, dressing for the day, putting up the tresses he'd taken down pin by pin last night. Was she thinking of him as she dressed? Thinking of his touch on her skin? His mouth on her mouth and other delectable parts? Would she sit at breakfast and break out in an unexplained blush over toast and tea? Would she daydream about last night? Most of all, would she be glad of what they'd done or would regrets crowd in?

Downstairs in the breakfast room, there was coffee, but there could be no basking over breakfast, not with his mother, his brother and

Violet at the table. Hazard took a swallow of the coffee, hot and strong as it went down in a searing gulp, aware that all eyes were on him. His family wasn't very good at subterfuge.

'Addy is having a tray in her room this morning. Apparently, she is tired from the festivities last night,' Rafe informed him with a smile as he forked his eggs. 'She has plans to spend the morning in the nursery with Max. I thought we might join her when we're finished.'

Hazard made quick work of his meal. Surely, the nursery couldn't be worse than the breakfast table. In the end, it was only Rafe who joined him upstairs, Violet and his mother opting to use the time to discuss menus with the housekeeper. Rafe was stiff this morning, taking his time on the stairs up to the nursery. Hazard offered his arm, but his brother pushed it away.

'I don't need help, Hazard.' Rafe shot him a surly look. 'I'm just slow. The damp does that occasionally. It's all right. I manage just fine.' But the fact remained that Rafe would be managing better if Hazard had worked faster, if he'd caught the error in the Spaniards' information sooner. If he had, none of it might ever have happened. He could not forgive himself for that.

Addy was already in the nursery and the sight of her did much to soothe him. She and Max were arranging soldiers up on the floor, intent on their strategy. She looked up when they entered and her smile warmed him. She looked as beatific in late-morning light as she had by rushlight. 'We're just getting started, would you gentlemen care to join us?'

Hazard took up a spot on the floor before realising the impossibility of that for Rafe, who pulled up a chair instead, far less bothered by the situation than Hazard was. 'Do you recognise the soldiers, Haz? They're ours. Vi had all our toys cleaned up when Max was born. They've been repainted, of course.'

Hazard picked one up and studied it. 'I remember this fellow, Max. This was my captain of dragoons. Do you know what a dragoon is?'

Max shook his head as Hazard set the soldier down. 'He's a mounted soldier who rides a horse to battle, but then fights on foot.' Hazard reached for another bright red soldier atop a black horse. 'This was the cavalry captain. Your father and I had splendid battles with this fellow. Sometimes we'd re-enact real battles, and other times we'd make up our own.'

'I want to be a soldier someday,' Max confessed, bright eyed. 'I'll be a hero like my father. I'll charge a fort and free it, just like he did.'

Hazard felt Addy's gaze on him. 'To be a soldier is a noble calling, Max. War is a serious undertaking.'

'What did you do in the war, Uncle Hazard? Did you fight? Were you in the cavalry?' Max was busy lining up his infantrymen.

'I broke codes so that our soldiers didn't walk into battle blind.' Hazard offered the little boy a half-smile. Toy soldier sets didn't come with codebreakers.

Rafe leaned forward. 'Your uncle was a great soldier, too. He helped break the Great Paris Cipher that helped us win the war in Spain.'

'We never really "broke" that code,' Hazard interrupted, uncomfortable with the acclaim. 'General Scovell was trying to break it when his men overtook Joseph Bonaparte's coach with the cipher table in it.'

But Rafe would not be daunted. 'Your uncle is too humble. Before that, he helped break the code of the Army of Portugal. He sent materials to General Scovell that helped him break it in two days. He was one of the best codebreakers on the Peninsula.' Rafe nudged him with the toe of his boot. 'Tell him some of your stories, Haz—how you could break *les petits chiffres* in moments.' Rafe glanced at Addy. 'Can you reach the paper and something to write with from the table?'

Addy handed him the supplies and Rafe wrote a short note. 'Now, Haz, put it into code and show Max how you did it.'

Hazard took it reluctantly. 'It's been a long time, Rafe.' He was aware of Addy's eyes on him. Did she understand how uncomfortable remembering made him? Max stood at his shoulder, expectantly, and he didn't dare disappoint him. Hazard took up the pencil and began the quick process, explaining as he went. '*Les petits chiffres* were the early French codes. They were meant to be deciphered quickly by those who used them, so you could send notes during a battle. Do you see what I'm doing, Max? It's based on using fifty numbers to replace letters and words.'

'There were fourteen hundred numbers, Max,' Rafe interjected, 'in the Grand Paris

Cipher, can you believe that?' The boy was clearly enthralled. Hazard handed the boy the paper. 'You can make up any code you want by assigning a number to a letter. You should practise with it. When your handwriting is good enough, you can send me a letter in code and I can write back to you,' Hazard suggested.

Max's face fell, rather surprisingly. Hazard wondered where he'd misstepped. 'You're leaving?'

'At some point. Not tomorrow, though,' Hazard assured the little boy. 'I am an inspector in London, I solve mysteries. I will be expected back there.'

Max frowned. 'But I want you to stay!' Max turned suddenly towards Addy and grabbed for her hand. 'I want Miss Addy to stay, too. For ever and ever. We'll pick apples and take walks and I can paint more rocks in the cottage. Please don't go, you're so much more fun than my little sister. All she does is cry and sleep. We have plenty of room, don't we, Papa?' Max turned his dark eyes towards his father, beseeching him to convince his uncle to stay.

'Uncle Hazard knows he can stay as long as

he likes, Max.' Rafe's gaze landed on Hazard. 'I've offered to build him a house.'

Max brightened. 'He can live there with Miss Addy, we can make it big enough for two!'

Hazard was definitely uncomfortable with the direction of this conversation. Rafe, Addy and Max were all looking at him, expecting something from him—different things, of course. He'd not spoken of any of this to Addy. It was Addy who came to his rescue. 'Max, I smell something delicious baking in the kitchens. Why don't you and I go see what it is?' She rose from the floor and took the little boy by the hand, giving the two men privacy.

'You haven't discussed anything with Miss Stansfield, have you?' Rafe said as Hazard eased himself off the floor. 'You'll take her "walking" in the orchard, but you won't offer her a future. I thought the Manning boys were raised better than that.'

'She has plans, Rafe. She's not in a hurry to surrender her freedom to marriage.'

'Have you asked? Don't make this about protecting her wishes. Don't assume you know her mind, or that what was once true is still true for her. She seems to like it here and she seems to like you quite a bit. What she doesn't seem like is a young lady who is loose with her morals. Were you her first? I'd wager Grandfather's pocket watch you were.' Rafe pulled the gold timepiece out from his waist-coat pocket, a twin to the one Hazard carried in his own pocket. They'd got them when they'd each turned eighteen, a reminder, their father had told them, that Mannings stand beside each other for all time. He'd done a poor job of it. He'd not protected Rafe when his brother had needed it most.

Hazard pushed a hand through his hair. 'Good lord, Rafe, what do you take me for? A cad?' He *had* been her first. He wanted to be her last, her only. But how was that to be managed without making her life difficult and dangerous?

'You tell me, Haz. What are you? I think you put the question to the lady and let her decide what she wants.'

'I can't possibly do that. She doesn't know what she'd be involved in. Inspectors walk out for a day at work and sometimes they don't walk home. A knife in the dark, or a bullet, can change everything in a matter of seconds. Catching and confronting criminals is dangerous work. The danger never ends. An inspector is always making enemies. Every crook caught is a new foe looking for revenge. Crooks have brothers, cousins, with long memories. I have enemies I likely don't even know about for reasons I can't begin to imagine. I do not want to make her a widow, or our children fatherless.' He had explained all this to Rafe before.

Rafe nodded, patently unbothered by the argument. 'Then don't. Leave your work. Come discover new work here, with me, as *I've* said before. I don't see what makes your choice so difficult. Mother, Violet, Max, we all want you here where you belong. Which leads me to conclude there are other issues at work.'

Hazard felt Rafe's gaze settle on him, serious and strong. 'You won't say it, so I will. You won't come home because of me.'

Hazard began to protest, but Rafe stalled him, rising from the chair and reaching for his cane. 'Do you think I haven't seen it in your eyes when you look at me? You pity me and you blame yourself. You can't own up to the past. You were decorated for your war efforts and yet you can hardly bring yourself to tell a couple tales to Max this morning.'

Hazard held his brother's gaze with his own, unswerving in its intensity. 'I failed you.'

'No one expected you to solve the Great Paris Cipher by yourself. The Spaniards thought their information was reliable, that the fort had no ability to withstand an attack,' Rafe argued. 'The other forts had fallen easily, ours should have been the same.' Rafe leaned heavily on his cane. In his eyes, Hazard could see long-ago battlefields. 'Besides, it was foolhardy to have gone. We could have waited. We knew we were low on ammunition. We could have waited for you to return, but we didn't. I talked the captains into the raid. I volunteered to lead the first party to the fort. *I* did that, Haz, all by myself. That was my choice. I could see the Peninsular campaign was nearly won and I wanted my piece of victory, my piece of history. It should have been easy.'

It hadn't been, though. The fort had been prepared to fight, thinking they would be reinforced. It had taken the sortie of four hundred by surprise. By the time Hazard had understood the reality of the situation and gone for help, it was too late. He'd come back to find

Rafe at death's door. 'I promised Father,' Hazard said.

'I know you did. What a ridiculous, impossible promise it was, too. How did you expect to keep it? I was headstrong, reckless to a fault. You knew that. You grew up with me.' Rafe laughed. 'How many summers did I swing too high on the orchard swing? Or climb too high in the trees, or swim out too far in the lake?' Only it had never been too far or too high. Rafe had always managed to emerge unscathed from those episodes until finally his luck had run out.

'Do you know how awful it was to wake up and know you'd left?' Rafe was pacing again in his uneven gait. 'I couldn't thank you for saving my life. If you hadn't been there to bring me home, I would never have made it. I was just another body to those overworked army surgeons. They had no time, no strength, to spare for the likes of me. You saved me, Haz. I remember that every day I wake up. You brought me home to Violet, to this.' Rafe stopped for a moment, overcome with emotion. 'Once the fever was gone and I could sit up in bed I asked for you, but you weren't here. For the first time in my life, I was without my brother. I didn't like it then any more than I have for the last seven years.'

'I couldn't stay, Rafe.' There'd been more than the broken promise to Father and the broken brother in the bed.

Rafe waved it away. 'Violet told me about what Father saw and what Father thought. Surely you know I never believed a word of it. Father was civil to Violet afterwards, and at times I think he realised his error, but it was never the same between them. That was entirely his fault, not yours. The point is, Haz, I've never blamed you for my wound. I've never thought you failed me in any way. I don't need your pity. I am happy. I have everything I need, except one thing. I *need* you to forgive yourself for crimes imagined and I *want* you to come home.'

Hazard turned away, looking out the window, letting the words wash over him. Was it that simple? To just let go of the narrative of failure? Either he continued to see the past through a flawed lens, a lens his brother disagreed with, a lens that required distance from the family he loved, or he could embrace the narrative Rafe offered him, a narrative of love and celebration, one that allowed him to consider making other choices, choices that he'd set beyond himself, the choice of a wife and a family.

He was not unlike Addy in that regard. Hadn't he encouraged her to trust herself enough to set aside the narrative left by Galbraith and create a new one where she embraced her own power? How could he expect her to take those steps if he was not willing to take the same steps for himself? For *them*. Moving forward with his life required it of him.

Hazard straightened, feeling lighter, as if a long-carried burden had been lifted from his shoulders. He turned back to Rafe. 'Thank you, Brother. I think that was exactly what I needed to hear.' Then they were embracing, laughing, Rafe thumping him on the back. It felt good to have his brother hug him and to hug him back with all that he was, with no reservations. In that moment, he felt, for the first time, the possibility for real joy come back into his world.

Chapter Nineteen

Early that afternoon, Hazard found Addy in the cottage working on the portraits. He stood in the doorway a moment, to watch her behind the easel, to take in the homely picture before him, of Addy painting, a little smile of contentment on her face, of the fire crackling in the stone hearth, of the comfortable, battered furniture set before it, of the rain that ran down the windowpanes and his collar. He'd got surprisingly wet running the short distance from the house to the cottage. But that's what fires were for. Joy still clung to him. It was time to share that joy with Addy, although that sharing didn't come without risk.

He'd sought her out as soon as he could. She'd been generous today, giving him the time he needed with his brother, even when he hadn't realised he needed it. He and Rafe had been long overdue for a real discussion. That dam had nearly burst this morning in the nursery. But Addy would perhaps have questions of her own after last night and this morning.

'Did it go well?' Addy looked up from her work, smiling at the sight of him.

'Yes.' Hazard came around the easel and kissed her. 'I didn't have time to offer you a proper good morning earlier. Too many people in the nursery.' He chuckled. When was the last time he'd ever felt this free?

Addy set aside her brushes and turned, her arms going about his neck. 'I'm glad you had a good talk with your brother. I've made a little progress on the portraits. What do you think?'

'I think I'm more interested in you right now.' Hazard kissed her, a more lingering variation of the first one. 'There's so much I want to say, to do with you, I don't know where to start.' Joy was bubbling out of him.

'Then let me decide.' Addy's eyes glowed with mischief. This time it was Addy who kissed him, reckless and hard. 'You handled last night, let me handle this afternoon. I've been thinking about this all morning since I left you.' She turned him about and danced him backwards to the vacated chair with the command, 'Sit. Take your shirt off.'

He sat, took off his shirt and tossed it, the garment landing on an old dressing screen set to the side of the hearth. He felt himself rouse as Addy knelt before him, her eyes shining, her hands reaching for the fall of his trousers. Never, in the wildest reaches of his fantasies, had he imagined what she intended now. 'Do you know what you're doing?'

'I think so. You're not the only one who can solve puzzles.' Her tone was coy, her hand was on him, his member hard and upright between them, straining as she gave a low, seductive laugh. 'Whenever I think back to last night, it occurs to me that what I liked, you might also enjoy.' She split her gaze between his rigid phallus and his eyes. 'It seems I'm right. This bodes well for my hypothesis.' It most certainly did.

Her hand slid up his length, sure and firm as she stroked him. 'As for knowing what I'm doing, I'll let you be the judge of that. Looks as though I'm doing well so far.' She gave him a look that rendered him speechless. 'And I haven't even begun to use my mouth.'

Her mouth. Sweet heavens. His body roused to the idea, but as erotic as the idea was, he was in no hurry. He was happy to linger here, with her hands, one of them working his shaft, the other cupping the sac beneath, making his pleasure a tandem effort as she explored him. A glistening bead formed at the tip of him, proof of that pleasure and perhaps a sign that it was time to move on. The sight of it brought a wide smile to Addy as she bent her lips to him, kissing the bead, then the tip itself, her mouth moving down the length of him with promising kisses that made him groan in anticipation of more.

She looked up at him, her lips wet, her eyes shining with erotic mischief and her own want, both of which served to ratchet his own desire. It was a heady realisation indeed to know that Addy revelled in the pleasures of lovemaking as much as he, that she shared with him the joy of giving pleasure as much as receiving it. She bent back down to him, her nails slowly, lightly, raking the tender inner thigh of him as she took him fully in her mouth this time, licking and sucking as he'd licked and sucked at her.

Was this how she'd felt? As if the world

was about to explode, that she might shatter from the inside out and welcome it if it would relieve the relentless driving pressure of the intimacy this act engendered? His heart raced with it, his blood pounded. His hands gripped the worn arms of the chair, his hips rising up to meet her mouth, not wanting to miss a moment of her touch. Even as his body raged, he felt it gather, like a storm chasing across the sky thundering towards completion. 'Addy.' Her name was everything, the sum of his world, a plea, a caution that his end was near.

It was warning enough. Addy gave him a final farewell, a gentle lick across the weeping well of his tip, and took him in her hand as he spent, a throbbing geyser of relief, of release that left him not shattered, not drained, as he'd thought, but complete, whole, sated. He gave her an easy, lazy smile as he passed her a handkerchief. 'I will give you pleasure soon, Addy. I just need a few minutes to recover myself.' Even his voice sounded drowsy.

'I'm in no hurry, Hazard.' She wiped her fingers and set the handkerchief aside. 'Perhaps I might ready myself for your attentions while you "recover yourself".'

She might just kill him, but he'd take the chance if it meant watching Addy undress in broad daylight. That was an entirely different fantasy than the one last night which had involved doing the undressing of her himself, but no less effective. Oh, no, definitely not less effective. Her hair came down and his phallus came up, starting to kindle again. Did she have any idea how tempting the simple gesture was—her arms raised, the fabric of her blouse pulled taut against her breasts as she sought out the pins in her hair? The movement had a domestic quality to it. A man might watch his wife do such a thing every night. Addy slipped behind the old screen and he heard the rustle of clothing being removed, the sounds of promise. A man might hear a wife make such sounds and know that pleasure was soon to follow. There was desire to be roused from the mundane, too. Not everything had to be a grand seduction.

Hazard eyed the sofa, a wicked idea of surprise taking root. Perhaps he would beat her to it. He stripped off his trousers and padded across the floor with a stealthy speed. He propped himself up on one elbow, his length aligned on the sofa facing the dressing screen, and waited, but when she emerged, it was his breath that caught. Addy wore his shirt. Was there anything sexier than Addy dressed in *his* shirt? The soft linen flowed over the curves of her breasts, ending mid-thigh and giving way to slim, bare legs—a reminder that she was naked beneath the garment.

'I see I'm overdressed.' Her eyes roamed him and he felt himself stirring closer to full life. She moved to take off the shirt, but Hazard shook his head.

'No hurry, Addy. Come lie down. I want to enjoy the sight of you in my clothes.'

No hurry. What delicious words. Addy cuddled against Hazard. 'I thought it couldn't possibly be as good as last night,' she confessed.

'Why?' he murmured the question against her ear, his hand warm on the bare skin of her stomach beneath the shirt.

'I was afraid it had been the fairy lights and the excitement that had made last night so wonderful. I thought that without the trappings, the magic might be lost.' Addy gave a soft sigh as his hand made an idle caress against her skin.

'We've just got started,' Hazard whispered.

'That's just it. *This* is wonderful all on its own. Just lying here with you, just touching you, would be enough, yet having you in the chair, well, that was spectacular, too. Even here in a cottage, being with you is extraordinary, Hazard. It's not the fairy bower that made last night memorable, it was the man. It was you.' The realisation was proving problematic. What did it mean for the future? For a time when there was no Hazard? She'd half-hoped this afternoon's experiment would fail in its passion. It would be easier to let him go.

Hazard kissed the back of her neck. 'It was *you*, Addy,' he echoed her words and she thrilled to them, to the idea that she pleased this man and he pleased her. 'Now that we've established that, what shall we do next?'

'Me?' She laughed and turned in his arms. 'Take me apart, Hazard, like one of your puzzles, and put me back together.' It was a reckless request, one made with passion rising in her, demanding its due. Broken things never quite mend the same. Only he wasn't breaking her, was he? Being with Hazard was like being whole. If that was true, what would she be without him when this was over? The unsettled future loomed on the other side of this. His brother had asked him to stay. Would he? They should talk about that, but not yet. For now, it was enough to enjoy the moment. It was all they'd promised each other when they'd begun this.

She should not be greedy and want for more, but she did, although it was impossible to give words to what that 'more' might be when Hazard made love to her on the ratty old sofa, the fire crackling in the hearth and the rain pattering on the windows. Autumn afternoons were meant to be spent just this way, curled up with Hazard, making lingering, uninterrupted love until they fell asleep in each other's arms. What a beautiful addiction this might become, if given the chance.

'Tell me about your talk with Rafe,' Addy asked quietly as she drew idle figures on his chest. His heart beat slow and steady beneath her ear. They were both sated now. The unbridled energy Hazard had brought into the cottage was contained in a more manageable form of joy.

Hazard shifted, moving one arm over his head. 'We made peace with the past. At least I did. Rafe has already made it. But it was something I needed to do, I realise. It was holding me back, placing limits on what I could do and be.' He drew a deep breath she felt beneath her ear as his chest rose. He lifted his head to catch her eyes. 'But now, Addy, anything is possible, I just have to claim it. Things I could not offer you before, I can offer now.'

Addy levered herself up on one arm, the words raising a certain amount of caution in her. She knew what those 'things' would be in his mind. Did she want him to say the words? Maybe. It was complicated and it was about to get more so. She tried to forestall the words. 'Hazard, you've offered me all that I've asked for.'

'You didn't ask for enough.' Hazard pushed her hair back from her face with a gentle hand. 'You should have. You undervalue yourself, Addy. You are worth the greatest honour a man can bestow on a woman.' He smiled. 'Addy, I am asking you to marry me, to be my wife, to share the life I can give you now, here in Sussex. We can raise a family, our children will have cousins to play with, you can paint, I can grow the estate with Rafe.' He was in earnest, plans spilling from him in his excitement. She *could* paint. He *could* look after the estate. Would that be enough to make them happy? Or would being together be enough to compensate?

Perhaps that was the price of their happiness. Perhaps that was the price of anyone's happiness: something must always be given up. For her it would be the chance to travel, the chance to pursue art her way, through historic exploration. More than that, if she should give up those small things, would she also lose the chance to discover who she really was? She feared very much that she would.

'But what about Bennett and the case?' Addy stammered, trying to get her mind wrapped around the proposal. There was so much on their proverbial plate, was this really the right time to think about something as life-changing as marriage?

'That will be resolved whether or not we wed. As you pointed out, how long do we put life on hold while we wait for Bennett to emerge, assuming he ever does? I don't want to wait, I don't want to give that man the power to define our happiness.' Nor was he apparently willing to let the danger of his Bow Street job define that happiness. Living here would require he give it up. She'd not missed that part. 'What do you say, Addy? Will you marry me?'

This time there was no skirting a direct answer, but she wanted to be sure of his motivations. Had Rafe badgered him into this out of an old-fashioned sense of decency? Or had the badgering come from Darius before they'd left Seasalter? 'Hazard, I am touched, moved beyond words, truly. But you don't have to do this because you think you should. I knew what I was walking into. I don't want a husband out of duty, or marriage for the wrong reasons.' When she looked in his eyes, when they lay close together as they did now, when he touched her, she didn't want to be without him. This was a golden opportunity to make sure she wasn't. She could have a life with him. She could have this passion always.

'It's not duty, Addy. I love you, you cannot doubt that.' No, she couldn't. He was not a man who would say the words lightly. She was surprised. More surprising was that she wanted to say them back to him. She *loved* Hazard. Maybe that was all that mattered. When two people loved each other, perhaps that was enough to build a life on. That was the fairy tale, she reminded herself as she gazed into his dark eyes.

Why did she baulk at happiness when it was handed to her so handsomely with this beautiful man, this beautiful life? So, what if the image of that life looked a bit different than she'd imagined? Dreams could change. Hazard's had as soon as he'd given himself permission to let go of the past. But he was letting go of so much more than that. Did he realise it?

'Are you sure you want to walk away from London, from Bow Street, for me?' Addy held his gaze, looking for any telltale signs of unease and found none.

'I'm not walking away from London, Addy. I am walking towards you. Will you meet me in the middle?' A slow smile took his mouth and she was convinced. She'd be a fool to turn this man down.

'Yes.' She would meet him anywhere, even the ends of the earth or at the altar. If it didn't feel completely right, it certainly felt mostly right and that was a good start.

Hazard drew her down to him and wrapped her in his arms. 'I am the happiest man alive. May I announce it at dinner tonight?'

294 *Revealing the True Miss Stansfield*

'Yes,' she murmured against his lips, his own certainty, his happiness was contagious. When he held her like this, she was certain, too. The sooner it was announced the better, there would be no backing out, no changing of her mind. She couldn't fathom disappointing his family. 'Max will be overjoyed.' She gave a breathy laugh as his mouth moved down her body.

Hazard chuckled. 'I'll let you in on a secret. His happiness cannot match my own.' But Addy wished hers did.

Chapter Twenty

It was to be a Christmas wedding. It was decided at dinner, by enthusiastic committee. It would give them eight weeks to make preparations, although based on the excitement demonstrated by Hazard's mother and Violet, eight weeks would be more than enough time to plan a simple affair. The banns would be called next week. They could be married on the twenty-third or on Christmas Day if they liked? Addy was quick to opt for the twenty-third, so that their wedding wouldn't take away from the festivities.

'Wonderful!' Hazard's mother beamed. 'We can decorate with evergreens and red bows and mistletoe, swags down the aisle of the village church and a big spray at the altar. We might even see if Mr Humphries could be talked out of his hothouse roses—he has the most beautiful white roses, just perfect for a winter wedding.'

Rafe laughed, pulling a cork from a champagne bottle. 'While you're at it, Mother, why don't you arrange for it to snow?' He sobered as he poured glasses for everyone. 'But really, Mother, we should let Addy plan a little bit of her own wedding.'

Hazard's mother took the chiding in stride. 'I just want you to know, dear…' she leaned towards Addy '…that you'll have help. You needn't do it alone, isn't that right, Violet?'

Violet raised her glass, a pretty smile flitting on her lips. 'Absolutely, Addy. We are here to help. Have you given any thought to a dress?'

In the last three hours? No. Addy shook her head, remembering exactly how she *had* spent the remainder of the afternoon. It hadn't included dresses unless one counted undressing. Violet rushed on, 'We have enough time to send to London for material if you want, or we can make over Grandmother Manning's gown. It's up in the attic and it's stunning.' Ah, the grandmother who'd been married to the ambitious grandfather responsible for the

Georgian staircase. Addy was barely keeping up.

Rafe shot her a humorously apologetic look as Violet went on about plans to remake the gown and Addy gave herself up to the swirling current of the family's laughter, letting it sweep her away as Hazard held her hand beneath the table. This beautiful family who'd welcomed her so completely—why not embrace it entirely, why not give over to the happiness and to the joy this celebration brought them? Maybe this was her place after all, maybe this was where her freedom led. Maybe travelling had just been something she'd reached for because she didn't know what she'd wanted. But now she knew. It wasn't a place she'd been reaching for. It was a person. She was reaching for Hazard and all he offered. She would get used to that, she *would*, and she would dedicate herself to making Hazard as happy as he made her.

The days that followed were the happiest Addy could ever recall knowing. There was the thrill of sitting in the village church as the banns were read that first Sunday, of meeting the people who'd made up Hazard's life: the vicar who'd baptised him was delighted to be the one who married him, the shopkeepers, the neighbours, the tenants who rented Manning fields.

There was the sweetness of an official courtship. Of walks along country lanes, weather permitting, or down by the lake, where she practised her stone-skimming with Hazard's help. There was the joy of being surrounded by a family in a way that was entirely different than the family she'd grown up in—an errant and absent father, an older sister who'd done the best she could, a haphazard household made up of her father's protégés and art students who came and went. Despite her father's knighthood, the Stansfields lived as bohemians at their core. She wondered what the more traditional Mannings would make of the Stansfields?

Her days were full. She spent her mornings with Violet and Hazard's mother, absorbed with their wedding plans. There were invitations to send and letters to write. She'd written a long one to Artemisia and a shorter one to her father. They would come for the wedding and stay for Christmas. She painted in the afternoons, more determined than ever to have the portraits done in time for Christmas, gifts for her new family.

But despite the planning, the painting and the fullness of new love, the happiness of these days was tinged with an edge of misgiving. She loved Hazard. She did not doubt his love for her. However, something was missing, somehow wrong. She tried to tell herself it was simply her anxiety over Bennett and that one last loose end. Though she couldn't quite convince herself that was the case. Even if that loose end was wrapped up, the concern would still be there. She and Hazard were giving up too much, changing too much to be together.

Hazard made it his habit to seek her out in the dusky hours between afternoon and evening, when the light made it too difficult to paint and they put the privacy of the cottage to good use. Today, though, he wanted to walk. Autumn colour still ruled the trees as they made their way to the far edge of the estate and climbed a hill. The climb was steep. She was glad for Hazard's hand, but the view at the top was worth it. In one direction, she could see the white steeple of the church and the neat High Street of the village. In the other direction, she saw smoke curl into the evening from the chimneys of Hazard's home.

'This is stunning,' Addy breathed.

'I was thinking we could build our home here.' Hazard wrapped his arms about her from behind, drawing her against him. 'There's a well for water, and plenty of flat land up here to clear for whatever we want. I wanted to ask you first, though. It has occurred to me that you haven't had much say in the decisions being made.' His chuckle was warm at her ear. 'We could build closer to the main house, if you preferred.'

'I don't mind, about the decisions. Your mother and Violet include me in the wedding plans and I'm easy to please.' Addy laughed, but his understanding and awareness of the situation touched her.

'I can say something to them if you like,' Hazard offered.

'No, I am grateful for them. I wouldn't know where to start.' She turned in his arms to see his face. 'You do understand that the Stansfield girls were not schooled in the domestic arts. We don't cook, we don't sew. I hope you know what you're getting into.' She was only partly teasing.

'We'll have help. You can hire a housekeeper, a cook, anything you need.' Concern shadowed Hazard's gaze. 'Would you rather we marry in London? With your father's title, and your brother-in-law's situation, perhaps you're expecting something fancier than a country village wedding.'

'Oh, no, a big wedding is not for me.' Addy was quick to dispel that idea. 'But I do wonder what I'll do all day with a cook and a housekeeper to see to things.'

'You can paint. We'll have space for a studio.'

'I *can*.' Addy cautiously approached the topic that had weighed on her mind since his proposal. 'I enjoy painting, but it's not my passion, Hazard. I paint because I can, not because I need to.' She played with the buttons of his greatcoat, choosing her words carefully. 'Do you really want to leave London and your work? Won't you miss solving your mysteries? Helping Monteith avoid fraudulent art?'

Hazard's smile faded. 'What are you saying, Addy?'

She grabbed her courage with both hands. It was now or never. The old Addy might have let it go, set aside her own need for the sake of another, but this new Addy, who understood she had value in and of herself, knew she had to stand up for herself, for them. 'Painting in the country was never my dream any more than running an estate was yours. We can do them, of course, but they are not our passions, they aren't the things that keep our souls alive.'

Hazard's dark brow furrowed. 'I cannot have you and Bow Street both, Addy. I thought you understood that? It's simply too dangerous. I had to choose and I chose you. I can provide for you here—reconciling with Rafe has made that possible.'

'I don't want you to have to choose between me and whatever dangers you think your job might put me in. You will come to resent me in time.'

'As you resent me?' Hazard was quick to infer. 'Because I am keeping you from the school with Artemisia? Because I am keeping you from your travels?' His voice was a growl in the growing darkness. 'Are you saying you want to call this off?'

She gripped the lapels of his greatcoat. 'No. When I said I loved you, Hazard, I meant it.

I've never known a man like you, who is so selfless, so honourable. When I watch you with Max and Caroline, I know I could want for no better husband to me or father for my children. You are the best man I've ever known. But I don't know that I can settle in Sussex and give up other dreams yet just when I've had a little taste of freedom. When I told Artemisia Bennett wanted to take me to Florence, she said, "Go on your own, go as your own woman." I think she was right. I don't need a man to travel. I have things I need to do before I can be a mother and raise children in the country.'

'You love me, but don't want to marry me?' Hazard's frown furrowed deeper. She was making a hash of this. She didn't want to hurt him.

'I love you, that's all I know,' Addy confessed. 'I'd been waiting for my life to start. Then you came along and it did. You made me feel alive and loved. You showed me I had worth, that I needn't settle for second-best. These weeks with you have been the best I've known, but I don't think I'm ready to stay here, to give up some of the things I *need* to do.'

Hazard disengaged her hands and stepped away, a hand running over his face. She was hurting him and she hated herself for it. But this was for both of them—surely he could see that? He stood for a while at the edge of the bluff, his broad back to her, the wind picking at his coat. At last he spoke. 'What do you suggest, then? Shall we call it off, go our separate ways?'

'I think we should live in London. You should continue at Bow Street doing what you love and perhaps Artemisia and I can figure out something I can do for the school in town, perhaps act as a recruiter.' It wasn't a perfect solution, it didn't entirely solve her desire to travel, but it did put her in close proximity to the English art world and perhaps opportunities would emerge to indulge her love of art history without leaving Britain. That certainly wasn't going to happen here in Sussex.

He turned with a shake of his head and she could see the angst she'd caused him. 'You are tearing me apart, Addy. I had it all figured out and now you've pulled the rug out from under me. You don't know what you're asking of me. Investigation is dangerous and if anything happened to me, you'd be alone, but that's the least of my worries. I'm more concerned about something happening to you. What if you became a target of revenge for someone I put away? I could not live with myself, knowing I'd failed to keep you safe.'

Addy went to him, wanting to offer him comfort. 'I do know what I'm asking, Hazard. I am asking you to trust me. Let *me* decide what I can live with.' She wrapped her arms about his neck. 'I already know what I can't live without and that's you.'

Hazard offered her a glimmer of a smile. 'At least that's one thing we can agree on.'

Bennett could have lived without the constant reminder that Addy Stansfield was going to land on her feet after betraying him. But in a small village where any news was big news, Addy and Manning's recent engagement was all anyone wanted to talk about. Oh, not to him directly, no one talked to strangers and he was careful not to be noticed, but they talked to each other in conversations between themselves on the street, at the inn, in the shops. He was an excellent eavesdropper. It appeared he'd got here just in time to interrupt her happy-ever-after.

Bennett motioned for another ale from his table in the corner of the taproom as the server went by. He'd arrived yesterday and taken the lay of the land quickly. It was something of a blow to his manly ego that Addy had got over him so rapidly, but it was an even larger blow to his sense of rightness that she should rise from this with a husband and a place in the world, with people thinking she was a hero while he risked imprisonment, all because of her. Did she have any understanding of what she'd cost him? He'd lost his place in the world. As long as England was looking for him, he had to leave.

True, he might be able to change his name and blend into the world if he stayed, but he couldn't work—not his work, anyway. He'd be damned if he'd become a clerk or some such middle-class position, slaving away for a few pounds. There was so much more money to be made in illegal trade. So, he had to go. She'd forced him from his own country. If he was going to rebuild his life, she was going to as well and she'd do it with him. But he would have to act fast.

He wouldn't be able to remain undetected for long. With news of the engagement, it seemed unlikely he'd be able to go in and get the painting. Even without the engagement, Manning would be on alert for him. Although, he did wonder just how vigilant Manning would be if he thought no one would find Addy here? Still, it seemed the best course of action was to assume that if he couldn't go in to get Addy and the painting, he needed to get Addy to bring the painting out to him.

The ale came and Bennett asked for writing materials. He had a plan for that. Just as soon as arrangements were in place, he'd send the note and, because Addy was Addy, she would take the bait. She'd do whatever it took to protect those she loved.

Chapter Twenty-One

～～～～

The fantasy was over the moment she saw the letter amid the post. Addy picked it up from the front console in the hall with trembling hands and slipped it into her pocket. From the looks of the pile, Rafe had not gone through the post yet. There was a good chance no one had seen the note's arrival. She pressed a hand against her pocket. The letter was from Bennett. She recognised the handwriting and all it meant.

He'd found her. He was coming for her, or the painting, or both.

The game was in motion, the idyll of these last weeks in Sussex could no longer obscure the reality she'd been trying so hard to forget. Bennett was still out there, Bennett could hurt her and the people she loved.

Addy hurried to the privacy of the cottage

before she opened the note. In some ways, it hardly mattered what the note said. The damage was already done in the finding of her. She sat down and slipped her thumb beneath the sealing wax and slit the note open. The prose was exaggerated, in the manner he thought a gentleman might write, as his letters usually were.

Felicitations on your engagement. I am in town and looking to finish the business that lies between us before your marriage.
If you could bring the painting...

This was blackmail, but even so, it impressed upon her a sense of urgency and a sense that perhaps the risk might be worth it. He wanted to trade the painting for her freedom and the safety of her family. All he wanted was the painting and he would never bother her again. Why not give it to him? The painting couldn't hurt her, it had her initials secretly hidden in the corner as proof she never intended to misrepresent it. But that painting would betray him if he tried to sell it. If it surfaced in the art world, if someone claimed to have a Perugino, it would damn him. However, the painting could do no good sitting in the studio. Neither could she while all she was doing was waiting.

Maybe, if this was to truly be over, this was the way towards closure. Even if it wasn't, what choice did she have? The letter was riddled with threats. Failure to comply would result in consequences, hence:

> *While I am eager, as I am sure you are, to conclude our business, I am happy to wait as long as needed to accommodate your schedule, although I would prefer not to become a burden to your family.*
>
> *Please come alone. Failure to do so will result in certain actions taking place against those you hold dear should my safe passage not be ensured.*

The last part chilled her. He would not leave her be until he had the painting. She would be forever looking over her shoulder, not just for herself, but for all of them: for Artemisia, Darius and Michael, for Violet and the children, for Hazard and Rafe. This was her last chance to keep this just between the two of them, the last chance to clean up her mistake, to keep them all safe. Even now, the ambiguity of the threat left it unclear as to whom he might harm.

Addy glanced at the directions in the note. Today at three o'clock at the crossroads at the entrance to the estate. It was simple enough. All she had to do was bring the painting and turn it over to him as he drove by. She would be safe, still practically on Manning property. What could he do if he did, in fact, intend to do anything? She could run. This did not strike her as a meeting place that was designed to take her unawares. It seemed, instead, designed to do the opposite, to ensure she understood how harmless the transaction was and to emphasize how quickly he wanted to be away.

Hazard's words from what seemed so long ago whispered their warning. *No one who values greed above human life will ever cease to surprise you.*

But this was Bennett. If she sat around and thought about it for too long, she'd overthink it. Sometimes simple could just be simple. It was what she had to believe. There was no time for anything else. Addy checked the clock on the mantel—a quarter past two. If she meant to go, she needed to go now. With luck, she'd arrive ahead of Bennett, which made her more comfortable. She'd have a chance to take in her surroundings. Oh, dear, she was sounding like Hazard now. She took a moment to hastily wrap the painting and grab her cloak before setting off. She'd be back before afternoon tea and all this would be over. No one the wiser, everyone the safer.

Addy stationed herself at the edge of the verge in clear sight of the road. There was no way Bennett would miss her, nor would she miss him. She had a clear view of all directions approaching the crossroads. In the distance a black speck emerged, coming closer. A carriage. Bennett. Right on time. Her stomach clenched and her palms began to sweat. The crossroads seemed more deserted today, every sound emphasised her aloneness: the rustle of squirrels among the leaves, the birds high in the trees. She couldn't even see the house from here. It was too late to rethink her decision now with the coach barrelling down the lane towards her.

'Miss Addy! Miss Addy! What are you doing?' The high-pitched sound of a child startled her, sending a hand to her throat as

Max came tumbling breathless through the tall grasses that preceded the verge. His fair cheeks were pink with effort.

'Max! What are you doing here?' Addy tore her glance from the road, worry swamping her.

'I saw you leave the cottage. I was coming to see if I could paint more stones. Daddy always says a gentleman never lets a lady go out by herself. I want to be a gentleman someday and a soldier, too.' Max cocked his little head to one side. 'I came to walk with you, but I had to run to catch up.'

She could hear the carriage rumbling closer. She needed to get Max away from here. 'I have a delivery to make. Someone is picking it up right here. It won't take long. If you could go back to the house, I'll meet you back there and we can paint our stones.'

Max nodded. 'I'll wait with you and we can walk back together.'

Addy knelt down beside the little boy and took him firmly by the shoulders. 'Max, you must listen to me. I cannot have you here when that carriage arrives.'

'Are you going away? Is it not really a delivery?' The child was too smart for his own good.

'I'm not going away. I promise. But the man in the carriage isn't a good man. I don't trust him not to hurt you if he knew you were here.' Addy was growing frantic now. 'I need you to run home as fast as you can. I need to know that you're safe. Under no circumstances are you to come back.' She turned the boy towards home and gave him a little push to send him on his way and then stepped out on to the road, her heart in her throat. She didn't dare look back to see what progress Max was making. It would give too much away. She hoped the tall grasses swallowed up his little form, that the men on the carriage were more interested in her and their mission than they were in terrorising young boys.

The coach pulled to a halt, the horses snorting. Men climbed down from the luggage rack on top, from the bench seat beside the driver, from their posts at the back. Bennett had not come alone despite his request that she do so. It was the first sign that not all was as he'd outlined in the note. This was not going to be a simple exchange.

The coach door swung open and Bennett emerged, stepping into daylight dressed in an expensive jacket of blue superfine and buckskin breeches, his golden hair brushed to perfection. One might mistake him for a gentleman—an *overdressed* gentleman. This was what young bucks wore about London in the Season, not a gentleman in the country. There was a tightness to his features that belied his guise of a gentleman at ease. How had she ever thought him handsome? Fun? Kind? There was only coldness and calculation about him now.

Bennett made a gesture to one of the men. 'Shoot into the trees. I want to be sure Manning doesn't have men hiding above.' She'd not noticed the weapons before. Now, men drew aside long coats and pulled out pistols, the driver pulled out a fowling piece. A cacophony of bullets fired into the trees, sending birds squawking into the sky.

Bennett grinned. 'Very good, it seems you followed directions, Addy-Sweet.' He pulled at his cuffs so that white linen peeped out from beneath blue sleeves and gave her a wink. 'Well, you almost followed them. You came alone except for the boy.'

Addy blanched. 'Did you think we wouldn't see him?' He nodded to a burly fellow with a scar on his cheek, one of the men who'd ridden on top. 'Alan here saw the little scamp.'

'Do you want me to go after him?' Alan looked up from reloading his gun with a wicked grin. 'I'm good-like with kids. They learn their manners real fast.' He spat into the grass.

Bennett waved away the suggestion and stepped towards her. 'No need, Addy knows her business. Isn't that right, *Addy-Sweet*?' His knuckles skimmed her cheek, a gesture that once would have warmed her. Now it turned her stomach cold. She should not have come alone. She was no match for this new Bennett. No, not *new*. This was who he had been all along.

'I've brought the painting.' Addy stepped backwards, moving towards the painting at the base of a tree. She wanted distance between she and Bennett. She did not like him touching her as if he had a right to. That proprietary nature of his was no longer appealing, no longer something she understood as a sign of his affections, but a sign of how he'd used her, how he'd tried to bind her to him and how easily she'd fallen for it.

Bennett motioned for one of his men to retrieve it. He unwrapped it and smiled. 'You

are good, Addy, just as I've always told you.'
He handed it to another man to stow in the
carriage and Addy breathed a sigh of relief.
This was nearly over. 'I need to go, before I'm
missed.' She took another step backwards, but
Bennett reached out and grabbed her wrist.

'So soon, Addy? I haven't had time to con-
gratulate you on your engagement, or,' he
drawled, 'to make good on my promise to
you. I told you I'd take you to Florence, to
make you rich and famous. I always keep my
promises, Addy.' His face was close to hers,
his eyes sharp. 'Perhaps I can remind you how
it used to be between us? How you used to
like my kisses until Manning came along.'

Addy tugged at his grip. 'I've done all
you've asked. I've come alone, I've given you
the painting.'

'You've done more than I've asked.' Bennett scolded. 'You turned on me, you helped
point the finger at me as the forger, the one
who had deliberately misrepresented your
work. Your efforts would see me rot in prison
or flee England. You have a lot to atone for,
Addy.' He reeled her to him, a fish on a line
until she was up against his chest. 'I've decided to give you a chance to make it up to

me. If you would just get into the carriage, we'll be off.'

Addy struggled, kicking Bennett in the shins above his polished Hoby boots. 'I am not going anywhere with you. We had a deal. Now, let me go.'

'Alan…' Bennett raised his voice, his eyes a steely green as they fixed on her, a cruel smile on his lips '…I think Miss Stansfield might need a companion on our journey. Perhaps you should fetch the little boy after all. Would you like that, Addy-Sweet? Alan can have him back here in a trice.'

'There's no need for that.' Fear for the boy made Addy decisive. She wanted Max safe. Not only that, but it occurred to her that Max was the only one who knew where she was and what was happening, the only one who could alert Hazard. Perhaps her best play was to get in the carriage and buy Max all the time he needed to get help. She counted the men out of her peripheral vision: five of them. She could not escape them here, but perhaps she could effect some kind of escape if she got Bennett one on one? Right now, they were all alert, waiting for trouble. She needed to catch them unawares. She needed to wait for a different moment.

Bennett smiled. 'That's better, Addy-Sweet. Let's be off.' He ushered her toward the vehicle, his hand light at her back as if he were escorting her to a ball. Dear Heavens, how foolish she'd been to think herself in love with a man who turned out to be a maniac. He held the door to the carriage open for her and followed her inside the dim interior. Her only thought as the carriage pulled away was that Max was safe. He would sound the alarm and Hazard would follow. But then another thought came to her. Surely Bennett knew that. Surely Bennett knew Max would raise the alarm indirectly if not directly, depending on what she might have told him.

'Hazard will come, you won't get away with this,' she voiced the idea as the horses picked up speed. What would his answer be? What was his plan?

Bennett chuckled. 'I hope he does. He'll be very disappointed. He'll either be outnumbered, or he'll be too late. I think it might be the latter. I can't imagine how he'll find us. The boy can tell him nothing about the direction we're headed.' He chucked her under the chin with amused familiarity. 'Don't worry, Addy. I am benevolent. Be nice to me, do as I say, and all the awfulness will be wiped away. You and I can start again.' He sounded entirely sincere, or entirely mad. 'I understand how you must have been scared when the inspector came to you. Perhaps the inspector threatened you with your own arrest for your part in all of this, or promised you immunity from prosecution if you turned on me.'

He grinned and leaned back against the squabs, his hands tucked behind his head, his pose one of confidence and power. He was sure of himself and sure of her. 'I can forgive you, Addy-Sweet, but forgiveness doesn't make the world go round. Money does and that is what I can't forgive. You cost me money and you'll need to make it back for me. I'll show you the world, you'll paint for me and we'll go bashing around the Continent just as we planned.' He winked. 'It won't be long now until we set out on our journey. Sussex is so conveniently close to the Channel, don't you think? We sail with the evening tide.' He closed his eyes. 'We've got an hour or so until we arrive. Feel free to take a nap, Addy. I'm going to—sailing can make for a long night, especially in the late autumn.'

He was far too cavalier with her. 'Aren't you afraid I might try to escape while you sleep?'

He opened his eyes, his gaze patronising. 'No, I'm not. For one, you would likely break an ankle or sprain it so badly you wouldn't be able to walk, let alone run away. But aside from that, you are your family's shield and mine. As long as you're with me, I am safe from Hazard and your family is safe from me. They can't get to me if they want you alive.' He paused, his new tone feigning incredulity. 'Do you think they'll want that? Or do you think they'll want justice more?'

'You can't do anything to them if you're in prison.' Addy refused to be scared now that it was just the two of them. He was playing with her and, by God, she was going to play him in return. But his next words dampened those prospects.

'Oh, Addy-Sweet, so little you understand. They can't expose me without harming you and without harming themselves, really. Artemisia will lose that silly little school of hers if this situation and your involvement in it goes public. I'll tell everyone where you've been. I'll tell everyone that you painted the pictures. I'll drag you through the mud. No one will exhibit your work or send their daughters to a school you teach at.'

'No one will believe you.' She rallied all Hazard's arguments, all his promises that Bennett's crime could not touch her, that she was not guilty.

'It doesn't matter. This is about gossip, not guilt.' His hand was at her leg, his body moving in the darkness as he took the seat beside her. 'Don't worry, Addy. It won't come to that. Your family will want you back more than they'll want justice. Of course, I can't speak for Monteith and Manning. They might want justice. The inspector can't enhance his reputation by letting criminals get away.' He was touching her again, his hand moving up her leg, to her thigh, lingering dangerously, indecently, at the juncture of her lap. She tensed. She did not want him touching her there, not anywhere, but especially not there. 'How did the inspector convince you to turn against me? We were together, Addy. I'd kissed you, promised you the world. Perhaps he didn't threaten you into turning against me. Did he seduce you, Addy? Are you no longer a virgin?' His hand moved against her. 'Do you like that, you little minx?'

Anger flared. Addy pushed him away, scrambling across the carriage to the empty seat. 'I will not sit here and be mauled by the likes of you. If you touch me again, I will kick you, I will scratch that pretty face you pride yourself on, I will bite you, punch you...'

'Yes, yes,' he drawled, feigning boredom, 'I get the general idea. You will wreak mayhem on my person.' Again that wicked laugh. 'Let me tell you a secret—I'd enjoy it very much, a right proper wrestle in the carriage. Let me tell you how that would end—with you on the floor, your skirts up and me pumping away to high heaven between your thighs. It would be glorious.'

'You are disgusting,' Addy retorted. Nothing she and Hazard had ever done resembled anything as crass as this imaging. How had she ever been taken in by him?

He gave a shout of laughter. 'No, I'm not, Addy. I'm a man—just a man. Do you think your Hazard doesn't have such fantasies or lacks imagination? I suppose some men might. As for me, I think it's exciting. There's nothing quite as erotic to a man as a challenge.' He leaned forward and Addy shrank back against the seat, thinking he meant to touch her again, but he merely laughed and looked out the window. He leaned back with a chuckle. 'We're making good time to the coast. How do you think Manning is doing? Do you think he'll guess right? Or will he think we took the London road?'

Addy glared. 'I think he'll come and when he does, you will be no match for him.' Hazard was a master puzzle solver, surely he would find her in time. She believed it with every fibre of her being. She had to—to not believe it was to surrender to fear.

Chapter Twenty-Two

Hazard would not surrender to fear, but it was deuced difficult. Max was gone, Addy was gone. Neither of them could be found at teatime. He could hear the others calling for them, Violet and Rafe's voices shouting for their son on either side of him in the distance. They'd quartered the grounds, dividing the acreage into sections among family and staff, calling for Max as the early dark began to fall.

Every possibility was running through his mind. Was Max with Addy? Had they gone down to the lake to gather stones? That conjured up a host of frightening scenarios Hazard didn't dare dwell on. Fear could paralyse a man, steal his ability to decide, to act. Or were they missing separately? Perhaps there was no connection, which raised different worries. Had Addy left? Had the discussion on the bluff at the house site changed her mind about marriage after all? Or had she been taken from the grounds?

Both prospects were equally awful. If she'd been taken, it meant only one thing: Bennett had found them. But none of the men out working and walking the grounds had reported any strangers. That didn't mean Bennett hadn't come for her. If he did not come in, it meant Addy must have been persuaded to go out. But first things first, they needed to find Max.

Movement caught his eye at the corner of the field followed by a small, breathless cry, 'Uncle Hazard!' Max stumbled forward, his cheeks flushed with extreme exertion, his little body breathing hard.

'Max!' Hazard shouted and then shouted again, 'I've found him.' He ran toward his nephew, fumbling with his pistol in his relief, and sent up a shot. The searchers would hear that. He fell to his knees, taking Max in his arms. 'Are you all right? What's happened?' The boy was clearly not all right. He was heaving with more than the exhaustion of running. The boy was frightened.

'Miss Addy left the house and I followed her,' the boy panted out his story. 'I ran all the way to the crossroads and found her, but she said I had to run home because a bad man was coming and she didn't want him to hurt me.'

Bennett. Addy had gone out to meet him. A whole new set of questions flooded his mind. He had to hold them back, had to think systematically. Violet and Rafe arrived, sweeping their son into their collective embrace as the staff joined them. 'He's just run two miles. He's come from the crossroads,' Hazard filled them in. 'Other than that, I think he's all right.' What a relief that was. Addy had been right to send him away. Hazard didn't want to think of Max in Bennett's hands.

'Did Miss Addy say anything else?' Hazard questioned gently. The boy had a fright. He didn't want to interrogate him, but he had to know every detail. Time was of the essence. How long had it taken the boy to run back? How much of a head start did Bennett have on him? Darkness would hinder them both, but him most of all. Clues would be harder to find. Where was Bennett headed? Was Addy all right?

'Did she have anything with her?' Hazard

asked. Did she have a valise as if this had been premeditated? But surely she'd not go with Bennett deliberately? And if so, for how long had she known? Before their quarrel? No, now he was imagining things. She'd not willingly go with Bennett, he knew that in his gut, his heart, his mind. She had no affection for Bennett. But Bennett could have forced her.

'Just a square package,' Max told him. The picture, then. 'She promised she'd come back, she said she wasn't leaving.' Max began to cry. 'She told me not to look back, just to run. I did even though there were gunshots. I heard the birds flying out of the trees.' Hazard's heart sank. He'd heard those shots, too. He'd attributed them to a late hunting party. How different things might be now, if he'd thought differently. But there was no time for regret at the moment. He focused his thoughts on how best to move forward.

What did he know?

Hazard pieced the facts, puzzle-like, together in his mind as Violet soothed the boy. Addy had met Bennett to give him the picture. No, not give. *Relinquish.* Giving implied she'd voluntarily turn the picture over and perhaps that she'd initiated the transaction. But she didn't know where Bennett was. That meant Bennett had contacted her and asked for it. She knew what he meant to do with the painting. She would not simply turn it over. But she might trade it, knowing that her initials were hidden on it, that the painting would eventually betray him should it ever be displayed.

Think, he urged himself. What would she trade it for? What would she risk her own safety for? He paced away from the group comforting Max. The safety of others came to mind. She'd had the wherewithal to send Max away for his own good. A few potential powerful threats formed. Had Bennett threatened her family? She'd do anything for Artemisia and the baby. Had he threatened Violet and the children? Or had Bennett threatened him? Any of those were reason enough for Addy to feel compelled to leave, to trade the picture.

But Bennett had not stopped at that. The picture was just a lure. He wanted more. He'd wanted Addy. That part was easy to reason out. Addy was his shield, the guarantee he'd get away. The harder, more pertinent part of piecing the puzzle was where would he take her? He returned to the group, forcing himself to take charge, forcing himself to be the inspector, not a man in love whose raison d'être had been kidnapped and even now was heading into the unknown with a dangerous man.

'Violet, take Max back to the house.' He ruffled the boy's hair. 'You've done well, Max, now I need you to go eat your dinner and stay with your mother.' He glanced around the circle. How many men did he have? It would determine how many chances he had. The crossroads went four ways. He had seven men: five grooms, a gardener, plus himself. Not enough to send them in pairs in all four directions. He did not want to send them alone and risk one of them encountering Bennett without support. From Max's account, Bennett had men with him and they'd been armed. But Hazard couldn't afford to leave any trail uncovered. He divided the men up, giving each partnership a direction. 'I'll take the road to the sea.'

That had been another difficult decision to make; which route did he take? Which route was Bennett most likely to choose? Was he going back to London? Was he headed to the coast? Or into the countryside? The latter made the least sense except that he'd have a lot of space to get lost in, to disappear. London was a strong possibility. His network, if he had one, and likely the sale of the picture lay in that direction. Bennett could put money in his pocket. But London was on the alert for him. Bow Street was on the watch. There was a large risk in going to London, but if the profit was big enough, Bennett might try it. The coast would take him out of England and into the wider world. Finding him would be difficult, catching up to him even more so. The coast was an hour and a half away. He pulled out his watch. He was already well behind Bennett. 'Saddle up, everyone, wherever this man is going, he's ahead of us and dark is falling. Ride out as soon as you're ready.'

The men dispersed until only Rafe and Hazard were left. 'I'll need you to run "headquarters" as it were,' Hazard told his brother. 'When people come back, you can take information and decide what to do next.'

Rafe shook his head. 'You're the only one without a partner. I'm going with you. Violet and the women can run headquarters.'

'Rafe, I need you here,' Hazard argued. He had Addy to worry about. He couldn't also worry about his brother.

'If the situation were reversed, if it was

Violet in danger, you would not stay home. Addy is as much under my protection as she is yours. She's family now, or as good as. I won't slow you down. I wouldn't volunteer if I thought that was the case. You need a partner. Those men are armed. You can't take them on by yourself.' Rafe was tenacious as they headed to the stable. 'My horse knows me, he knows how to ride with me. I'll keep up.'

Hazard stopped and faced him. 'I know you will. It's not your leg I'm worried about. It's about bringing you home safely to Violet and the children. Soldiers and criminals are very different things, Rafe. Soldiers have a certain code. Criminals do not. Bennett will stop at nothing to secure his own freedom. This is a zero-sum game for him. If he does not flee England, his life is over. He is out of business here and he will be caught eventually. He will not care what you have waiting at home.'

Rafe opened the stall where his horse was kept and threw a saddle pad over the big roan's back. 'Then that absolutely settles it, Hazard. You cannot possibly face such a man alone. I'll be in ready in five.'

This was the nightmare come to life—not the one that haunted his sleep, but the one that walked his waking hours with him, the one where his loved ones were in peril. The realisation galloped through Hazard's mind as he and Rafe raced down the sea road as fast as failing light would allow. In half an hour, it would be entirely dark. They would have to slow then, but for now they were taking all the advantage they could of the remaining daylight. Beside him, Rafe flashed him a grin meant for reassurance—reassurance that he was with him, reassurance that they would find Addy, that Addy would be safe and home with them before sunrise, perhaps even before midnight.

How many times had he offered such reassurances to the people he'd helped, each time knowing that the reassurances were just words? He couldn't guarantee them anything, just as Rafe could not guarantee anything to him now. There was no way of knowing if Addy was safe, no knowing if one of those bullets he'd heard earlier today had been for her, that she wasn't wounded or worse, in Bennett's carriage. He tried to tell himself it was unlikely, that she was little use to Bennett hurt or dead. Why take her just to shoot her? There was no shield, no leverage in that for Bennett. A wounded woman would slow him down.

Damn it all, but his mind was too good at games, framing and reframing every scenario until it spawned new scenarios, each one more terrifying than the last. He had to stop thinking, but that was dangerous, too. This was what he'd wanted to avoid, this was the peril he'd warned Addy and Rafe about. This was when it got dangerous, when there was something on the line besides the event itself. This was no longer about simply apprehending the criminal. This was about getting a man back safely to his family, about getting back the woman he loved and starting their life together. This was when men made different types of decisions. This was when they compromised their integrity, their rational thought, even unintentionally their safety and the safety of those around them.

Compromise. The wicked word whispered across his mind along with condemnation. This was what he feared—an attachment that would become more important than doing what was right. What wouldn't he give to have Addy home safe in his arms? Another man's freedom? Was that worth the price of Addy's life? Worth the price of his own selfish happiness to have her back? A fraud would go free. But Addy would be safe. All he wanted was Addy back, a chance for a life together, to see her walk down the aisle towards him on December the twenty-third.

Do not think about it. Do not think about what comes next.

It was a basic rule. It was bad luck to look beyond the moment. He'd never had a reason to before, but then, he'd never had Addy.

In the distance, light bobbed. A carriage? His hope rose as did a litany of cautions. It might be any carriage. Just because it was on the road shortly after dark didn't mean it was Bennett. Hazard drew a breath, taking in the night scents, assessing his surroundings. It had begun to rain a few miles back and now the wind was picking up. The coast was near. He could smell the salt of the sea on the breeze. He ran through the geography of the region. Shoreham was the biggest town in this direction. Bennett would be able to find a boat there. The tide would come in early in the evening, making a night sailing possible. *If* Bennett had travelled in this direction. They would not know until they caught up.

As they closed in on the carriage, his hopes deflated. If it was Bennett, he was in no hurry to make time. This carriage was *not* speeding along to its destination. It pulled over too easily, the gentleman within happy to comply. There had been a carriage earlier, though, he informed Hazard. It had been barrelling along just as the weather started to turn. They'd been forced aside to let it pass. Rafe and Hazard exchanged looks. *That* would be Galbraith. The speed suggested he understood this was a race. Nothing but the road to Shoreham and the sea lay between Galbraith and freedom and Galbraith knew it. All he had to do was reach the sea first and he was safe. Hazard and Rafe thanked the man and put spurs to their horses' flanks. Shoreham was close. They would be in time, Hazard told himself. He couldn't afford to think otherwise.

Hazard would come. The thought had sustained Addy right up to the point they'd arrived in Shoreham after a racing, rocking journey at top speed down the road to the sea. Too late, she saw the flaw in her sustaining litany. It was true. Hazard *would* come. Even Bennett knew that. He knew Hazard would try. It was why they were *flying* down the road. He just wanted to be gone before Hazard arrived. It wasn't a question of *if* Hazard would come, but *when*. Bennett not only needed Hazard to be too late, he *wanted* him to be too late. It was another way to make Hazard suffer.

He *would* suffer. She knew all too well how this would play out in Hazard's mind, like some kind of allegorical parallel to his brother in the war, of being too late to deter Rafe's ill-fated ambush on the fort. There was his other fear, too, that his work and his personal life would eventually collide, and now they had— through her. This was the very thing they'd argued over on the bluff the last time they'd been alone. She'd not believed him.

Addy shifted in the carriage seat, grateful for a chance to release her tight hold on the grip as the carriage slowed. She wasn't grateful, however, for the reason. Slowing meant they were in the town now, the streets and buildings confining their ability for speed. Slowing meant they were near their destination, a ship that would take them out of England. She managed a look out the window, surprised to see raindrops on the panes and to feel the rise of the wind against the carriage. All the rocking hadn't been just the road then, but the weather, too. Perhaps they would not be able to sail if the weather worsened? She would stall for time any way she could, to give Hazard every chance she could.

Across from her, Bennett roused himself. If he'd really slept was anyone's guess. For the moment, however, he was doing a fair imitation of someone waking from a nap. He stretched and gave her a wicked smile. 'We're here, Addy-Sweet.' He leaned forward and peered out. 'Ah, no Inspector Manning yet? How disappointing that must be for you. Do you think he's just late or do you think he's not coming? You might never know, that's the problem with being late, so much ambiguity.' He tut-tutted.

The ambiguity raised other unknowns. Had Bennett intended that to raise her anxiety? What if Hazard *did* make it in time? What happened then? Bennett would not go quietly. What happened if Hazard *didn't* make it in time? She shuddered to think about it—life with Bennett, doing his bidding, all to keep her family safe, to keep herself alive, to keep alive the hope that Hazard would somehow find her, that he wouldn't give up. But nowhere in that scenario did it end with a happy-ever-after. If she got on the boat, if that boat sailed away, even if Hazard found her, there would be no happy ending. How could Hazard want her then? Used goods in the possession of a known criminal, helping that criminal perpetuate his crimes, even under duress.

The bottom line was that she could not get on the boat and yet she would if it kept Hazard alive. If he made it in time, it would put Hazard's life at risk. She loved him too much to let him die for her. She loved him enough to go with Bennett if that was what it took to protect him.

The carriage rolled to a halt and Bennett jumped down before he turned back to haul her out. They were on the docks, a packet bobbing none too gently at its moorings, the only ship looking to sail that evening. The wind blew her skirts flat against her legs as fat raindrops fell from a cloud-darkened sky. A night storm was blowing in. The five men who'd accompanied Bennett earlier were already on the gangplank, eager to be out of the weather. 'Best get on board, we won't want to delay.' Bennett's grip was tight on her arm.

She wasn't ready to give up hope yet. She

struggled, digging her feet into the ground and gripping the side of the coach with her free hand. She would make this as difficult for him as possible although she didn't expect to win, not with five men nearby to assist him. She screamed, only to have the sound swallowed up by the wind. She kicked and she clung while Bennett cursed, trying to get a grip on her.

'Drive on!' Bennett yelled to the coachman and the horses began to move, forcing her grip on the door to slip as Bennett tightened his arm about her waist. With a final scream, her grip failed as the coach moved off into the dark. Bennett had her now, stooping to heave her over one shoulder, an arm wrapped firmly about her thighs to stifle her kicks. She pounded on his back with her fists. 'Stop it, Addy,' he growled, his feet on the first steps on the gangplank. She wished she could see more than the ground beneath her. 'You're making a scene. What will everyone think of you? Be still, or I'll accidentally knock your head against something hard. I would think being unconscious is the last thing you'd want at such a moment.'

It was. She needed all her wits. Addy stilled for a moment, debating the merits of fighting and risking injury or preserving herself to fight another time. Either way, it seemed she was bound to end up on board the ship. There was a sound on the wind, the jangle of harness and a hoarse cry. She craned her neck upwards as far as she could, straining to locate the sound.

Suddenly, Bennett pivoted, hard and fast, the ground whirling beneath her from the sharpness of his turn and the rocking motion of the gangplank stretched between ship and shore, choppy waves dark and menacing between the boards. She could see them all too well. Her stomach lurched as her head bumped the railing of the gangplank, the world blurring. She fought for consciousness as she heard a familiar voice make a most welcome demand.

'Put her down, Galbraith, you're under arrest for art fraud and kidnapping.'

Relief swept her, almost as debilitating as the blow to the head. Hazard had come! Everything was going to be fine. But the relief was short lived.

'I like my chances with her on my back better,' Bennett drawled. 'I fall, she falls. You won't take us both alive. The water's too rough for that.'

Chapter Twenty-Three

Hazard dismounted and threw his reins to Rafe, taking a careful step towards the gangplank, slow and steady. His gaze did not leave Bennett. To let his gaze slip from Bennett was to let his gaze slip from Addy, to let his thoughts slip the disciplined leash of control, to entertain horrifying what ifs—what if he'd been too late? Five more steps and Bennett would have been on the boat and Addy with him. Hazard knew his advantage was slim as it was.

The wind was in his face, the rain coming down in earnest now. The gangplank lurched from the waves, keeping Bennett off balance. The weight of Addy on one shoulder couldn't be helping that cause either, he reasoned. He didn't need Bennett losing his footing and dropping Addy into the churning harbour. 'Set her down. You can't win this, Galbraith.' His voice was steady with the bluff. He drew his pistol, loaded and ready.

Bennett laughed. 'You won't shoot me. You can't, not without risking hitting her. The way this gangplank is shifting, you'll hit her right in her fine arse.' He squeezed and Addy squealed. Hazard fought hard not to let the little scene get a rise out of him. It was what Galbraith wanted. Angry men were rash men and rash men made poor decisions. He took another step forward. At least Galbraith couldn't easily draw on him while he held Addy. It would be a slow clumsy draw, leaving him plenty of time to respond.

'I might shoot you in the leg, though. I could manage that as long as I'm not too picky about where—kneecap, thigh…wouldn't matter. Any shot would disable you.' He might have to resort to that. He was nearly there at the base of the gangplank. He'd prefer to get close enough to overpower him instead, though. It would be safer for Addy and he meant to bring Galbraith in, not kill him. A shot to the thigh might do that, though, if it pierced an artery. Killing did not serve justice, violence did not serve justice.

The gangplank pitched violently and Galbraith lost his balance. His free hand reached out for the rope rail, but too late. The pitching brought him to his knees. In a mixture of horror and hope, Hazard watched Addy seize the moment, struggling to be free of her captor. She wrestled with Bennett, the roping giving dangerously with their weight.

No! Hazard saw the danger in slow motion. 'Rafe, cover me!' He charged the gangplank, feet pounding up the lurching wood, pistol thrown to the side. He hadn't the hands for it, he'd need them both for Addy. Bennett had her by the waist, pushing them both forward, over the ropes, into the water while the storm raged. 'Addy!' Hazard fixed his eyes on the spot where she'd gone under, Galbraith's weight pushing them both beneath the whitecapped surface. He whipped off his greatcoat before diving into the churning waters. It was not going to end this way.

This was how it ended, without a breath, without a scream. The water closed over Addy, angry, cold, disorienting and rough. Whoever said death by drowning was peaceful had never done it in a storm, never done it with the man they loved yelling her name above the surf. Whoever had said that hadn't wanted to live. She did. She wanted to live with Hazard. In London, in Sussex, in Florence, it hardly mattered where, only that they were alive and together.

Bennett shoved away from her, her last dubious anchor in the storm, letting her fall towards the harbour bottom, drawn down by the heavy wetness of her skirts. She kicked against the inevitable, struggling upwards in the dark with all that was in her, but the surface remained elusive and soon her strength was, too.

She gathered her courage and her thoughts, fixing on Hazard: Hazard smiling down at her, Hazard eating sweets on the beach in Seasalter on ginger biscuit day, Hazard teaching her to skim stones. Hazard's body against hers. Her eyes closed. She could almost feel him now, that body so strong, so broad, a physical fortress. She'd felt so safe when he'd wrapped his arms about her. Nothing could touch her in his arms. It was the perfect memory to go out on.

Her strength failed, but her body was moving, an arm carried her up through the waters, the waters she'd not been able to penetrate on her own. Her head broke the waves. She gasped, taking in a long, painful breath of air, choking on the shock of it, on the darkness, the wind. A strong arm towed her through the waves, to the pebbly shingle of land at the shore's edge. A body collapsing beside her before rising to loom over her, to shake her, to draw her against him, to envelop her in his strength. Hazard. Only one man felt like that. He'd come and she was alive because of it.

'Addy… Addy.' His voice was hoarse against her ear.

'I'm here, Hazard.' She found the strength for a few words.

'Thank God…thank God.' He rocked her and she clung to him. Rafe was beside them, offering a blanket. Hazard wrapped it about her and thrust her into Rafe's arms, rising.

'Where are you going?' she croaked, reaching for him. He was heading back into the water, back into the storm.

He turned, his eyes lingering on her for a moment. 'I'm going back for Galbraith,'

'No! Hazard, please don't. He'll kill you!' Addy's scream was a raspy panicked plea. She tried to rise, tried to chase him down, but Rafe held her tightly, stopping her from following even if she'd had the strength to stumble after him. She watched in horror as Hazard disappeared into the water. Fear rose—what if he didn't come out a second time?

She forced herself to watch the water, agonising minutes passing. 'Why? Why would he do such a thing?' she pleaded with Rafe.

'Because his justice demands it, Addy. Because you demand it.' Rafe's jaw was tight in the dark. 'He'll bring Galbraith in dead or alive because you'll never be free if he doesn't. You'll always be looking over your shoulder, wondering.' Or he'd die trying.

'Bennett isn't worth the life of a good man,' she murmured, the tears starting as the minutes passed.

'No, but you are, Addy. Remember that. He loves you.' Loves, not loved. Rafe still held out hope. She would not give up either. Still, she would sit here all night. As long as she sat here, watching, there was still a chance. To move from this beach was to admit Hazard was gone, to admit hope was gone. Addy shivered beneath the blanket and Rafe urged her to find shelter from the storm.

'I can't leave him, Rafe,' she whispered. But as the time passed, she thought she might have to. How long could someone last in the storm? Even Hazard's strength must have limits.

A form moved on the edge of the water, dragging another with it. Addy staggered to her feet. Rafe was already in motion, moving in his laboured gait towards the water. 'Hazard!' They reached him together, Addy getting her shoulder beneath Hazard for support while Rafe managed to drag the sodden form of Bennett Galbraith to the beach.

'Is he alive?' Addy asked, as Rafe dropped the body on to the shingle.

'Yes, just barely.' Hazard sank to the ground, breathing heavily. 'Rafe, find the local magistrate. He can take over from here.'

Rafe had done better than that. The Manning brothers were quite the force of nature, Addy reflected an hour later. Rafe not only brought the local magistrate, he also arranged for dry clothes and a parlour at the inn in which Addy and Hazard could recover themselves in privacy. Clothes and a hot drink went quite a way in that recovery. But they didn't go all the way.

Silence descended on the warm little parlour as Addy cradled the mug of hot wine between her hands, aware of Hazard's gaze on her. She'd wanted to go to him, to wrap her arms about him and hold him close, convince herself that he was safe, but something in his demeanour had held her at arm's length.

'I thought I'd lost you tonight.' Hazard's voice was low, quiet, his words momentous. 'I saw Galbraith go over with you and I've never known such fear, that I wouldn't be able to find you, that I'd be too late if I did.'

'But you did find me.' Addy reminded him.

'I did. This time.' He shook his head, his dark eyes sad. 'This is what I warned you about. It could happen again. I can't expect you to live like that, Addy. This is why we can't go to London. I wanted to believe you were right, that maybe we could try it, that it would be different. Tonight has shown me otherwise.'

She nodded slowly. He wasn't just asking her to live with the risk to herself, She'd experienced that tonight, but she'd also experienced that other risk—the risk of losing him. He'd gone back in for Bennett because justice demanded it. He was required to risk himself for the good and the bad. If she married him, she'd be required to accept that or to accept that if he left his job, marriage to him would be marriage to half a man, a man who had settled for less than he could be for her sake.

She drew a deep breath. 'It's not fair to make me decide between marrying half a man and marrying a man cloaked in danger.'

'I know.' Hazard rose from his chair. 'So, I am not asking, Addy. Tonight has shown me the impossibility of my two worlds co-existing. I think this is where I leave you, knowing that you're safe, knowing that Galbraith will face a trial, knowing that my job is done. Perhaps it's simply the best we can do.' He strode quietly to the door and leaned for a moment against the frame, 'I will always love you, though, Addy.' His body sagged with a momentary nod to defeat before he shut it behind him, leaving her cold to the bone in the warm parlour.

No. The word galvanised her. She'd not endured tonight for him to walk away because he thought it was best for her. She'd waited for her life to start and now that it finally had, she wasn't going to let go, not without a fight. She was done with waiting. Addy threw open the parlour door and stormed into the taproom, crowded with people waiting out the weather.

'Hazard Manning, you stop right there.' Her

voice carried over the noisy conversations, stifling them into silence as Hazard turned from the door. 'You are not walking away from me. You asked me to marry you and I said yes. For better or for worse, that's how it goes, doesn't it? Well, tonight we had a bit of the worse. But we conquered it. *You* conquered it.' She made her way towards him, winding her way past crowded tables. She'd never wanted to be the centre of attention, but she held everyone's now. 'You feared that when faced with a crisis you would compromise your ethics. Tonight you saved me and brought a criminal to trial. Tonight, you compromised nothing on the beach. You beat that demon. So how dare you be willing to compromise our happiness, our chance at a life together?'

Somewhere a barmaid called out, 'You tell 'im! Men need a woman to point out the obvious to 'em.'

It emboldened her. She reached Hazard and wound her arms about his neck. 'I want a life with you, Inspector Hazard Manning, wherever that might be, with whatever danger might follow, for however long we have. If tonight taught me anything, it was that one should not wait for happiness or it might slip past you. I would rather have one week with you than a lifetime without you.'

She kissed him full on the mouth in front of everyone with all the conviction, all the passion within her on display. If he walked away from her now, she'd follow him into the rain and she would continue until he saw reason. For a moment, she thought she might have to. Then the rigid, unyielding hardness of him gave way. His mouth moved against hers, his arms came about her, drawing her to him.

'Addy, are you sure?' The soft murmur was for her alone, private words in a public place. 'I don't think I could let you go again.'

'I don't intend to let you.' She framed his face with her hands. 'You are mine for ever, Hazard.'

'And you are mine. For ever, Addy. For better or for worse,' he whispered, just before he kissed her again to the applause of onlookers.

December 23rd

In many ways, Hazard thought that night in the Shoreham tavern had been their first wedding. There'd been vows of a powerful sort, a public pledge and a public kiss, not to mention a public intention to bed the 'bride'

when he'd carried her upstairs to a room moments later. They'd promised themselves to
one another that night. Today, though, in just
a few moments, they'd pledge themselves to
one another more formally and officially before family and friends.

Hazard fought the urge to fidget beneath
the stares of all those friends who peopled the
pews in the village church. Villagers sat next to
Bow Street comrades who'd come down from
London despite it being Christmas. Family
crowded the pews as well. Sir Lesley Stansfield in a deep-purple tailcoat sat beside his
son-in-law, the Viscount. Darius and Artemisia
sat beside Violet, Michael and Caroline sleep-
ing quietly for the moment in their mothers'
arms while Darius discreetly entertained Max
with a hand magic trick that involved a separat-
ing thumb. Rafe stood beside him at the altar
while Hazard's mother beamed at her sons and
cast more than an occasional look at Sir Lesley
Stansfield, who definitely looked back.

The pre-Christmas wedding was a tribute
to the season; evergreens caught up in red
bows lined the aisle and a beautiful spray of
evergreens and mistletoe with white roses at
the centre stood behind the altar in pride of

place, an exquisite backdrop for an exquisite ceremony.

Rafe nudged him and all thoughts of decorations fled. The doors at the back of the church opened and he saw Addy for the first time in her bridal gown. It might have been his grandmother's once upon a time, but it was Addy's now, wholly and completely. The full cream skirts of winter white were set off by a new blue sash and seed pearls had been added for further embellishment at the hem. A bouquet of white roses and evergreens was held in her hands.

She was the consummate winter bride. But it was her eyes that drew him. They always would, no matter the season. Those soft eyes glistened with love, with commitment and contentment as she walked down the aisle. On her own, he might add. His mother had been scandalised. His mother had thought her father should give her away, but unconventional Sir Lesley Stansfield had supported his daughter's wish that she alone decided who she gave herself to.

It was the right choice. Hazard smiled warmly at Addy as she slipped her hand into his and the service began. Knowing that Addy came to him of her own accord lent a new beauty to the words, a new importance to them. This was their life, their decision. Together, they'd decide to live with whatever the future brought. When he kissed his bride, it was with full knowledge that whatever came, they would weather it together.

It was a day for celebration. Friends and family gathered for the wedding breakfast back at the house where they ate and drank and danced. It was the first of many celebrations. Tomorrow was Christmas Eve and Christmas Day after that. After years of spending Christmas alone in London, Hazard was looking forward to a family-filled festive season. There would be some privacy, of course. They would spend their wedding night in the cottage. While the ladies had been planning the wedding, he and Rafe had been planning the honeymoon, such as it was. They had transformed the cottage from art studio to a honeymoon abode. It would be their refuge. Addy had finished the portraits of the family and was looking forward to presenting them Christmas morning.

Hazard spun Addy about the makeshift

dance floor in a country dance, catching Rafe
out of the corner of his eye. His brother was at
the door, taking something from a messenger
and making his way towards them. Rafe waved
the letter in his hand. 'It's from Monteith.'

Hazard led Addy from the dance floor and
took the note from Rafe. 'Felicitations, no
doubt.' He flashed her a smile of assurance.
He scanned the contents, his body going still
as he read it a second time to be sure.

'What is it? It's not bad news, is it?' Addy
leaned forward, trying to read the letter, concerned.

'No,' he said slowly. 'Not bad news. Very
good news, actually.' He looked from Rafe to
Addy. St Helier and Artemisia and Sir Lesley
Stansfield gathered about them, a little thrill
of excitement jumping between them. They
knew! Hazard felt himself flush with gratitude for his new family. 'Monteith says I've
been offered a post at the British Museum,
as an inspector of antiquities.' He glanced at
Addy. 'And my wife has been invited to assist
me.' He would remember for ever watching
Addy's face change with amazement. Hazard
cleared his throat against his rising emotion.
'We are instructed to take a post in Florence,

Italy this spring and use it as a base for our travels about the Mediterranean.'

Addy was hugging him and all joy broke free as the family took turns clapping him on the back. He and Addy had decided to live with the dangers of his work, but now they didn't have to. Now, they could live within the scope of their dreams, together, pursuing their passions—all of them. He beamed at his new in-laws. 'Thank you, I don't know how you managed it, but thank you.'

'It's where you belong.' Darius slapped him on the back. 'Monteith put it in motion. He told my father and we all took it from there.'

'I am grateful, *we* are grateful.' Hazard leaned down and kissed Addy. They were both vibrating with excitement and with something more. The afternoon shadows were lengthening, the time to celebrate alone would soon be upon them.

Not long after, he and Addy said farewell to their guests and slipped off to the cottage, all thoughts of Florence and spring relegated to the future as they focused on the present in each other's arms.

Epilogue

London—January, the New Year

Addy thought they might be on a permanent honeymoon as she and Hazard walked among the stalls and the street artists with Artemisia and Darius. Christmas was pleasantly behind them and they'd come to London to meet with Monteith and the museum, as well as to be on hand for Bennett Galbraith's trial when the court session opened. It had been short, uneventful and straightforward, resulting in his transportation. That episode was now truly past them and Addy had emerged as something of a hero in the art world for her part in bringing him to justice thanks to her historical expertise. It was an unlooked-for slice of fame.

Artemisia stopped to watch a few of the

street artists at work, making comments to Addy. 'Oh, no,' Artemisia muttered under her breath as they moved through the market. 'Look who's here.' Addy stifled a groan. Approaching them was Sir Aldred Gray, a member of the Royal Academy who'd strongly opposed Artemisia's nomination. Gray tipped his hat, forcing them to acknowledge him and engage in small talk.

'How is your little school, Lady St Helier? Any budding Raphaels?' He chuckled, his belief that the school was a whimsy and incapable of producing any real talent evident. Addy felt Artemisia stiffen.

'We have some promising girls,' Darius supplied, stepping in, hoping to diffuse tension. 'Mrs Manning and Lady St Helier are excellent instructors and mentors. I could not be more proud, especially now that Mrs Manning is a special envoy to Florence,' he offered as a sharp reminder that the school benefitted from the patronage and support of the Earl of Bourne, a viscount, and a highly valued member of the art community. One ought to think twice before crossing them.

'I think it's a risky business to let the students get their hopes up and then, when their talent outstrips the instruction and they need more, there would be no place for them to go. You will have brought them up to a certain height and then dropped them. That's hardly fair,' Gray insisted.

'So you do admit they have talent? If they can be raised to such heights as you claim.' Addy chose that moment to speak up. She would not stand by and let Gray malign her sister.

'They can do nothing with it,' Aldred Gray commiserated.

'They could if the Academy would permit them to,' Artemisia joined her. 'But my skill and the skill of my sister will suffice in the absence of the Academy.' Artemisia linked her arm through hers.

Aldred Gray looked dubious and patronising. 'Well, I don't know about that. We have masters.'

'Addy and I are masters,' Artemisia all but snarled. 'Are you a gambling man, Sir Aldred?'

'Yes, at times, but…' Gray spluttered.

Addy was enjoying watching Artemisia put him on the hook—right up until Artemisia nudged her with an elbow.

'Addy, you've a good eye. Pick one of these street artists. Any one of them. Offer them a place at the school. Sir Aldred, I wager one hundred pounds I can turn an artist of my sister's choosing into a prize-winning painter in five months for the May exhibition.'

'Arta!' Addy gasped. These were street artists, people with some natural talent, but no schooling, no understanding of what they did and how they did it.

'Do it, Addy. Pick one,' Artemisia insisted as they began to stroll once more among the artists, Sir Gray sputtering beside them, but Addy swore Hazard was chuckling beside her.

They walked past several artists whom she discarded immediately. She needed someone young, someone who didn't have terribly ingrained practices, which ruled out most of them. They'd never rise above their bad habits. They'd given up on real excellence, real nuance, years ago. Someone female, preferably, but there were few choices on that account. Except…wasn't there a black-haired girl in the corner, under the arcade when they'd arrived?

'This way.' Addy retraced their steps and found her, the slender, olive-skinned girl with the black hair. She stood behind the girl's easel, watching her work, aware of Hazard at her shoulder, his very nearness making her blood thrum. Would it always be that way? Three weeks of marriage suggested it would be.

The girl Addy was interested in was good, there was some skill in her work that spoke to more than natural talent. 'This one,' Addy announced, causing the girl to turn.

'I have a name, *signorina*.' The girl's accent was apparent beneath her use of English. Her dark eyes flashed.

'Lei come si chiama?' Addy replied in formal Italian, meeting the girl's sharp tone evenly.

At the sound of her own language, the girl softened. 'My name is Josefina—Fina to my friends,' she offered.

'I'm Adelaide Manning and this is my sister, Lady St Helier. We have an art school in Seasalter for girls. We'd like you to come study there.' Addy could see the girl was dubious. She felt Artemisia step forward, ready to bombard the girl with arguments. She put a quiet restraining hand on her sister's arm. Artemisia would only scare her off. Of the two of them, she was the one with the people skills.

'Just for a short while, come and see if you like it. If you don't, you're free to leave.' Addy shrugged as if the girl's decision was inconsequential. 'The market is cold in the winter, customers are few. It's hard to paint in the rain. Why not spend the winter indoors, with three meals a day and a warm bed, all at no cost to you, just your time?'

'I've heard of the school,' the girl said cautiously, obviously weighing Addy's words. 'I'll come.'

Artemisia fished a card from her reticule. 'Here's our address in town. Come to us there in the next two days and you can travel back with us.'

The group moved off, Artemisia grinning wickedly at Sir Aldred Gray. 'Have your money ready, Gray.'

'You are incorrigible,' Addy scolded her sister once they moved away from Sir Aldred. 'Do you think you can do it?'

'Of course. It would be easier with you there to help, but you'll be in Florence.' They laughed and Addy felt good, alive. She hugged Hazard's arm and looked up at him. A man had once promised to make her rich and famous. What a small dream that had been. She had so much more now.

* * * * *

MILLS & BOON

Coming next month

A MARRIAGE OF EQUALS
Elizabeth Rolls

'I'm sorry it's so dull here and not at all what you're used to, but—' Psyché fiddled with her skirts.

'No.' Damn it. Now he felt guilty that she could possibly think her home, her very bed, inadequate to his finicky needs. And he liked this room. It was comfortable, soothing with the delicate watercolour paintings on the wall, plain furnishings and pretty, feminine oddments scattered about. 'It's not that at all. You've been more than kind and—'

'He would have shot me. It was Carshalton. He fired at me deliberately, thinking I was Kit.'

Memory flooded back.

'It was nothing.' Oh, God! The last thing Will wanted was her gratitude, for her to feel any obligation. 'He might have hit either of us.'

She reached out and took his hand. 'It wasn't nothing. And he couldn't have hit *me* because you deliberately dropped back to shield me.' Her smile trembled, doing strange things to his insides. 'Knowing that you would have done the same for Kit, or any other friend, only makes you more special.'

The blush, curse it, burned hotter than the fever. She was making him out to be some sort of hero. What kind of man let a woman take the risk she had taken?

But he couldn't say any of that because her eyes were wet, her mouth trembling and—

'Especially when it was my fault,' she whispered.

Her fault?

'It was mine,' he said. 'I should never have allowed you to come at all, let alone in that blasted cloak.'

Some of the tears turned to smoke as her eyes narrowed. *'Allowed?'*

He winced.

'Just how did you propose to stop me?'

'I have no idea,' he admitted. 'Your logic was unarguable. That doesn't mean I have to like it. Or that I don't want to—' He broke off. She didn't need to hear that he wanted *her*. Or that he wanted above all to protect her. Even from himself.

'What do you want?'

He wanted…he wanted… He shifted uncomfortably as his want manifested itself in a very physical way.

'Are your pillows uncomfortable? Here. Let me.' Psyché leaned forward, bending over him to adjust the pillows at his back. And her mouth, that gorgeous, lush, warm mouth, was closer than temptation and a wish.

He braced himself carefully with one hand, reached up with the other and clasped it on the tender skin of her nape under the riot of spiralling curls. 'The thing is,' he said, 'this is not how I ever envisaged being in your bed.'

Continue reading
A MARRIAGE OF EQUALS
Elizabeth Rolls

Available next month
www.millsandboon.co.uk

COMING SOON!